Mr. Pickwick's Guide to
Marriageable Young Ladies

Jill M Beene

Mr. Pickwick's Guide to Marriageable Young Ladies/Jill M Beene. -- 1st ed.
ISBN 978-1-7347993-0-9

For Jamie,
who thinks that I can,
and tells me I should.

Table of Contents

Prologue

In the ballrooms and drawing rooms of the great houses, tumult was stirring. There was a current of change, of upset. Everyone in the upper classes knew it was happening, but they soldiered on and did their best to pretend that things were serenely the same, much like how a baker spreads too much frosting to disguise a broken cake. But the earth had shifted; an eruption had occurred. Everywhere in high society, one name was spoken. It was murmured behind the lace-gloved hands of bosom friends in the park, hissed in the privacy of bedrooms by irate mothers, wailed into tear-soaked silk pillows by beautiful ladies who had suddenly lost their stampede of beaux...

Mr. Pickwick.

It started, as things usually do, in the servants' quarters. A lady's maid or a secretary or a literate footman spent a few coins for the promise of good, reliable gossip. In London, gossip was a currency all its own. When the servant skimmed the first few pages and realized the value of what they had, they looked to be sure no one was watching, bundled the small booklet into an inner coat pocket or at the bottom of a basket, and hurried home.

Late that night, that servant huddled by the dying kitchen fire and read page after page to the rest of the downstairs staff, who listened avidly to catch the murmured, forbidden words--as dangerous as contraband, as delicious as chocolate. They clutched their sides and shoved fists against their mouths in order to muffle their hysterics.

It took weeks for Mr. Pickwick to reach the upper floors of the townhomes and palatial estates. But like a silent flood, the waters finally rose high enough for those upstairs to notice. Perhaps it was a careless maid, leaving her copy in a bedroom she was cleaning. Maybe it was a concerned butler, who thought the master of the house needed to know what was being written about his beautiful, vacant daughter. Whatever the instigating spark, the dam between the lower and upper classes cracked, and within a week, the floodwaters of Mr. Pickwick's writings crashed over the cobblestones of St. James' place, seeped up through the inlaid floorboards of ballrooms, sloshed down gilded hallways, and stained the silk walls of drawing rooms all over London.

Chapter 1

London, 1824

From *Mr. Pickwick's Guide to Marriageable Young Ladies-*

Lady B.T. is beautiful as a flower, but speaking to her is a trial. Her vacant smile is admittedly lovely, but the depth of her character leaves much to be desired. She is like a spoonful of sugar on the tongue--sweet for a moment, then cloying and distasteful.

"Have you seen this?" Percival Waldrey, the Marquess of Salisbury, tossed a booklet onto the great mahogany desk.

It skidded across the polished surface and onto the ledger where Edward Dain Montclief, the Duke of Devonshire, had just made several neat markings. He frowned at the smudged numbers, then glowered up at his closest friend.

"Hello, Percy," he drawled. "Lovely to see you. Thanks for showing yourself in...again."

Edward was used to his friends coming and going as they pleased. He wasn't quite sure why they felt so entitled to his house, his horses, his liquor. Percy had even appropriated a pair of Edward's boots once. His friends just seemed so *comfortable*, where everyone else treated him with standoffish respect. Edward thought it was good that he only really had a couple of friends, otherwise his estates would be overrun with drunken, carousing people who treated him with insouciant sarcasm when he hinted that they should go elsewhere. As if on cue, Percival crossed to the carved sideboard, selected a crystal decanter, and poured himself two fingerfuls.

"It's nine in the morning, Perce," Edward said.

"Montclief, read the damn book," he said, taking a deep drink.

Edward picked up the booklet, even as he blotted the smeared ink on his ledger. "*Mr. Pickwick's Guide to Marriageable Young Ladies*? What is this drivel?"

"Are you familiar with Harris' List?" A blush dusted Percival's cheeks, and he cleared his throat as he yanked at his crisp cravat. "You know...the one that rates, erm... ladies of the night?"

"I've heard of it," Edward said, a frown fixed on his face. "You don't mean that someone is reviewing ladies of the peerage in the same manner?"

That would be a grave insult, indeed. Although dueling was largely out of style, if someone was reviewing the parts of a lady covered by her dress, no one would blink an eye when an angry father or brother took his justice at the smoking end of a pistol.

"No," Percy said. "Thank heavens it's not that. Although... I don't know... maybe this is worse. Just... just read it."

Worse? Worse than some scoundrel writing comments on the figures and bedroom talents of ladies of society? Edward raised his eyebrows and flipped open the front cover.

Lady A.A., lately of St. James, a fair-haired beauty with remarkable blue eyes, charms her suitors with a tinkling laugh and an exceptional singing voice. Let the buyer beware, however. The lady is short-tempered, prone to private, vicious fits. Servants and hounds alike flee in the wake of her tantrums. Any husband of hers will find ample reason to travel for business.

Lady B.A. has auburn tresses with a tight curl. This shy dove is often found seated at balls and against the wall at salons and parties. But lo, if you can coax a smile from this secret beauty, you will be half in love already. She is a lady of purity, gentleness, and grace. The gentleman who captures her heart will have found a precious, hidden gem.

"I'm not quite sure what the calamity is, Percy." He tossed the book back onto the desk. "This sounds like a collection of entries from the local society pages. Harmless nonsense for the gossips."

"Harmless? *Harmless?* Turn to page forty-three."

Edward sighed and obeyed.

"No. Read it aloud," Percival demanded.

"Lady C.W. is a fair flower with her reddish blonde hair and flashing green eyes..." Edward paused and looked up into the male equivalent of the description. "Ah, your dear sister."

"Read it," Percival demanded, his lips thin.

"Lady C.W. is a fair flower with her reddish blonde hair and flashing green eyes. She is charming, with a pleasant demeanor. Although not as accomplished as many of her peers..."

"You see?" Percival said. He slammed his empty glass down upon the credenza and began to pace.

"Although not as accomplished as many of her peers," Edward repeated, "...she is all that is lovely, both inside and out. Her virtue is above reproach. Any gentleman would be lucky to have her as his wife." Edward looked up from the book. "*This* is what you are upset about? This is a glowing review."

Percy stepped forward and jabbed the cover. "Not as accomplished? *Not as accomplished?* Candace can speak some French, and she plays *several* sonatas passably well on the piano. What more do you want in a woman?"

Edward tried very hard not to smile, but something about his expression betrayed him.

Percival's expression turned into a scowl. "Of course *you* aren't concerned. I've got two unmarried sisters, but your sister's already made a good match."

"My agreement with that statement depends on the day of the week," Edward said, dryly.

Percival rolled his eyes. "Lucas is a good chap. He adores Amelia. He's sensible, from a good family, and has that enormous goat fortune."

"It's wool, as you are well aware."

"That's not the point," Percival said, slicing his hand through the air. "How is dear Candace supposed to find a good husband with this review hanging over her head like, like…"

"A lovely compliment? An advertisement to her virtue? A glowing endorsement?" Edward supplied, helpfully, steepling his fingers.

"An albatross," Percival hissed. "A shroud."

Edward chuckled. "Candace has received two offers of marriage already, and she isn't even through her first Season. You and I both know that she is waiting for the Marquess of Shelbourne to declare his intentions. And if he doesn't, the Duke of Canterbury is waiting in the wings."

"Ugh, the old lecher."

"He's four years older than you. Don't be ridiculous."

Percival slumped into a chair in front of the Duke's desk and grumbled, "He's been married before. He has a child."

"Don't be petulant," Edward said. "It's unbecoming. It isn't Canterbury's fault that his wife died in childbirth. Besides, you can tell a lot about a man by how he treats his children. I have it on excellent authority that he's hired a nanny and a tutor for the boy."

"The boy can't be more than five years old," Percival said. "What's the point of a tutor?"

"He's four. Canterbury believes that it's never too early to start an education, but that's not the point. The point is that most men would see a nanny and a tutor as an excuse to spend less time with their progeny, especially at such a demanding age. But Canterbury spends every morning, afternoon, and evening with his son. They share most of their meals together, unless Canterbury has another engagement. He is loyal, even when it is not always easy to be so. *That* is the kind of man to whom I would happily give my sister's hand."

"*See?*" Percival said, waving his arm. "This is why I brought you the book! You seem to know everything. You can find out who wrote this scurrilous nonsense."

Edward laughed. "And deprive the peerage of this gem of social commentary? Why would I do that?"

Percival winced. "Turn to page twenty-three."

Edward pursed his lips, but complied. As he read, his face grew white, his knuckles tensed around the pages. By the time he was finished reading the entry, he completely agreed with Percy. He needed to find the author of the book, immediately.

Chapter 2

From *Mr. Pickwick's Guide to Marriageable Young Ladies-*

It is a sad state of affairs when Lady J.O. is not chaperoned carefully around champagne. Many ladies monitor their own consumption lest they miss a step on the dancefloor, but she prefers to have a glass in each hand. There was a furor at a recent dinner party in which the lady was found in a state, out in the formal gardens. Unlike other, similar scandals, the lady was found quite alone--her only companion was an empty bottle of Merrit Spécial.

Lady Eleanor Gilbert's umbrella did little to shield her from the driving rain. Her brown hair was wet and coming loose from the neat chignon she'd pinned that morning. Wet tendrils clung to her smooth cheeks and neck like seaweed on a dock. Raindrops dampened her lush eyelashes, and she blinked the moisture away, only to have a fresh sheet of rain blow in and obstruct her vision once more.

She quickened her pace, dodging puddles as best she could, though her serviceable leather boots were already soaked through and the hem of her fashionable velvet walking gown was muddy. The clatter and splash of a covered load pulled by miserable horses was the only noise that rose above the pounding splatter of the rain. There were a few other people running toward cover in this downpour, but the streets of Cheapside were mostly empty. Even the most desperate of the whores and cutthroats had taken shelter.

Dim light peeked through the cracks in the shutters in the forlorn house that was her destination. Mr. McAffrey was ancient and cranky, slow to fix roof leaks and stingy with coal in his grate, but he was a rarity all the same. It was rare for a male landlord to respect the boundaries of single female tenants, even rarer for a landlord to feel protective, but Mr. McAffrey had served with her father in the war. He remembered the late war hero, Major Matthew Gilbert, with far more familiar tenderness than the rest of the nation did.

"Ellie, girl?" A croaking voice from the open door to her left said, once she let herself in the front door.

"Yes, it's me," she said, stamping her feet on the worn rug. "You didn't have to wait up, Mr. McAffrey."

"'Course I did," he groused. "Now double-check the lock on the front door and close my door on the way up. It's well past my time for bed."

"Goodnight," she said, jiggling the closed front door so he could hear it and be comforted, and closing his door as he asked.

She lit the candle waiting on the chipped yellow table by the front door and trudged as quietly as possible up the sagging stairs. The other tenants were long asleep. The flickering candle illuminated the faded floral wallpaper. Eleanor was sure that the roses on a green background were once cheerful, but they had long since faded away. It reminded her of her life. Her future, once bright and incandescent with possibility, had faded. There was no returning to the kind of life she'd known, not unless she married well. And even that dream had slowly dissipated into nothing, like fog in the sun.

She would never again live in a fashionable townhouse on St. James, or spend the summer in a countryside manor. Her sister-in-law had seen to that. But Eleanor wouldn't spend the rest of her days in this tenement house, either. Or maybe she would, but she would see it returned to a level of comfort that hadn't been enjoyed in decades.

She had moved in with nothing. No furniture, no household supply, just a paltry twenty pounds a year, and the clothes she owned, the gowns that were too out of style to be sold for the debtors. Mr. McAffrey sent her down to the basement, told her that there was at least an old bed down there, and she was welcome to anything else she'd found. Eleanor had found the bed, a brass monstrosity that she'd wrestled up to her room in pieces. She'd also unearthed something most unexpected. Beneath a large canvas tarpaulin, she'd found a machine.

"That old thing?" McAffrey had replied, when she'd asked about it. "Always meant to get the scrappers in here to take it away. Doubt it works, but you're welcome to fiddle with it, if you're interested in that sort of thing."

Fiddle she had. It was a printing press, an old one. But whoever stored it had drenched it in oil before covering it, so it still moved. Barely at first, but with application of more oil, it articulated more smoothly, until it was as functional as one could wish.

Those days, Eleanor spent a lot of time in the basement, just staring at the machine, nibbling her fingernails, and thinking. It was like she had discovered an answer, but she hadn't figured out the question yet. It was no surprise that her mind was working slowly. She was still mourning her brother, still raging at her sister-in-law. Above all, she didn't want what had befallen her family to happen to anyone else.

It was months later that the idea came to her. She remembered the errant thought that eventually grew like a seed in her mind-- *They have reviews on whores. If only they reviewed debutantes, then maybe my family wouldn't have fallen into ruin.* She had been washing her face at the time. She had bent down to the bowl of water as one woman, and straightened as another. She'd stared into the mirror with wide brown eyes, rivulets of water running down her skin.

Eleanor pushed open her door. Things were already better. Not nearly as comfortable as they once were, when even thinking about economies was beneath her. But she had bought a new feather mattress, the one creature comfort besides hot baths that she missed most from her previous life. And she'd received a note from her runner that said they were low on booklets. She'd need to do another printing soon.

The thought made her excited and tired, all at once. She was going to raise the price on this next printing. She didn't want to count her chickens before they hatched, but she hoped to buy a new cloak and boots, and maybe have the railing along the stairs repaired. Eleanor wasn't an idiot. She knew that she would never return to the ballrooms of St. James' Place with her pamphlets. But even this, her first year of printing, had brought success beyond what she'd hoped for.

Mr. McAffrey didn't question the coal that appeared in his bin, nor the fresh bread and milk that were delivered three times a week. It was the least she could do. She'd been penniless, homeless, one breath away from an abbey or a brothel. Eleanor still wasn't sure which would have been worse. The brothel, probably. But she couldn't decide. Was it better to spend one's days in endless, monotonous toil and punishment, or sell her body and soul? Were endless hours of silent regret better or worse than a short, brutal life? She didn't know.

And thanks to Mr. McAffrey and the fictional Mr. Pickwick, she hopefully never would.

Eleanor bolted the door firmly behind her, sat on the little bench by her door, and pulled off her damp boots. She set them before the grate, where they would steam and dry, then deftly removed her dress and petticoats and hung them to air.

Eleanor's apartment was two rooms, delineated only by an archway between the two spaces. Her brass bed was pushed against the interior wall that was closest to her small, potbelly iron stove. Her very first expense, once she had an income, was to have a chimney sweep come and service the apartments in the building. She was terrified of fire, ever since she'd been a small child and the hayloft she'd been playing hide and seek in was set ablaze by a careless groomsman. She could still remember the blistering heat, the way the smoke made her eyes water and her throat close.

She wasn't immune to the fear of having the highest apartment in the building. She knew that those were the least likely people to get out or survive, were there a fire. After all, fire burned *up*. But the chimney sweep came once a month now, and Eleanor slept a bit easier for it. Her bedroom was little more than an alcove with one narrow bed, an iron stove, and a massive cedar wardrobe. The wardrobe had been relegated to the attic long before she had resided there; it was too large, took too much precious space for the families who'd once inhabited the building. But it was perfect for her. Her livelihood depended upon the dresses within being preserved.

After all, Eleanor's bread and butter was gossip. And gossip was served hot in several places. One was in the bowels of kitchens of every great house across London and beyond. Since Eleanor couldn't be in every kitchen or hear the whispers in every larder, she had good friends. Her old maids, Ida, Beatrice, and Emily, had been her friends long before the hag her brother married bankrupted the family, broke him body and soul, then abandoned him on his deathbed.

Emily and Ida couldn't write to send messages, but it didn't matter. They both had Sunday mornings off for church, and enough time for luncheons after. Every week, Eleanor dressed herself in the manner of a servant attending services, then met them for lunch in a small tavern.

One of Eleanor's tenets in publishing *Mr. Pickwick's Guide to Marriageable Young Ladies* was that she never printed something she didn't have a first-hand account of, or hear from multiple sources. Eleanor didn't put much stock into the criticism of competitors, for example. She put even less trust in the claims of mothers whose daughters were shunned in favor of a brighter social star. It was easy to claim that Lady so-and-so was a harlot, a ne'er-do-well, a hussy. But the truth was more often that Lady so-and-so had caught the attention of a man in that mama's sights.

Eleanor had a system. Positive things were most believable when reported by servants. They had no 'skin in the game' so to speak, when it came to the marriage mart. Positive things were nigh on unbelievable when spoken too often and with too much vehemence by someone invested in the outcome of a debutante--by a mother, for example, or a desperate older brother. Negative things were most reliable from multiple sources--eyewitnesses were best. But servants were only reliable when conveying negative stories if they had not been fired or otherwise dressed down by their employer. Neutral sources were important, Eleanor constantly reminded herself.

The other source of her information was far more dangerous than her Sunday luncheons with her erstwhile maids. Eleanor was still a Lady, but only in breeding and title. Long gone were the days of sleeping in and being tended to by a bevy of servants, but Eleanor still had the nobility of her birth. Little else was prized by society, except for looks and wealth and youth. Eleanor would slowly lose the battle to time, but she had her looks and her smarts, and she was determined to make something of herself.

And she still had her friendships. To her shame, her closest friend was now her greatest source of information. The Marchioness of Millen was better known to Eleanor simply as Jane. But she was as charming and beautiful as her name was simple. And she adored Eleanor. Jane did not care that Eleanor no longer had fortune or family. In fact, she asked Eleanor so little about her circumstances that Eleanor often had to fight down the rising bitterness in her throat.

But then Eleanor reminded herself that she'd never offered the information. And when she had lived on St. James' row, she'd never wondered how others got by. The poor were the poor, and she did her duty by them--food baskets at the holidays, regular donations to worthy charities, her castoff dresses donated--but she'd never really *thought* about it. She'd known about the mechanics of poverty in the same way she'd known about the planets--that is, in passing theory only.

But now that poverty was close enough to blow hot breath upon her neck, and the possibility of homelessness nipped at her heels like an invisible wolf--now, she understood. In those grey, bleak days after what Eleanor internally called *the downfall*, she had stayed with Jane and her husband, the greying Marquess of Millen. They treated her with kindness and sympathy, but a month into her stay, she'd overheard a conversation between them that let her know they wished her gone.

Eleanor had tumbled from one misfortune into the next, spending hours writing letters to everyone in her father's address book that she personally remembered. In those letters, the memory of which still brought the warmth of shame to her cheeks, she hinted at her impossible situation, all but begging for help. She'd received several responses, much of which were expressions of bland condolences, and empty wishes for her good health and fortune moving forward.

Only Mr. McAffrey hadn't ignored her thinly veiled plea. He'd offered her a private room in his tenement and his support. Eleanor was now ashamed when she remembered how long it took her to respond. She'd been waiting for someone else to offer assistance--a better address, a member of the peerage to reach out, one of her recently fled friends to have a change of heart. And when it finally came time to move, Eleanor told Jane that a long-lost cousin had invited her to stay indefinitely across town. Jane had smiled, kissed her cheeks, wished her well, and did her best to hide her relief at seeing Eleanor's trunks stacked neatly by the door.

The Marchioness was her very last friend, and Eleanor saw her at least twice a week--once for tea on Tuesdays, and for dinner on Thursday nights, when the Marquess was at his private club. Though it pained her to admit it, Eleanor knew she was Jane's charity friend. She was the grateful recipient of Jane's castoff gowns, the tag-along guest on the many invitations where the Marquess found himself unable--or more often, unwilling--to attend.

It was at these events, the tea parties, salons, balls, and dinners, where Eleanor stood, mostly silent, at Jane's elbow. She was there for Jane's amusement, that the Marchioness need never to be lonely or bored, never need to be without someone to compliment or soothe her, as need arose. Eleanor *was* grateful, just not in the way that Jane would expect. Eleanor used the time to listen and observe, and she was thankful.

The Marchioness surrounded herself with like-minded ladies of the peerage whose main occupation was, at their current stage of life, making heirs for their titled husbands and whispering delicious tidbits about others behind their fluttering, hand-painted silk fans. It was here, pressed against the walls in overly fragrant ballrooms, seated at the far end of long dining tables, and hiding behind potted ferns in a salon, that Eleanor heard and saw things. Valuable things. *Printable* things.

Eleanor's future depended upon printable things.

Chapter 3

From *Mr. Pickwick's Guide to Marriageable Young Ladies-*

Lady L.O. has very few bachelors paying attention to her, for good reason. Her unpleasant countenance would be helped with the application of a genuine smile, but those are in short supply for someone as ill-tempered and spoiled as she. It would be wonderful if, under that lemon-sucking expression, there was kindness or wit. Alas, the opposite is true--the lady is as unpleasant as she looks--short-tempered, conniving, controlling, and manipulative. It seems the only positive thing that can be said about the lady is of the massive dowry her father has agreed to--perhaps he is as anxious to

be rid of her presence as any future husband
would be.

"Any news?" Percival asked him, shaking rain from his reddish curls onto the marble floor.

They were in Edward's London home. It was a large, indolently sprawling manor, built before space in London was at a true premium. The entryway, in which they now stood, was larger than many apartments in Cheapside, and richly furnished.

"I apologize, Huntley," Edward said to his stoic butler, who watched Percy's slovenly antics with a neutral expression. "I've tried to tell the Marquess that if he acts like a dog, I'll relegate him to the stables, but he's yet to listen."

"Think nothing of it, Your Grace," Huntley said, the hint of a smile tweaking the corners of his mouth.

Huntley had been around long enough to remember when Edward and Percival were nothing more than knee-high ruffians of the lowest order. Their mothers had been dear friends, and they'd grown up playing hide and seek together in this very house. Edward wondered what it was like for long-term servants; if watching your master grow from an infant squalling in his own filth to a respected member of the peerage made it more difficult to respect them.

"That's unkind, Edward," Percy said, frowning. "After all, it was raining out, and I'd forgotten my hat and umbrella."

"I doubt you forgot them," he said, handing his coat off to Huntley. "You hate wearing a hat and can't be bothered to carry an umbrella."

Percy laughed. "True, but it's a deuced easy way to meet the ladies. They all wait rainstorms out inside fancy shops. If you happen to be near one, just bop in and comment on how you forgot your umbrella. They're all too happy to commiserate until it's sunny again."

Edward rolled his eyes. "As if you need any help in *that* area. I'd think an umbrella would actually be handy in warding off eager misses and their mothers."

"Did you know that the Lady Wainberry invited me to yet *another* dinner?"

"You have to sympathize with the woman," Edward said, leading the way to his study and closing the door behind them. "She has four daughters to marry off, and none of them all that pretty. You lucked out with your sister. She's charming and lovely."

"If you like her so much, why don't *you* marry her?"

Edward raised an eyebrow. "I think of her as a younger sister."

"I know, I know," Percy said, his shoulders sagging as he slumped into one of the chairs near the great stone fireplace. "But it's terrifying that she's *out*. She's having a *Season*. I can barely keep myself from baring my teeth at some of the gents who speak to her. Did you know that Lord

34

Allsberth asked her to dance a *waltz* at the last ball?"

"I saw that," he said, trying to keep a smile from his face. "If I recall, she didn't encourage conversation during the dance."

"It doesn't matter." Percy sat forward and wrung his hands. "It was the fact that he had the nerve to *ask*. After what I've seen that man get up to at the club? You think I'd let Candace marry someone like him? I have two unmarried sisters. Thank goodness only Candace is out, and Sophia is still safely in the country with her governess, but what will I do next year, when they are both having Seasons? You're lucky. Your sister's already married, and you won't go through that with Henry."

He wouldn't have to marry Henry off, but that didn't mean he didn't worry. Edward stood, moved to the sideboard, and poured each of them a small snifter of brandy.

"I'm sorry, Edward. I know that you have your own worries in that regard. I shouldn't have said that."

Edward waved away the apology. "No need. My concerns for Henry are unique, that is to be certain.

But I well remember the stress of having a sister in the marriage mart. You're worried that they won't find anyone they fancy. Worse than that, you're worried that they *will*."

"Exactly," Percy said, gratefully. "And what if she fancies the wrong sort? What if she's *ruined*?"

He laughed. "You know as well as I do that Candace is more concerned with marrying well than you are. She's had offers; she'll have more by the time the Season's up. She's just waiting for Shelbourne to return from the countryside. I predict you'll have a new brother-in-law within three months."

"Ugh." Percy swallowed the brandy in a large gulp. "Forgive me--have you heard any news on our Mr. Pickwick?"

"None," Edward said, his voice grave. "I've contacted every printing house in London, by various means, and none of them seem to be the source of the booklet."

"How can you know that?"

"I have a list," he said, patting the small notebook in his pocket. "But essentially, many of the printing houses are owned by peerage who have daughters included in the booklet. I cannot see any of them risking such a printing. I've bribed employees of the others, even sent one of my men into a couple when they were closed."

"Has it really come to breaking and entering?" Percy said.

"It's been nearly a month, and I'm no closer to finding out who our dear Mr. Pickwick is."

"The name is obviously an alias." Percy leaned forward in his chair.

"Undoubtedly."

"I just don't understand why anyone in the peerage would risk printing such drivel," Percy said.

Edward frowned. "What makes you think it's a member of nobility?"

"Dear heavens, Edward. Have you even read the booklet?"

"I made a list of all the named ladies, but other than that..."

"It isn't all negative reviews. Some of them are absolutely glowing. Rumor has it that the new Baroness of Chauncey has Mr. Pickwick to thank for her title. You know that they hadn't been introduced a fortnight before she received a proposal. Most people thought the Baron would never remarry, but the Baroness' review in the booklet specifically mentioned how kind she was, how she was so talented at gentle pursuits, playing the piano and such. Everyone knows how much the Baron enjoys listening to music. And, forgive me for speaking ill of the dead, his last wife was a shrill harpy."

Edward scoffed. "You expect me to believe that the Baron of Chauncey, a man I know personally to be steady and reasonable, was talked into marriage by a pamphlet that was published by some anonymous individual?"

"I'm saying he was tempted." Percy held up his finger for emphasis. "And sometimes, all it takes is a little nudge. Besides, he isn't the only one."

"What? Who else?"

"That Duke, the one from Scotland?"

"The Duke of Nimburgh?"

Percy snapped his fingers. "That's the one. Turns out he dropped Lady Anne Burnswith without nary a by-your-leave, after the pamphlet tattled on her for disliking children. He's got two little daughters waiting at home, from his last marriage, and he needs an heir. Rumor has it, he's now courting Lady Josephine Milton, who was reported as being 'an angel to everyone around her, whether animal, child, servant, or peer'."

Edward was stunned. He'd considered the booklet as nothing more than the kind of drivel made to entertain, more salacious gossip like what was already found in the society page of any London newspaper. To hear that individuals were actually putting stock in such a book was shocking.

"The thing is," Percy continued, with a thoughtful expression. "There is some truth to the book. Obviously, I don't know *every* lady mentioned..."

Edward raised his eyebrow sardonically, but Percy ignored him.

"But the reviews for the ladies I *do* know are spot on." He ticked them off on his fingers. "Lady Patrice is lovely but dumb as a sack of hair. Lady Georgette has a temper worse than any drunk you've ever met. Lady Ainslee is a mean spirited gossip. Lady Celia is shy, unless you get her alone, and then she reveals a surprising wit, which probably stems from all those books she reads. The point is, I am more inclined to believe the reviews after having some of my own experiences repeated by Mr. Pickwick. If other readers are having the same experience as I, it's no wonder that the damned book is getting credence."

"That's a good point." Edward frowned.

"You've seen the quality of that booklet. Do you really think it was made by one of the printing houses? I think you should be looking at the source of the gossip, not the source of the booklet."

"Gossip is everywhere. Everyone gossips." Edward, himself, tried not to pay attention to much of it.

"That's exactly my *point*." Percy leaned forward, earnestly. "Most of the time, gossip isn't worth the air used to speak it. But Mr. Pickwick seems to have some very valid sources. I would bet my favorite horse that those are harder to come by in London than printing presses."

Edward tapped his chin. "You may be right."

"Edward, you are one of the brightest men of my acquaintance in many areas, but in terms of gossip, both creating and listening to it, I am the far superior being."

He laughed. "I'll read it. This very evening."

"Good. Because I have a theory about our Mr. Pickwick, but I want to see if you come to the same conclusion. You are a quick reader," Percy said, standing. "The book will take you a few hours' time to get through. I shall call upon you tomorrow morning for breakfast, and we can review notes then. Be sure to let Mrs. Gardner know that I will break fast with you. She knows I love her brown sugar bacon. I shall show myself out."

"Always a pleasure, Percival!" Edward called to his friend's retreating back.

Edward dug his copy of Mr. Pickwick's Guide out of his pocket and settled himself at his large desk.

"Would you like some tea, Your Grace?" Mr. Huntley stood just inside the open doorway.

"Yes, please, Huntley. I will take a tray in here for my dinner as well. I have some work to attend to. And please inform Mrs. Gardner that Percival will be joining me for breakfast in the morning."

"Very good, Your Grace."

Edward opened the booklet and set to reading.

It was late that night, after a pot of tea, a picked over dinner tray, and pages of hastily scribbled notes when Edward closed the back cover on *Mr. Pickwick*. He ran a hand through his dark hair. His notes were mostly questions to be answered. *Who knows all of these people? Are all of these reviews correct? How can one person have such a vast knowledge of all these ladies?*

"Basics, Edward," he muttered to the empty room.

It was printed in booklet form, using a printing press. That required paper, ink, binding material, and space to work. All of those could be had from many sources. In fact, several pages of the book he held looked to be different paper, as if the individual had taken precautions to avoid discovery by such means. Which meant his quarry was clever.

No, not just clever. Book smart, too. The thought came to him as clear as a rung bell. He opened the book. Everything was written well, with attention to grammar and punctuation. He hadn't seen one word misspelled; even Lady Hendricia von L'Allstead's name was abbreviated correctly. This meant that the writers, or at least the editors, were well-educated, both socially and in terms of schooling.

Edward also surmised that the individuals had been involved in the London social scene for years, as some of the ladies mentioned had already gone through several Seasons. The *Guide* did not discriminate in regards to age or number of Seasons, either, which could be considered odd. Most attention was normally given to ladies who were either just coming out, or the wealthiest, or the most beautiful. Instead, the longest entries seemed to be dedicated to the 'diamonds in the rough'--the ladies who possessed high value characters rather than beauty and social clout.

Special care was also given to ladies who held high value, by society's standards of beauty or wealth, but whom the authors deemed lacking in character or morality. There were some entries that had surprised him. The entry on Lady Helena deGaunt, for example, was most enlightening. Edward had been introduced to her only months ago, but he had thought her lovely and agreeable. Page twenty-seven served to abuse that notion, calling Miss deGaunt, 'an actress of first order, whose pretty smiles are naught but lures for wealthy bachelors; she spares none for her servants or peers'.

Edward sighed. Mr. Pickwick was a puzzle that would not be solved tonight. He pushed his notes and the *Guide* away and pulled out his stationery. Edward comforted himself with the knowledge that little Henry resided comfortably in the countryside with his governess and tutors.

In addition, his sister, Amelia, and her husband, the Lord Lucas Wilcott, were in residence at the great house with Henry, in Edward's absence.

Once Henry was a bit older, Edward would bring him to London while he sat in Parliament. But the countryside was healthier for a small child. Not that Henry's health was the only thing Edward was concerned about. It was Henry, after all, that had prompted him to begin the search for the author of *Pickwick's Guide* in the first place.

Still, his brother expected regular letters from him. At five years old, Henry could not read, but Amelia, Lucas, or Miss Gresham, the governess, were sure to read any missive to him. Edward did his very best to write at least twice a week. He included descriptions of the park, the large buildings, the carriages, horses, and anything else that might delight Henry. He wrote, honestly, about how he wished he were still at home. Writing Henry had been a struggle, at first. Like most men he knew, he wasn't used to writing descriptions for others' pleasure. Lists, ledgers, instructions--those he knew. But writing social letters and descriptions usually fell to the lady of the house, not the man.

Edward stilled, the errant thought freezing him in place for so long that a blot of ink dripped from his pen onto the crisp parchment. Hurriedly, he blotted the error, finished the letter, and signed his name. With new eyes, Edward opened the booklet once more.

Chapter 4

From *Mr. Pickwick's Guide to Marriageable Young Ladies-*

Lady D.T. is lovely and talented, and attracts suitors as a brightly colored flower attracts bees. However, it seems as if it is impossible for her to choose which among the gentlemen is her favorite. Her father has approved of no less than three suitors, but the lady still dithers. With multiple proposals looming, one wonders if the lady has no favorite--or perhaps she prefers being the center of so much attention.

"It's a woman, the writer," Edward announced to Percy the next morning over breakfast.

"Ah," Percy said, putting a finger next to his nose. "I wondered if you would come to the same opinion."

"I can't believe I didn't see it sooner." Edward shook his head.

"I read that booklet for two weeks before I wondered about it." Percy took an enormous bite of sugared bacon and continued with his mouth full. "Don't feel bad about it."

"Thank you," Edward replied, dryly.

"Welcome," he said, popping a piece of biscuit into his mouth. "I only figured it out when I threw the drivel down one night, frustrated. It doesn't note any of the sorts of things men would list in their descriptions."

"How so?" Edward said.

"Well, it doesn't talk about fortune or the prestige one might get from marrying a lady. It spends most of its time talking about who the ladies actually *are*. That's not how a gentleman, especially the young ones, typically go about things. Men are often too busy trying to suss out what a lady looks like beneath all those frills and ribbons and bobs and whatnot to pay attention to their inner attributes."

"That's a sad assessment of our sex," Edward said.

"I'm not here to sugarcoat things for your tender feelings," Percy said, stabbing a piece of bacon in the air. "My father warned me of the power of a good bosom in a pretty dress--it distracts a man from what's really important. And before you know it, you're leg-shackled to a pernicious harpy for the rest of your days."

"And a dour assessment of marriage," Edward said, dryly.

"The happy ones are the *exception*, Edward. The exception."

"Back to the matter at hand. So not only am I looking for a bootleg printing operation in all of London…"

"Or surrounding areas," Percy interrupted, helpfully.

"…But I'm also looking for a member of the peerage, a *lady,* no less. Who in their right mind would write this?"

"I've thought on that," Percy said, breezily. "I haven't any good ideas."

"I can safely assume that any lady who was maligned in the *Guide* is safe from my scrutiny. I should focus on the ones who have glowing reviews."

"Or none at all," Percy said. "Maybe who *isn't* in the booklet is an even better clue."

"I'd thought the same thing. But I will admit that even some of the ladies with glowing reviews aren't good suspects. Lady Beckinridge, for example," Edward said, turning to a dog-eared page. "She has a wonderful review. It notes that she is kind, generous, and patient, as well as being lovely and talented, if a bit shy." He flopped the booklet closed onto the table. "But you and I both know that her elder brother would never leave her unchaperoned long enough to accomplish this."

"What do you mean?"

"Think of the *time* this must have taken, Percy. Not only in writing the damned thing, but in cultivating sources, distribution, finding a printing situation that would agree to what is a very dangerous activity."

"Why dangerous?"

"You got your knickers all in a twist about Candace's review, and it was a good one! Can you imagine how upset Lord Alberry is, or for that matter, the Duke of Earn? Both of their daughters were absolutely lambasted."

"You're right," Percy said, nodding thoughtfully.

"In fact, I'd be surprised if I were the only one looking for her. I wonder if anyone else suspects that the writer, at least, is female."

"I doubt it. You know we're very forward thinking about the gentler sex. On account of our mothers, and all."

Percy was right about that. In a day and age where many still viewed ladies as nothing but ornamentation or little better than a broodmare, the late Duchess of Devonshire and the Marchioness of Salisbury had been ahead of their time. They'd quickly realized that they shared common viewpoints regarding their own treatment, and what they wished for their sons and daughters. While their husbands were in Parliament or off hunting, the two schemed ways to make things better for women in general, whether that be by encouraging their husbands to become patrons of charities for girls, or gently steering their husbands' votes on issues pertaining to women's rights.

"After all," Percy continued. "Candace and your dear sister Amelia were educated right alongside you and me. That could hardly have been a common occurrence. Even our late mothers did their best to keep that quiet."

"Rightly so," Edward said. "Our mothers wished for their daughters to have an education greater than their own, but they didn't wish to preclude Amelia and Candace from marrying well, either."

"I don't think it would have kept that goat herder away from Amelia. He's smitten." This last statement was delivered with a sarcastic shake of the head, as if Percy couldn't condone such foolishness as love within a marriage. "He's worse than my father was with Mother."

"Let's call it a tie," Edward said, chuckling. The late Marquess had loved his wife dearly.

"Regardless, I think you are correct about the level of danger that this book has presented to its author. I wonder if *she* knows that, or if she's just some dunder-headed ninny who's doing it as a lark or rebellion."

"This is too much work for a simple act of rebellion." Edward tapped the cover for emphasis. "My grandfather took me to watch a printing press in action, once. It takes forever for the type to be set, the ink to be blotted, the pages to be inserted, printed, and dried."

"Yes, but she's not doing *that* part."

"Maybe, maybe not," Edward said. "At this point, nothing would surprise me."

"True." Percy was on to the eggs now, but kept glancing back toward the sideboard, where a huge pile of sugared bacon lay waiting.

Edward suppressed a smile as a footman took the hint and carried the tray over to Percy. "More bacon, sir?"

"Don't mind if I do. Thanks, Jeeves."

Edward sighed. "They're not all named Jeeves, you know."

"I can hardly be expected to remember all their names, can I?"

Edward chuckled, then his glance fell upon the booklet at his elbow and he sobered immediately. "The other thing I have wondered is whether this is a social move, or a fiscal one."

"What do you mean?"

"Is the lady in question doing this to set down a rival? Or is she trying to earn some extra money?"

Percy looked thoroughly scandalized by the thought. "You think the writer views this as some sort of *trade*?"

"I don't know. I keep trying to think of what would cause a lady of some intelligence--for you must admit that some of the entries are written with high wit, Percy--what would make a lady who is familiar with the nobility on this level to do such a thing?"

"Ah, motivation. The murkiest thing to deduce," Percy said in a terrible, affected Scottish accent.

Edward raised an eyebrow. "Been reading *Sir O'Connor's Mysteries* again?"

"They're better than you give them credit for," Percy sniffed.

"They're written for children," Edward answered, dryly. "But once again, back to the point. What would make a lady do such a thing? Where would she even get the idea?"

"Well, there's always Harris' List. You can't ignore the similarities."

"Do you really think that a lady of good breeding has encountered such garbage?"

"Based on my experiences with my sisters alone, I think that young ladies often have much more worldly knowledge than their male protectors wish they did."

"That's the other thing I cannot figure," Edward said. "Who would agree to print this, if they knew the young lady was protected? I certainly hope that my sister couldn't have something of this nature distributed without someone contacting myself or her husband."

Percy tapped his chin, and resumed his horrible excuse for a Scottish brogue. "So y'er sayin' the lass be canny, but unprotected. Educated, but unsupervised. Noble, but poor or *deranged*."

"Despite your poor imitation of Sir O'Connor, yes. That is correct."

"I think you may be right," Percy said, tilting his chin. "I have to believe that someone in my household would alert me if Candace was trying to have *anything* printed, let alone something that could destroy our family's name."

"That's another thing," Edward said. "Who would take that risk? It makes no sense. Everyone knows that you cannot insult a Duke's daughter with impunity, no matter how awful she is. And to put such a thing into *print*? It's unfathomable."

"So maybe it isn't a member of the peerage at all," Percy said.

"Maybe not. Or maybe the writer has little left to lose. Regardless, the outcome is the same." Edward snapped the book shut. "I shall have to do the thing I dread the most."

"And what is that?"

"Be a part of the social scene of London."

Chapter 5

From *Mr. Pickwick's Guide to Marriageable Young Ladies-*

On S.P.- this lady is all that a potential wife should be--on the surface. She is beautiful, full of bashful smiles for her beaux, and accomplished in all the arts. A word of caution, however, is in order. Although the lady comes from an excellent family, rumors of a disturbing nature have escaped the well-run household--this lady is prone to fits of rage. A large footman is assigned to her bedroom door, but not for the lady's protection. It is said that her last maid left the great house with a large severance, a letter of glowing recommendation, and a well-blackened eye.

Eleanor woke, splashed cold water on her face, put on a walking dress, laced her sturdy boots, and tucked a pair of slippers into her velvet reticule. It was Sunday, which meant church and then lunch in the corner of a tavern near the docks that didn't see much business before nightfall. She picked up her skirts just enough to keep them from brushing the muck and stains that coated the cobblestones. The walk took the better part of half an hour, but she walked briskly, enjoying the sights and sounds of a day already well underway in London.

She'd never realized, before, how many people lived and worked within the miles of property that was called London. Eleanor had known about her own servants, of course, the ones who built fires, prepared meals, cleaned, and kept her in absolute comfort. She'd known about the ones who visited the house, too--the doctors, dressmakers, chimney sweeps, peddlers. But she hadn't thought about the market stalls, where servants bought food for large houses, the beggars on the street, the flower girls, the whores, the dock workers... she'd had a very narrow view of London before--like gazing through a gilded keyhole.

Her view was wide open now.

Ida and Emily were already waiting at the regular table in the back. They smiled in greeting as Eleanor stomped the mud from her boots and dried them thoroughly on the mat.

Emily was lady's maid to the Marchioness of Windgate. A petite blonde, the Marchioness was the veritable toast of London. Invitations to every sparkling ball and flower-laden dinner party she hosted was coveted. The crème de la crème of society were invited, and with the large property with all those places to sneak away to... there was always good gossip.

Ida was parlor maid for the Duke and Duchess of Interwile. The Duke was nigh on seventy, and the Duchess scarcely twenty-five. She'd born him an heir and a spare and never returned to their bedchamber. Not that anyone could blame her. Her title and immense wealth opened doors to every social function in London. Her boredom at home with the husband who snored before the fire immediately after his early supper nightly caused her to accept every invitation she could. She had decided that Ida was her bosom friend. The Duchess chattered endlessly as Ida worked; Ida remembered it all, and repeated it to Eleanor.

Beatrice was lady's maid to the young Lady Elizabeth Walters, the only daughter of the Duke of Winscote, and the shining diamond of the current Season. Lady Elizabeth was vivacious, kind, and immensely wealthy. To top it off, she was the paragon of the current ideal of beauty-- short, somewhere between curvy and slender, ice blonde hair, crystal blue eyes. She'd had six offers of marriage already, but it was rumored that she was trying to break the Duchess of York's record for offers within a Season, which was eleven. Beatrice assured Eleanor that was not the case; Lady Elizabeth wasn't proud. Rather, she was secretly, madly in love with the second son of the Viscount Amberley, who had just taken a commission in the army.

"Don't expect her to settle down anytime soon, mark my words," Beatrice said, the last time they'd met. She'd sipped her cider. "He's got two years before he can make it back to society, with his father buying his promotions 'n all. She reads me his letters at bedtime. Such pretty words, too. I'd bet a year's wages that she stays steadfast. No one's turned her head; not even the Viscount Mathers, and I know of four girls who would poison their mothers to be the next Viscountess. So handsome, that one, and such a talker. No. My Lady Elizabeth is pure of heart and deeply in love."

Eleanor believed her on that account.

"Hello, lovelies," Eleanor said, kissing each of them on the cheek in turn. "Beatrice not in, yet?"

Emily rolled her eyes. "You know how long-winded her preacher is. 'Tis why we go to the church on Second Street now."

"But she's got a terrible crush on the Vicar's son," Ida added, unnecessarily.

Eleanor smiled. She'd heard how Beatrice spoke about the young Micah Kent.

"Then I wish her all the luck in the world," she said. "But let's order some cider while we wait."

Eleanor waved the barmaid over and placed their order. At this time of the morning, it was the tavern owner's daughter who took their order. But judging by the careful watch the man kept over the girl, and by the fact that her dress was buttoned primly to the bottom of her chin, Eleanor thought that she probably was closeted away by the time the sailors and dockhands arrived in the evening.

"So, anything new?" Eleanor asked, once the girl had retreated.

"The Duchess had a dinner party this week," Ida said, leaning forward, her freckled cheeks bunched with her smile. "At least thirty people."

"Did she?" Eleanor said, though she'd already heard as much from Lady Allen in Jane's drawing room on Thursday. "And how did it go?"

"I was in the servants' dining room. You know the Duke and Duchess always put a huge spread out for us and the visiting servants when they have a party. Very generous. Anyways, apparently the Viscount Preston's house was in a near uproar this week when their daughter ditched her chaperone and arrived back at the house... in *disarray.*"

"What do you mean?" Emily leaned forward, eagerly. The only thing she loved more than free ciders and a meal was the gossip served at their meetings.

"She was *rumpled.*" Ida delivered the word with relish, and let it hang in the air for them to savor for several moments. "I heard that she wasn't upset, neither. Came back to the front door, cool as you please, and apparently, their butler was the first one to see her. And he says that she was smiling."

"So it weren't no criminal who'd put her in dishabille," Emily said, with a sly wink. "It were someone known to her."

"In the *Biblical* sense, is my guess," Ida agreed.

"Do they know who on earth she might have been meeting in the park?"

"Well, once her ladyship was well into her bath, her maid comes running up to the servant's entrance, carrying on and crying about how she'd lost dear Lady Bella. The Viscountess had her straight into her chambers, and questioned her thoroughly. It turns out that the maid, Sheila, had been strolling right behind Lady Bella when a tall man with dark hair waved from a nearby barouche. Lady Bella ran to him, and I've seen Sheila at the market. Likes her biscuits, Sheila does. She couldn'a kept up with the girl for nothin'. And the two of them's rode off without her, laughing."

"My goodness," Eleanor said, sipping her ale. "Did she recognize the man?"

"This is the best part," Ida said, a sly smile on her face. "It was Lord Avery."

"Ugh. That knave?" Eleanor said.

Lord Avery, second son of the Earl of Winterson, was well known as a deflowerer of young maidens. The problem was, he was too handsome and charming for his own good, not to mention a crack shot with a pistol. It would take a brave father, indeed, to demand pistols at dawn over his daughter's honor.

"Yes," Ida said, bouncing in her seat. "But he's not getting away with it, this time. The Viscount marched out, four of his biggest footmen with him, and came back two hours later with Lord Avery and his father. Lord Avery proposed to Lady Bella, then and there, in front of both their fathers. They're to be married once the banns been read."

Eleanor had already heard a more sedate version of this story, one in which Lord Avery and Lady Bella were to be wed after a whirlwind romance. She'd wondered what about the young girl had finally ensnared the known womanizer. This was why at least two sources to corroborate any story was so important.

"I bet Lady Bella is very happy," Eleanor said. "There have been many a young Lady who've seen the inside of his barouche *without* the benefit of a marriage contract afterward."

Emily laughed. "Maids too. That barouche should be burned. 'Tis not fit to sit in."

"Oh, I don't know," Ida said, a dreamy look in her eye. "I saw Lord Avery once. I wouldn't mind sitting in his barouche, myself."

Emily and Eleanor laughed, with Ida joining in a half-second later.

"And what's all this, about?" Beatrice said as she bustled in and tucked herself into a chair. She removed her Sunday hat, a straw, narrow-brimmed bonnet with mounds of bows. "Started without me, eh? At least no one's been sipping my cider."

"We wouldn't dream of it, Beatrice," Eleanor said, kissing her on the cheek in greeting. "We've been discussing Lord Avery's well-worn *barouche*."

"I've heard it's huge, that barouche," Beatrice said with a wink.

They dissolved into laughter once more.

Later, when Eleanor was back in her rooms and alone once more, she jotted down notes. She'd asked her friends questions and listened to what they said, how they hinted. Though there hadn't been anything new that she'd heard, she'd had several rumors confirmed, and that made for a very good day. She would need to revise *Mr. Pickwick's Guide*, or she would have to print an insert. There were a dozen ladies, at least, who had been left out of the initial printing, because she'd lacked sufficient information about them.

Eleanor stretched her back and began to write. If she proofed and typeset tonight, she could print and dry the rest of the week. She guessed that she might be able to sell a hundred copies or so within the week--business had been good, and her distributor, the head of a gang of local street urchins, was asking for more of the entire booklet. She'd start with an appendix and then revise the entire book. Some people might buy the appendices and the new version, after all.

The next morning, she tucked her work apron and leather gloves over her arm and went downstairs, unlocking the door to the basement with the key that Mr. McAffrey had given her. She locked the door behind her, lit a gas lamp, opened the window that was barely large enough for a rat to slip through for some ventilation, and started type-setting.

It was a slow job; there was no getting past it. But Eleanor found that setting the type made her consider each and every one of her words. It sunk in that these were *permanent* things she was putting out into public for consumption; they shouldn't be taken lightly. After all, whispered rumors had destroyed many a lady's future-- printed ones were given more credence.

Words had power, and the words she wrote were no different. They entered the mind and worked their power, for good or for ill. Eleanor had heard the stories, the rumors--that *Mr. Pickwick's Guide* had been the downfall of several debutantes, while launching others to marriages far above their reach. All it took were twenty-seven letters, arranged in the proper order, to cause nagging doubts or the fulfillment of wild dreams. Eleanor didn't do it flippantly.

There were times when she doubted herself, doubted what she was doing. What if she'd gotten something wrong? What if she'd heard a false rumor that was posed as truth, from two or more sources? Eleanor did her very best to make sure that every entry in the guide was as truthful as possible. But what if...? It was times like those, when her doubts rose around her like floodwater, that she called her brother's wife into mind.

Her visage was easy to remember. Too easy, some days. Full, flowing black hair, blue, nearly violet eyes. Eleanor could remember the sneer that had curled the lady's full lips when her brother lay dying, weakened by grief and stress. Eleanor had asked that his wife go to him, reconcile, and nurse him back to health. But she had been a cold, heartless woman. Once she had stripped Lord Thomas Gilbert of all the family's carefully curated wealth, she had no interest left for him. So he'd died, overwhelmed by debtors, shame, and a broken heart. The woman had died soon after, and the paltry remains of the estate had gone to Eleanor's distant cousin in entailment. Eleanor was left to the charity of friends, friends who were quick to leave her alone.

Grief was such a messy thing, Eleanor reflected wryly. Some people could not navigate it, even if the grief wasn't their own. It was too hard for some people to come alongside in a time of great need--after all, it wasn't pleasant to think or speak of. It was a rare friend, indeed, who would take one's hand and wade through the murky waters alongside you.

So in the moments when she typeset, when guilt and fears and doubts started creeping in, she shut them out firmly. If she could spare even one family from the hell that had descended with her brother's marriage to that scheming harlot, she would take any risk. And she comforted herself by saying that if she printed a false review, those close to that Lady would know better.

She worked until her stomach was growling, until her fingers ached from pinching the small metal letters in and out of place. Then she dabbed on enough ink for a test run, placed the paper in the cradle, and pulled the lever. Eleanor loved this part, when hours of tedious, back-aching work culminated in a crisp sheet of paper with professional type. But she had to proof carefully, as the letters in the press had been laid backwards, and it was difficult to read entire passages thus. She'd gotten better at it, but she'd only done a page without mistakes once.

Eleanor closed the window, setting the latch firmly, hung her apron and gloves to dry, turned off the gas lamp, and pinched the proof on the corner where it was free of ink. The ink she used stained fingers, and she didn't want to have to explain herself when she visited Jane the next day. Jane already thought that she was clumsy enough.

When the door was locked, and she was seated at her apartment desk once more, Eleanor spread the pages out before her and read.

Lady C.B. was difficult to assess, as she is shy, and prefers books to people....

Chapter 6

From *Mr. Pickwick's Guide to Marriageable Young Ladies-*

Lady R.Y. is new to the London Season, and has already attracted several beaux. Although she has fit in well with the hustle of the city social calendar, it must be noted that her first love is the nature available only in the countryside. An avid gardener and equestrienne, she prefers long walks and cultivating roses to any ball or formal dinner.

"Come in, darling girl," the Marchioness of Millon called to Eleanor the next day.

Never mind that Eleanor was a year *older*, Jane still insisted on calling her pet names that insinuated she was much younger, or much lower in rank. Which, Eleanor supposed, she was. Not that anyone needed reminding of that, Eleanor thought.

Jane was seated in the room she called her pink parlor. Everything in the large space was either cream or a shade of pink. Between the cream-colored paneling were insets of pale pink silk. The carpet was abloom in tufted roses. The settee upon which she sat was a pink so pale it was very nearly white. And Jane herself was in an overwrought gown of burgundy satin and pink lace. It was enough to make Eleanor dizzy upon entering the room, but the entire tableau was meant to set Jane in the best light, to display the wealth of the family, and to make visitors feel inconsequential.

It certainly worked, for most people. But Eleanor and Jane had been friends since their coming out, five years earlier. That was Eleanor's first and only Season, and her brother's marriage and the tumult that followed, had cut it short. Jane had snagged her Marquess that very year, and had proclaimed herself Eleanor's dearest friend and savior ever since. Eleanor often wondered if Jane realized that she treated Eleanor much like one of her little dogs--a companion at her beck and call, who was only as valued as how entertaining or pleasant she acted at any given moment.

"Eleanor, my dear girl. I've been waiting all morning for you to arrive."

Eleanor approached the velvet sofa and gave a deep curtsy, lingering in the depths of it longer than she would have for the queen herself. She knew that Jane was easily gratified by such showings of flattery. Sure enough, by the time she straightened, Jane was smiling again.

"I'm so very sorry I kept you waiting, Jane. Cousin Bertrand's carriage was in use, and I had to hire a hack."

Jane made a little moue of distaste with her lips. "Poor dear. I sent for tea as soon as Stephens announced you. It should be here soon. You'll take yours with extra honey, to revive your spirits after such a dreadful journey."

"Thank you, Jane." Eleanor hid her smile.

If Jane only knew--Eleanor hadn't taken a conveyance at all--she'd walked all the way from her little apartment in Cheapside. Though she had the money to hire a carriage, she was now well aware of how quickly circumstances could change, and she'd never take income for granted again. She meant to save every last farthing she could while her Mr. Pickwick scheme was still working.

A maid with a stern face and a starched white cap bustled in with a tea service. Jane poured, and added a large dollop of honey to Eleanor's cup without asking. Eleanor would never tell Jane that she preferred her tea with cream, not honey--she took the cup and thanked her warmly.

"So, I'm glad you've come. I'm all a dither. Guess who is hosting a ball? Everyone who is anyone will be there. And this family hasn't thrown a ball since his mother passed. His sister and her husband, I wonder if they're in town? You shall come with me, and you shall have the aubergine gown that makes me look sallow. The Marquess cannot come, obviously, as he is in the countryside."

Eleanor was used to her friend's way of speaking, where questions were given with no room left for replies, where numerous threads of different subjects were woven together haphazardly to make a tapestry that only Jane could make sense of. It was frustrating at times, but Eleanor reminded herself that Jane was the only lady of consequence to show her any kindness.

She knew that Jane liked to excite, so she tried to sound breathless. "Thank you, Jane. How very kind of you to think of me. And I cannot possibly imagine whose ball we will be attending."

"The Duke of *Devonshire*," Jane said, with great relish, her blue eyes wide.

Eleanor frowned slightly. "I apologize. Is he the one with the red hair?"

"No, you ninny," Jane said, swatting at the air between them. "Devonshire is tall and broad, with dark hair. He's two and thirty, and has never married. Never seriously courted someone. Can you imagine how the mothers will be in a positive lather? The modistes will be absolutely swamped this week. Rumor has it, he prefers light blue gowns."

Eleanor thought she might remember the man, now. There were only so many single Dukes in London, after all. She thought she might have seen him across the ballroom several years ago. She remembered he was tall and handsome and well-dressed, but that was all she could gather at the time. There had been a sea of swirling humanity in between her and the man, and it had appeared, even then, that he was in danger of being overcome by the sheer number of silk-swathed ladies heading in his direction. It had reminded her of a painting she'd seen once, of a ship being swamped in a storm.

"And where did that rumor originate, I wonder?" Eleanor murmured, sipping her too-sweet tea.

"He once danced with Lady Susan, the earl's daughter, at a ball. Very rare for him. Very rare. Anyways, she was wearing a light blue gown, and he called it a 'fetching' color. I doubt London will have any light blue silk left by tomorrow."

"It is lucky that you have so many gorgeous gowns to choose from, Jane. It would be terrible to have to tramp down to the dressmakers this week. What a crush that will be."

That was another thing Jane liked--when Eleanor repeated her own ideas back to her as though they were facts. Eleanor sometimes wondered if her flattery were not *too* obvious, but Jane seemed to like it, and Jane was the only link Eleanor had to society. Were it not for Jane, Ida, Beatrice, and Emily, Mr. Pickwick simply would not exist.

"Ah, yes. I prefer to order enough gowns at the beginning of the social season so that I do not have to go back, no matter how many cotillions and salons I'm invited to. I don't want the modiste to rush my order along with six others. Did you know that Lady Anne and Lady Francis arrived at the Viscount of Hearthby's dinner party last week in the *exact same shade* of silk charmeuse? And green, of all colors! What either of the ladies were thinking when they ordered that fabric is beyond me. They looked like twin hills of Ireland."

"How embarrassing." Eleanor said, even though Jane had already told her the story. She made her eyes go wide. "What happened?"

"They were mortified, of course. Lady Francis finally had the presence of mind to fake a headache and leave before dessert was served. If she'd been smarter, she would have left before the soup."

Eleanor nodded.

"Now, you must help me choose which gown I must wear on Saturday. I'll need you to arrive before luncheon, and Hettie will help do your hair as well. I already have her taking in the aubergine."

"How wonderful," Eleanor said. "Thank you. Is it rare, the Duke giving such short notice for a ball?"

"It is. But then, it's rare that he invite anyone over at all. He's quite the hermit. Only stays in town long enough for Parliament, and is gone the very next day. Back to his manor. Chatsworth, I think it's called. Although, I'd probably leave London if I had a palatial estate to retire to, as well. I've heard the manor and the grounds are stunning. Also, if rumor has it, the house isn't quite so empty as it was in years past."

"How so?"

"Well," Jane said, leaning forward with a whisper. "It seems that a young boy now resides there. No more than five or six years old. They say that he's the product of a tragic love affair between the Duke and one of his servants."

"Oh, goodness," Eleanor said.

She knew better than to speak her true feelings, which was that it was amazing that the Duke was so popular with the ladies if this rumor was widespread. After all, who wanted a husband who philandered with the servants?

"It is exciting, is it not? The fact that he is hosting a soiree definitely signals his interest in society, which is more than he has ever shown before. He may be looking for a wife." Jane waggled her well-groomed eyebrows for emphasis.

"I'm sure that he will find many willing candidates among the *ton*," Eleanor said, taking another sip of tea.

Jane's butler, Stephens, appeared at the door. He was an aged man, with grey hair and a lined face, but his posture was as flawless and straight as one of the pillars in the corner.

"My lady, Lady Anne Sheffield, Lady Priscilla Downte, and Lady Millie Effens here to see you."

"Oh, how wonderful. Thank you, Stephens. Please have someone bring more tea and refreshments. Lady Anne does love cook's little scones, so please remind her. Eleanor, dear, would you mind giving up your seat for Priscilla? You know she likes to sit closest to me."

"Of course," Eleanor murmured, immediately standing and moving to stand behind Jane's settee.

She'd wait until all of the other ladies had chosen their seats and take the one left that was the least obtrusive. In the beginning, when

Thomas had first died, it had taken her by surprise to be set down by people she'd once called equals. But as a woman in London society, her value was directly tied to the highest-ranking male who had ties to her. And Eleanor had no one left who came close to filling that role. So, as she'd done a hundred times before, she stood and moved aside for those of higher rank. The sting, once fresh and painful, had been muted by time and repetition.

Stephens returned with three ladies. They were already chattering in the hall, and ignored him as he announced them to Jane. Each one was clad in the finest silk, feathers and trim, from head to toe. They looked like a trio of very expensive pastel birds. These were Jane's *real* friends, or at least, that was how Eleanor thought of them. All daughters of the peerage, they were all also married to men of means and titles--titles their sons would inherit someday.

Eleanor gave her best false smiles as Jane reminded the ladies of her name. They'd met dozens of times before, but it was a signal of how little they thought of her that Jane mentioned it. Eleanor took a seat at the far end of the grouping and settled in to listen with her lukewarm teacup.

"Can you believe that the Duke of Devonshire is throwing a ball?" Lady Priscilla took the closest seat to Jane. "I'm all abuzz."

Lady Priscilla fluttered her delicate, lace-covered fingers to accentuate her words. Then she patted her perfectly coiffed blonde hair to make sure none of it had escaped during her effusions.

"Eleanor is to be my companion for the evening," Jane said. "She didn't even know who Devonshire was--she thought he had red hair."

The ladies laughed.

"You've never been introduced?" Lady Anne said, with false sympathy. "You poor dear."

"No, which is why you will have to tell me all about him," Eleanor said. She was adept at turning veiled insults into opportunities.

"They call him Midas," Jane said, leaning forward. "Because everything he touches turns to gold."

Eleanor looked skeptical. "Surely not *everything*."

"It's true," Lady Anne said. "There are many who have taken to copying his investments, to try and replicate his success."

Eleanor wondered if Lady Anne was speaking of her own husband. Lord Sheffield wasn't known for his creativity or intelligence. Copying someone else's fiscal moves sounded like something he would try.

"Goodness," Eleanor said. "That sounds like a sound plan, if the man really is as gifted as you all say."

Lady Priscilla nodded. "He's legendary in monetary manners. Well, just look at Chatsworth, his country estate! It's said that the gardens there rival those of Versailles."

"I've never seen it," Eleanor said.

"Pity," Lady Priscilla said, shaking her head.

"So you have seen it, Priscilla?" Lady Millie said.

"Well, no, but I've *heard* all about it," she said, a bit defensive.

"Descriptions really are nearly as good as being there yourself," Eleanor said, trying to smooth her feathers. She'd learned that these ladies were prone to turning on the weakest if they felt cornered. "And proof that you have friends in high places. Versailles! Who can imagine?"

Priscilla pursed her lips, looking mollified.

"Darling, what are you wearing?" Lady Anne cooed, from her spot across the table. She glanced down at the half-spent tea service and pouted her full lips. "Where's the tea? Is it coming?"

Jane nodded at Anne. "I cannot believe Devonshire is having a ball, either. Has anyone a notion of why he's suddenly decided to break his social fast?"

"None at all," Lady Millie said. "I wondered if his fortunes were failing. You know that is part of the reason he has eschewed all society and gotten away with it. The man is richer than Croesus; he can do whatever he pleases. But I asked Lord Effens, and he said the man is wealthier than ever. Apparently, he invested in some scheme on the Continent that is doing exceptionally well. So it cannot be that."

"Maybe he's going to choose a wife at last," Lady Anne said, leaning forward in her excitement. "Why else would he have a ball?"

"I'd thought that, myself," Jane said. "Didn't I say that, before these ladies arrived?" She asked, looking to Eleanor for confirmation.

"You certainly did," Eleanor said, nodding dutifully.

"Exactly right," Jane continued. "But I just wonder about the *rush* of it all. And Lord and Lady Sheldon were supposed to have a dinner party that evening. But now it has been cancelled, and they will be attending the ball as well."

Lady Anne snorted. "Of course they wouldn't miss that chance. They've got five daughters, and only one's married off. Huge teeth, those girls, and terrible fashion sense. I don't envy the challenge of getting them married. They look like a bunch of horses dressed in last year's curtains!"

"Oh, but I grew up with Lady Dianne," protested Lady Millie. "And she's absolutely lovely. Did you know that she spends her Saturdays assisting at the orphanage attached to her church? She works right alongside the commoners they have working there."

"Well, that's no loss to her," Lady Anne said. "It's not as if she has other social engagements to attend to, no hordes of beaus waiting to take her to the park or ask her to go riding."

Lady Millie frowned at Lady Anne's cruel words, and Eleanor began to construct a new entry into her Appendix. She had heard that Lady Dianne Sheldon was kind, but that was only from a passing source. Eleanor made up her mind to inquire about her work at the orphanage. Perhaps there was room for one more entry before she published.

More tea was brought, with a tiered plate of scones, tea sandwiches, and delicate cookies. Jane poured in her theatrical manner, and Eleanor received a second cup, this time without the glob of honey, as Jane was too distracted. Things were looking up for her, until Lady Priscilla spoke up.

"Do you think that it is because of that blasted Mr. Pickwick?" she said.

Eleanor's throat seized up; she choked on her tea, but did her best to recover silently.

"Whatever do you mean?" Lady Millie asked.

"Do you think the Duke is throwing his ball because of Mr. Pickwick?" Lady Priscilla said. "There have been several gentlemen who have abandoned their seeming intendeds because of that book."

"And several more who have proposed, out of the blue," Jane mused. She narrowed her eyes and tapped her chin with a manicured finger. "You know, you might be right."

She pronounced this last statement with great surprise, as if Lady Priscilla very rarely had insights worth sharing. Eleanor schooled her face into bland neutrality, but Lady Priscilla beamed as if she'd been given a compliment.

"If you don't mind my asking," Eleanor said, her tone as gentle as she could manage. "I am not as well connected as you ladies. Pray tell, how many proposals do you ascribe to this Mr. Pickwick? Is he a matchmaker of some kind?"

Lady Millie's mouth dropped open in a decidedly unladylike manner. "You've never heard of Mr. Pickwick? He's absolutely all that anyone has been talking about."

"He's the writer of a review book that targets unmarried ladies," Lady Priscilla said. She'd leaned forward and wiggled her eyebrows for emphasis, to accentuate the scandalous nature of her report.

Eleanor endeavored to look appropriately scandalized. "I've never heard of such a thing!"

"And what's more," Jane said, looking eager to bestow new information. "Gentlemen are taking the advice in his booklet!"

"There's been *five* engagements so far that can be attributed to the infamous Mr. Pickwick. And at least as many courtships broken off."

"My goodness!" Eleanor said, shaking her head.

"I think that Priscilla may be right," Jane said. "Perhaps the Duke has chosen a bride from the pages of Mr. Pickwick and intends to begin courting her at the ball! Can you imagine? And everyone will be there to witness it! The ballroom at Netherton Hall is the largest in the county."

"I've heard that there are many rumors about how big the Duke's *house* is," Anne said with a sly smile.

The other women tittered, and Eleanor gave a smile, all the while thinking that sometimes, there was very little difference between people of the upper and lower classes. The same tawdry jokes, the same gossip...

"So you all are invited?" Jane asked. "You all are going?"

"Of course we are," Millie said, simpering. "It will be the premier social event of the Season. Especially if the Duke is finally going to single a lady out. You know that we may not be the only ones who have come to this conclusion; everyone will be watching him with bated breath."

"And the mothers will be doing everything in their power to put their daughters in his path. Especially my own," Anne said, rolling her eyes. "She's quite put out that my dear sister hasn't yet had an offer."

"Such a *shame* about her entry in Mr. Pickwick's Guide," Jane said, holding up her teacup to hide the smirk that Eleanor knew was there.

Eleanor suppressed a smile. Anne's sister was lovely, but there was no getting past her terrible personality. The girl looked as if someone were forever shoving pickled cod beneath her upturned nose--her lips were always twisted into a sneer, her chin lifted, and she looked down her nose at everyone and everything. Eleanor couldn't imagine a man who would shackle himself to that kind of attitude for as long as they both should live.

"Father has consulted an attorney," Anne said, her expression pinched. "He says that the besmirchment of Fannie's good name is a besmirchment of the family."

Eleanor's stomach flipped. Unlike the gossip rags who had the funds and lawyers to fight libel charges, Eleanor was alone. If the true identity of Mr. Pickwick were ever discovered, she would face charges in court. She'd be lucky to avoid transportation overseas, or even the gallows.

"I'm sure that Mr. Pickwick will be routed out, soon." Millie looked sympathetic. "And when he is, he won't be able to print any more of that scurrilous drivel. After all, they don't have paper and ink in prison."

"Although," Priscilla said, tapping her chin and pursing her lips. "It is interesting how many of the entries *are* accurate. Not the one about your dear sister, of course," she hurried to add, for Anne's benefit. "But the entry about Lady Miranda..."

Anne smiled, a wicked gleam in her eye. "Oh, *that* entry was well written. Miranda Mongarten is every bit the tart the book says. Surely *she* isn't the one that Devonshire has chosen as his intended."

The other ladies launched into an examination of which entries in the Mr. Pickwick Guide were correct. Oddly enough, they seemed to side with Mr. Pickwick on most of the negative entries, which wasn't odd at all when one considered that they had been the source of some of the information. As for the assertion that the Duke of Devonshire had singled out a bride simply because of the Mr. Pickwick Guide, Eleanor didn't know. It was possible, but she wasn't arrogant enough to think that a grandly titled man with extensive holdings and even a modicum of good looks would need to read a silly publication to decide on a wife.

The other men who had taken wives, she understood. Those men were ready to get married, ready to settle down. They just had buyer's anxiety, which was more than understandable. So many men found themselves married, for better or for worse, to a wife who had been better before the contract was signed--but who was now much worse. Those were the men she aimed to help--the ones who needed to marry, as her brother had, who had no clue that a beautiful face and figure did not equal a beautiful person; that marrying a beautiful woman did not guarantee connubial bliss.

"And have you heard about the scandal with Lord Avery?" Lady Anne asked.

"I heard he was newly engaged, but what on earth could have prompted him to do that?" Jane said.

And they were off, discussing the possibilities that may have caused Lord Avery to trade in his carefree days in the back of a barouche to marital responsibility.

Chapter 7

From *Mr. Pickwick's Guide to Marriageable Young Ladies-*

Lady W.P. is one that may be overlooked by all but the most astute observer. Recently from the country, she is not as accustomed to the London scene as others, and may not be suited to someone looking for a commanding hostess. But gentlemen, let me advise you--a kinder lady, one would be hard-pressed to find. Although her plumage is not as flashy as those surrounding her, she is a secret delight. The man who marries her will be continually gratified at the quiet, gentle care his household receives at her hand. She is one of the greatest hidden treasures of this Season--

compassionate to all those who cross her path, devoted to good works, and kind beyond comparison. She would be an excellent wife to one who values domestic tranquility over social flair.

Netherton Hall, the Duke of Devonshire's London home, was far grander than anything Eleanor had seen before. The house was made of smooth stone, with a grand facade of four stories and nearly a hundred windows facing the street. Eleanor had ample time to do the counting and calculation in her head while the carriage jostled and inched towards the front door. A steady, but slow parade of elegant carriages drove the long cobblestone drive and turned a lazy circle into the portico. Each one divested itself of its richly-attired passengers at the entryway. The massive front doors were open, and the golden light, strains of music and gaiety of the party spilled out onto the wide front steps, a tantalizing hint of what was to come.

Jane gave a smug smile as Eleanor let the carriage curtain drop to cover the window once more. "It is quite the sight, isn't it? I've been here before, when I called upon the Duke's younger sister after my marriage, otherwise even I might be overcome with the grandeur, too."

"It is impressive," Eleanor said. "You are very lucky to have seen it before tonight. I suppose that is befitting of your elevated station, however."

"Just so." Jane's chin lifted; she always had been prone to being swayed by flattery. "But I have never seen the ballroom, and I've heard that it is stunning. I was indisposed with my own wedding preparations when the Duke's younger sister had her wedding ball."

Meaning she wasn't invited, but Eleanor nodded. "I cannot imagine a busier time in one's life than preparing for a wedding."

"Maybe someday you will, dear," Jane said, with no real conviction, and patted her hand.

"Perhaps."

It was one of Jane's favorite pastimes, to remind Eleanor that she was one who *had*, while Eleanor was one who *had not*. It was an unfortunate social custom, a way of dressing down those around, and a way to make herself feel better. But Jane wasn't the only one who did it. The custom was not relegated just to those who had money or titles; mothers incessantly pointed out their ability to breed to wives without children; wives pointed out their own marital status to ladies who were still single. It was a disgusting form of self-assurance, and one that Eleanor abhorred.

"At any rate," Jane said. "We are very nearly to the front of the line. It shouldn't be long before we both have experienced all that Netherton Hall has to offer. I, for one, cannot wait to test the dessert buffet. Rumor has it that the Duke has two pastry chefs from France in residence."

"How wonderful." Eleanor fixed a serene smile on her face, as if she had nothing better to think about than French pastries.

The door was opened, the steps let down, and a gloved hand attached to an impassive footman was offered for their assistance. Eleanor allowed herself to be helped down out of the conveyance, and looked around with bright eyes. She tried not to smile as Jane smoothed down her dress incessantly. Jane was wearing light blue--a stroke of chance, no doubt.

Jane's gown was of the latest *mode*, with beading at the bodice and at the nearly off-the-shoulder neckline. The glittering jewels drew attention to the decolletage that Jane had assiduously lotioned and perfumed before they got dressed. Eleanor's dress was not nearly as stylish as Jane's, in color or pattern, but it was lovely all the same. It was dark purple, nearly the color of eggplant, with a rich sheen and full skirts. The neckline was high but wide, showcasing Eleanor's collarbones, and it had a line of cloth-covered buttons down the back.

Eleanor wasn't sure that she had ever worn anything quite as fine. If anything, it highlighted her dark hair and eyes in a fetching manner. Perhaps a little too fetching, as Jane had frowned at her for several moments before waving her off and telling her she looked 'fine enough'.

The carriage trundled off, waking Eleanor from her momentary reverie. She took one more look at the front of the house, then followed the Marchioness into the hall. There, they were divested of their wraps, but Eleanor was too distracted by their surroundings to pay much attention to the servants or the other ladies making ready. The front entryway was at least four times as large as her own apartment, and two stories tall. Wide windows were visible all the way at the other end of the house, and the floor was marble intricately set into a quatrefoil pattern. The walls were handsome wood paneling and covered in stately groupings of oil paintings.

Before she had collected herself, they were being ushered through a set of double doors. Eleanor stepped to the side to take a better look. Six crystal chandeliers, each the size of a small carriage, hung above the growing throng. The floor was sheets of bookmatched marble, with inlaid brass between. Three stories of windows faced the back wall, and the ceiling was coffered, with glints of what appeared to be real gold applied to the trim in a geometric pattern. The room could have felt cavernous because of the size, but the warmth of the candles and the gold detailing made it soft and romantic.

"Even I am impressed," Jane said, standing at Eleanor's elbow. "They say that his great-grandfather built this house as a gift for his second wife. Rumor has it, his first wife, who died in childbirth, was a terrible woman. The second wife, he loved."

"He must have loved her very much, indeed," Eleanor murmured. "This is beyond anything I've ever seen."

At both ends of the massive room, long tables spread the breadth, covered in crisp white linens and mounds of pastries on silver servers, here and there punctuated by a crystal punch bowl. Strains of music came from a large string section set up at the far side, and dancing had commenced. Below the music was the muted whisper of rustling silk and satin. Ladies' jewels glimmered in the candlelight, punctuating the fact that these were the most exclusive members of society.

"Oh, there is Lady Millie," Jane said, patting Eleanor's arm. "You don't mind if I leave you for a moment?"

Jane swept off without waiting for a response, but Eleanor was used to it. At every party, Jane asked her to come along for support and friendship. At every party, Jane found other people she'd rather spend time with, leaving Eleanor to fend for herself. Eleanor preferred it that way. She moved slowly toward one of the tables, letting her attention and her ears open.

It never ceased to amaze her how quickly people forgot that they were in public. If a grouping of ladies, or gentlemen, for that matter, were facing each other, they forgot that their words could often be heard by those behind them who cared to listen. And Eleanor always cared to listen. On her way to the punch table, she heard murmurs of the Duke's motivations--some people thought him searching for a bride, others claimed he was to announce a betrothal, or perhaps the birth of a nephew, as his sister and her husband had not been seen in London for a year.

Others spoke of Lord Avery's betrothal. It seemed that by now, most people had heard the story that the young lady's father had forced him to agree--some people thought it had been at the end of a rapier, others thought it was a pair of loaded pistols. But Lord Avery was set to be married in two weeks' time. There was also fevered speculation about whether the marriage would go uncontested, as it was rumored there was a dowager countess who had retired to the countryside. It was suspected that she was in confinement, and that the most likely father was Lord Avery.

By the time Eleanor reached the punch bowl, she was tired of hearing vicious rumors from the same prattling mouths. She accepted a cup of punch gratefully, and moved out one of the side doors, into the gardens. She always found a little time at any party to slip away alone, hopefully unnoticed, and just enjoy the quiet. Eleanor found she needed it sooner than usual on this night.

Truth be told, she was tired. Tired of fake friendships, looming bills, and being set apart. She didn't belong mingling with the *ton*, not any longer. She had once felt at home in grand houses, at frivolous parties, where she engaged in as much idle gossip as anyone. She had been born a lady, so now they tolerated her presence, as long as she followed their rules and stayed mostly silent. But these people would shun her if they knew her true living situation. All it would take was for one person to see her entering her tenement house. Or worse, for someone to discover that she was the infamous Mr. Pickwick! Were that to happen, she would be lucky to escape with her life.

But she didn't fit in with the people of Cheapside, either. Her manners were too fine, her habits and viewpoint too different. Granted, those people usually accepted her as long as she had coin. But even with Beatrice, Ida, and Emily, she felt the separation. After all, they had once been her servants. She was glad that she had been kind to them, that they had been true friends, even before her brother's death and the downfall of her family name, but she longed to be able to tell someone everything about herself without fear of rejection and ridicule.

She breathed in the night air that smelled of rich earth and jasmine, listened to the breeze as it gently ruffled the ferns around her. The cold of the marble bench was beginning to leach her warmth, but it was worth it for the peace alone. One of the reasons she loved gardens at parties was because they were an excellent source of gossip. But young lords and ladies sneaking off together usually happened later in the evening, once waltzing and secret flasks loosened the bonds of propriety.

Gardens were beautiful. It was nature, subdued. Eleanor could enjoy the sights and smells of nature without fear of wild animals or brigands. If anyone overtook or molested her here, she would scream, and then demand restitution or marriage. In the early days, she'd thought of doing that, of finding some poor, unmarried lord alone in the garden and forcing him into being caught in a compromising position. But she had no father, brother, or male relatives to force the man to do the right thing. She might find herself divested of her virginity, or worse yet--pregnant, without anything to show for it.

Now, she mainly thought of whether she could become a governess, a paid companion for an elderly peer, or maybe even a lady's maid. She snorted at the thought--she was nearly a companion for the Marchioness, but under the guise of friendship it was difficult to request payment. What did her future hold?

Chapter 8

From *Mr. Pickwick's Guide to Marriageable Young Ladies-*

It has been said that Lady L.O. has impossible standards for a match, but that is not the truth. After the passing of her late husband, the lady has come into her immense dower, and is wealthy in her own right. This, naturally, has attracted the attention of every penniless cad in the country, and several from abroad. However, if they had hoped to find a dim-witted lady in search of a smooth-speaking companion, they were sorely disappointed. The denied gentlemen have retaliated with the usual complaints against the lady--that she is sharp-tongued, a harpy, a cold and bitter woman. The real truth is that the lady wishes to make a match with an intelligent man of her own age, or none at all.

The Duke of Devonshire had been presiding over his ball for nearly half an hour, though no one could see him doing so. He was in an upper alcove of the ballroom, hidden behind velvet curtains, peering through a crack in the heavy fabric like some kind of peeping knave. As he was a Duke, it was his prerogative to arrive to his own party late, though his internal manners poked and prodded at him to get downstairs and greet his guests. But he knew it would be much more difficult for him to observe once he was swarmed by unmarried young ladies, as would be the case when he stepped foot downstairs.

It was a frustrating task. He didn't know quite what he was looking for, or whether he

MR. PICKWICK'S GUIDE TO MARRIAGEABLE YOUNG LADIES

would be able to spot it if it walked right in front of him. He didn't know if Mr. Pickwick *were* a woman, as he and Percy suspected, or if it were a man. Or maybe it was a grouping of individuals. He didn't know. His reasoning for throwing the ball instead of just attending one was thus--he could be sure, that should the individual responsible for the guide be a peer, they would be attending this function. Much to his chagrin, there was too much allure around his grand title and wealth for anyone to want to stay away.

He never threw social functions. He abhorred the inevitable cooing, the posturing, the falseness of the smiles. But he had a list of all who were here--his butler at the front door had asked for every name as they arrived. If Edward saw anyone looking suspicious, he could note it and investigate them further. Right now, though, it just looked like a regular ball. Nothing stood out as odd, except that an inordinately large percentage of the female population was wearing shades of light blue.

He frowned. "Huntley?"

"Yes, Your Grace."

"Did we include a dress code of any sort on the invitations?"

"No, Your Grace. It is assumed that most of the peerage know what to wear to a ball."

"Then why do you think they're all dressed in blue?" Edward said.

Huntley coughed, a sound that sounded suspiciously like it was trying to cover a laugh. Edward's eyes narrowed, even as he continued to study the crowd.

"I have heard it rumored that you prefer that color on young ladies, Your Grace."

Edward snorted. "You cannot be serious."

"I ascribe to always be serious, Your Grace. I can assure you that I am not jesting."

Edward rolled his eyes. "I cannot begin to imagine where some of these rumors get their foundation. I don't prefer light blue more than any other color, I assure you."

"Duly noted, Your Grace." Huntley sounded a little bit more amused than Edward would have liked.

"This is the problem with throwing a ball--everyone thinks that means you are interested in socializing. Or worse--getting married."

"A woeful idea, indeed, Your Grace."

Edward turned to scowl at the man, then remembered he only had a quarter hour or less before his absence would go from being fashionable to being flat-out rude. He studied the crowd, watching as silk and velvet draped ladies glided into the room and chose conversational partners. The young men congregated near the dance floor, where several groupings of hopeful young debutantes lingered, waiting to be asked for the next dance. The elder men were either dutifully at their wives' elbows, or were grouped together near doors, as if to make an early escape.

He nearly chuckled at that--at least he wasn't the only one who wasn't looking forward to the evening. But then his attention was arrested by two figures coming through the door. One was in the ubiquitous light blue with strategic glittering baubles to draw attention to her ample bosom. The other wore purple--a dark eggplant color that in this crowd, looked like a blot of oil in a light blue puddle. As he watched, the lady in blue excused herself from the lady in purple, and found a grouping across the room.

But instead of finding her own group of ladies, as Edward expected, the lady in purple meandered across the room, taking her time in doing so. Was she lingering on purpose, to try and draw a beaux's attention? Was she looking for people known to her? But no. Her head wasn't turning to look; her eyes weren't seeking out a familiar face. She was just walking slowly... and *listening?*

Edward's back stiffened. "Huntley, do you know that lady? The one there in the purple dress?"

Huntley dutifully approached the curtains and looked. "No, Your Grace. I don't recognize her."

"Please check with the doorman and see if he has her name."

Edward barely heard Huntley exit, so rapt was his attention. Yes, as he watched, she paused, tilted her lovely head, gave a small smile, then continued on. She was listening, and all of the groups that she passed by had no idea that they might be feeding the rumor mill that was Mr. Pickwick's Guide.

He studied the lady more closely. From his vantage point, he could only see the broad points of description. She had an abundance of dark, loose curls arranged artfully on the top of her head. A narrow waist, a pleasant figure, a modest yet beautiful gown. She wasn't dressed to garner attention, the way every other woman in the room was, and that was enough to convince Edward that she was different, at least. Different was enough to raise his suspicions, under the circumstances.

Edward watched her get punch, then walk to the double doors leading out to one of the side gardens. Was she the famed Mr. Pickwick? Was she meeting someone? Did she have someone who was in collusion with her? He straightened his cravat and turned toward the door. He aimed to find out.

"Pleasant evening, is it not?"

Eleanor jerked out of her reverie at the sound of the deep voice at her elbow. She looked up, then up again. The man standing at a slightly-less-than-respectful distance was tall, broad in the shoulders, and the kind of handsome that made Eleanor distrust him immediately. It was a masculine sort of handsome; far different than the current style of men looking like over-watered, under-sunned plants with feminine features. No, *this* man's brand of handsome was rugged, strong, and altogether too effective on her pulse for her liking. Her eyes narrowed.

His hair was full and dark, and disarmingly attractive because it was a bit overlong and swept to the side. Full lips were currently stretched into a blandly interested smile. He had a strong jaw, a prominent nose, and masculine eyebrows. But the truly arresting part of him were his eyes--a piercing green, ringed with thick, long eyelashes-- those were eyes that looked as if they wished to strip her soul bare.

"Do you speak to all the strange ladies you find lingering in the gardens alone, my lord, or am I a special exception? And if so, should I feel honored or alarmed?" Eleanor let the ire she felt at being surprised seep into her voice. She'd found that most men didn't like ladies who displayed intelligence, or worse, wielded it against them in conversation.

But the man just laughed. It was a deep, melodious laugh, one that told her he was genuinely amused. He wasn't laughing for politeness or to garner her favor. The way that her stomach twisted at the sound made her think that he was dangerous, and she needed to find the quickest exit to this conversation possible. She straightened her spine.

"I typically speak to whomever I choose. Whether you should feel alarmed or not, well, that depends on *your* motivations, not mine."

"*My* motivations, my lord?" Eleanor raised an eyebrow. "My motivations are to be left alone in the peace of this garden. We have not been introduced, and this conversation is quite improper. Good evening to you."

She turned her back, hoping that outright rudeness would succeed where her barbs had failed. She did her very best not to garner any attention--especially not attention from a large, attractive male. So far in life, she had succeeded.

But not with this man. Instead, she stiffened as she felt him sit on the bench next to her. She felt as tense as a drawn bowstring. She turned to him, her eyes wide, her mouth agape.

"Are you hard of hearing?" Eleanor snapped. "Or just daft?"

"I noticed you in the ballroom and followed you out here," he said, his voice low, intimate.

His words were warm and slow, like the syrup she used to drizzle over sweet cakes. Eleanor's eyebrows shot up. No one had ever spoken to her in such a tone, but she had heard that manner of speaking in many an overheard seduction attempt. Eleanor ignored the flutter in her stomach; it was deeply unsettling. Her frown deepened further.

"You must have me mistaken for someone else," she said, scooting away on the bench. "If we are caught out here together, it will go poorly for both of us. I am not looking to be married, and I am not the kind of lady one wishes to trap into a visit to the altar. I have no fortune, I can assure you."

"I have fortune enough for both of us." He slid closer and placed his arm along the back of the bench, behind her.

Eleanor could feel the heat coming from his arm. She could see deep into those green eyes that were inches from her. Were those flecks of gold, just around the iris? And why did the cool garden suddenly seem so *warm*? Her heart pounded in her chest, and her breathing increased. It was a very remarkable sensation--she'd never felt anything quite like it before. She felt cornered, provoked. She didn't understand what was happening, and it was happening too fast. Eyes wide, she panicked.

She drew back her fist and punched him in the face. "Get back, you great, big lummox!"

"Ow," he said, clasping his eye. "Why did you do that?"

Eleanor stood and shook her hand. "You...
you were trying to seduce me, and I cannot allow
that."

"I was trying to talk to you, you infernal
woman! I was merely flirting. Hasn't anyone ever
flirted with you before?"

She scowled. The truth was, no one ever had.
She'd been barely out when she was called away
from her Season for her brother's marriage. By
the time she'd returned to the social gambit, her
family's fortune was gone, and the scandal of her
sister-in-law had turned her invisible. No
gentleman wished to be attached to her in any
way, even if it was as simple as flirting. Now that
the scandal was years old, Jane was sure to
remind any single men who wandered in
Eleanor's direction that her circumstances were
'uniquely difficult'. And no man was looking for a
'uniquely difficult' wife who was on the cusp of
spinsterhood.

"Good heavens," he said, blinking up at her.
"No one ever *has* tried to flirt with you. I can
assure you, madam, your virtue was always safe

with me, but especially now. And for the record, flirting is often the best way to get information."

"Poppycock," Eleanor said. She set her fist upon her hip. "The best way to get information is to ask."

He studied her with narrowed eyes. Eleanor thought the sensation much alike to when Jane had taken her to see the royal menagerie. She'd stared deep into the eyes of a lion and had thought that he'd seen and noted all her secrets in a glance.

She looked away, discomfited by the notion. "What on earth could you possibly want to know? Who are you, anyways?"

"I suppose we are past the normal introduction phase," he said with a wry smile. "What with the fisticuffs, and all. I am Edward Dain. You are?"

"Eleanor."

She didn't wish to give her surname; at the mention of 'Gilbert', his attention would be snuffed out like a suffocated flame. And heaven help her, she didn't want this interlude, strange as it was, to end quite yet. Not that there was any hope in it. She'd *struck* the man. She racked her brain for any memory of an Edward Dain, but came up lacking. Surely, someone would have mentioned a young lord with his physical makeup. It made her positively breathless to look at him. He was too gorgeous, and she hated herself for noticing. If she stayed in his presence long, she was bound to do or say something else stupid, so she resolved once again to escape as soon as possible.

"Well, Miss Eleanor," he said, rising from the bench. "It is lovely to meet you."

He took her hand and leaned over it in a courtly bow. The heat from his hand seeped through her glove, and she was struck momentarily speechless. She couldn't even find the wherewithal to curtsy. All she could do was give a feeble nod and stare up at him. Goodness, he was tall. Broad in the shoulder, too. His silk brocade vest and fine wool jacket were impeccably tailored to his frame, and she would bet the buttons on her best coat that he wasn't wearing one of those silly male corsets, or padding along the shoulders or biceps. No, that was all *him* under the expensive fabric.

A blush dusted her cheeks, and he smiled at her as if he knew what she was thinking, knew that she was dazzled. That thought broke the spell. *Stupid height. Stupid broad shoulders. Stupid handsome face.*

She yanked her hand from his and stepped back.

"You said you wanted information, that was why you were flirting with me. What did you want to know?"

"I said I was *attempting* to flirt with you. Flirting is a two-way street, you know."

"Well, your attempt failed. What is it you want from me?" she demanded.

Eleanor felt overwrought from even several minutes in this Lord Dain's presence. She had broken all her own rules--never be noticed, never make a scene, no impropriety. Her access to the upper echelons of society was constrained to whether she could curry enough favor with the Marchioness. Though Jane said she was fond of Eleanor, she'd drop her like a hot iron if Eleanor made her look bad.

Then there was the man himself-- too tall, too broad, too handsome, too rich. He was too much of everything, and the ladies of the nobility would delight in eviscerating her if she and this man were even seen together. Men of his ilk were too highly valued for their attention to be wasted on someone like Lady Eleanor *Gilbert*. As of now, Eleanor was a barely visible, barely tolerated charity project of the Marchioness. If she smelled like even a whiff of competition for the attention of the small pool of male peers, she would be ostracized. Everything would be ruined.

"I want to know who you are," he said.

"Like I said, I'm Eleanor."

"Last name?" he said, his eyebrow raised in challenge.

"Gilbert." She said the name as if the gallows waited. She looked to see the inevitable change in his expression--the slamming of a door, the sliding on of a polite facade that masked the judgement--but he just frowned in thought.

"*Lady* Eleanor Gilbert?"

"Yes."

"Sister to the late Lord Thomas Gilbert? Daughter of Major Matthew Gilbert?" he said, his face a cool mask of indifference.

There was the change that she'd been waiting for. Before, his face had been alive with expression. She'd seen the range of it, all the way from interest to amusement to anger. But now, it was like looking at a painting.

"Yes."

"Very well," he said. "Enjoy your evening."

And he spun on his heel and left.

Eleanor staggered to the bench and slumped down upon it. She didn't know why she felt so disheartened at his reaction. Lord Dain was obviously a well-bred, wealthy man. Why shouldn't he ignore her, the second her identity was made known to him? But oh, before he knew... She shook her head. Her actions had been quite shocking, but who knew how frightening it was to be flirted with? Every lesson in deportment she'd ever had flew out the window when he'd looked at her with those piercing green eyes. It had triggered a reaction in her--she'd felt the need to defend herself, or flee.

Danger, that's what the feeling was. She felt that she was in danger--not of physical harm, per se, but danger of doing or saying something rash. Of laughing like a giddy fool. Of leaning into his large frame. Of running her hands all over his chest. Of kissing him.

So she'd smacked him in the face, instead.

"Oh," she murmured, her face in her hands.

She'd be thrown out of the party, any moment now. At the minimum, she'd be whispered and laughed at, and the Marchioness would sever any contact between them. At the worst, she'd be scorned and ridiculed. Either way, as soon as the story of her and Lord Dain in the garden got out, she'd lose one of her most valuable information sources. Mr. Pickwick would be ruined. *She* would be ruined. And the worst of it was, it wasn't because of her brother's death or her sister-in-law's treachery. It was because Lord Dain had *flustered* her.

Chapter 9

From *Mr. Pickwick's Guide to Marriageable Young Ladies-*

Lady N.H. is rather like a butterfly, both in beauty, fragility, and social habits. She enjoys the social whirl in London, and is uniquely talented at being liked by all. However, any man hoping to marry this lady must be gentle and patient, as she is sensitive and feels deeply. Much like the aforementioned butterfly, if you try and pin her down with rules and drudgery, you will kill her spirit.

Edward stalked toward the ball, heedless for a moment that he hadn't yet made an appearance there, and that his guests were waiting. He'd gone outside to follow a Mr. Pickwick lead, and had ended up with an even larger problem. *That* was Eleanor Gilbert? When had she grown up? He remembered the scandal better than others did, as Major Matthew Gilbert had been a childhood friend of his father's.

Edward's own father had passed before the death of the son and the ruin of the Gilbert title, thankfully. The title and lands that had been bestowed upon Major Gilbert were now entailed to a distant cousin. But he hadn't heard much of what befell the daughter. He remembered her only as she'd been as a toddling infant, before Major Gilbert had moved his family to the countryside for his wife's failing health. He might have glimpsed her upon her debut, years ago, but he remembered only a fresh-faced girl, still with the full cheeks of childhood.

She was no longer a child. Her form was slender and lovely, although maybe a trifle *too* thin. Edward wondered if she was eating well, if she was well taken care of. Then the thought, right on the heels of that one, was *Why did he care?* The lady was nothing to him, of course. Their fathers had been friends, long ago, but that was all. Still, the memory of her hitting him, *hitting* him, had him touching the small mark on his cheek with a smile. She had a fiery temper, a plain way of speaking that he enjoyed, and she had no desire to play the coquette with him.

She didn't even know who he was! Eleanor had sat, cool as you please, in *his* gardens, and demanded to know why he was bothering her. Of all the nerve! But through his irritation, he found himself wondering if she'd hurt her hand when she'd struck him, how she'd feel when she found out who he really was, and if and when he'd see her again.

It was a wonder they'd never met in society before. It was a wonder no one had married her. Although, perhaps the scandal was too great for some to forgive, even if she'd had no part in it. Did she have a fortune? How was she living? Her dress was fine enough--closely woven purple silk with a subtle sheen that set off her creamy shoulders and neck to perfection. In hindsight, he wasn't sure which would be softer to the touch, the expensive cloth or her flawless skin. Or maybe it was all those shining, dark curls that would be the winner. They certainly caught the dim light well. And the smell of her--soft and sensual, like lilacs and jasmine.

He hadn't meant to flirt with her. He hadn't meant to slide too close. And it wasn't like him to be overcome with the urge to do so. But when she'd scowled at him, when she'd turned her back, he'd found himself drawn to her--not because she didn't want him--he wasn't the kind of man who just enjoyed a chase--but because she was so honest in her reactions. There wasn't an ounce of guile within her. She showed what she really felt, and what she'd felt was irritation and confusion. When was the last time a lady had been irritated with him? He couldn't think of an example, except for his sister.

Edward caught his train of thought and frowned. He opened the door, and blinked. For a few moments, he'd forgotten that he had a ballroom full of curious guests awaiting his arrival. Then the wall of sound and light and smells hit him, and he schooled his features into pleasant aloofness.

"I say," Percival said, gently bumping his elbow. "Are you not looking forward to an evening of being pecked over by London's finest? I've been asked by no less than eight women when they might expect your presence, and four gentlemen want to speak to you of measures in Parliament or various business ventures. And those are only the ones who had the courage and dexterity to trap me into conversation as I dodged and weaved through this cacophony of humans. I swear, being your closest friend is trying sometimes."

"I'm sure," Edward said, dourly.

"But the free food and drink go a ways to repair things between us. And there *are* a bunch of beautiful ladies tonight." He frowned. "Although, it is deuced difficult to tell them apart when they're all wearing the same color. Ah, here is my sister. I took the liberty of assuming that you will dance your first with her. That way, you will both be safe from the social piranhas, at least for one song."

Lady Candace Waldrey shared her brother's reddish blonde hair, but their personalities could not have been more different. Where Percival was playful and sarcastic, Candace was gentle and kind. Edward wondered if she felt she must make up for her elder brother's carousing by striving to be good. It was a safe thing, this idea of dancing with Lady Candace. They had grown up together, and had a sibling-like affection for one another.

Every other dance would have to be managed with careful analysis, lest he pay too much attention to one, and not the other. Dancing with the daughter of a political supporter, for example, was sure to please, as long as the lady in question didn't set too high of hopes on him as a match. Then, she would be heartbroken, and that father would show less support. It was a delicate balance, all of it, and Edward had seen individuals fall from grace for small, stupid social gaffes.

Edward bowed over Lady Candace's hand. "You are looking exceedingly well, tonight, Lady Candace. May I please have this dance?"

"You may, Your Grace," she answered, with a smile.

He led her out to the dance floor, which was already crowded with couples. "I hope you are enjoying yourself?"

"Of course. We were ever so grateful to be invited."

"And is your dance card full, my lady?" Edward teased.

Candace was a favorite with the gentlemen this Season, to the everlasting chagrin of her brother. It was a hard thing, being the brother of a young debutante. After all, an older brother was cursed with the knowledge of the motives and thought processes of all the men seeking the sister's attention. And no one wanted their sister to be *snubbed*, but having her be the center of an ever-increasing crowd of young beaus was difficult to stand as well. It was all a brother could do to not flail into the fray of bodies, throwing kicks and elbows, when one of them looked at her too long.

Candace blushed prettily. "Nearly, Your Grace, but Percival was insistent that I save one for you."

Edward was grateful for the minutes of music, for him to clear his mind of that blasted Lady Eleanor. He had a long night of socializing in front of him, when all he wanted to do was look for the Mr. Pickwick writer or corner Lady Eleanor in the gardens for a far more delightful outcome than their first meeting. Eleanor was wearing gloves past her elbows, and he had a sudden, vivid image of him plucking at the fingertips of those gloves and pulling them slowly down her arms.

"Your Grace?" Candace's question brought him out of his reverie.

"My apologies, Candace. I was thinking of something else."

"Obviously," she said, a smirk on her face. "You didn't hear my question about your new horse at all."

"Oh, you mean *Percy's* new horse." Edward nearly rolled his eyes. "He talked my groomsman into purchasing the thing, supposedly under my orders. I told him that it wasn't my fault that his stables are completely full. He says he is going to sell one of your mares, after she's done foaling. Pardon me, my lady, for mentioning that."

It was an empty apology, they both knew, as Candace was as passionate about horses as her brother. She was often present for such events, but that was the only thing about her which may be thought of as unladylike.

"Not at all, Your Grace."

"Regardless, he insinuated that I would be selling Peaches to him as soon as he had room to accommodate her. The knave. Between you and I, I'm going to allow him to sell his mare. Then, and only then, will I inform him that I've grown accustomed to Peaches, and that I'm keeping her."

Candace's tinkling laughter rose about the dancers like a silvery mist. Several heads turned in their direction, speculation warm in their gazes, but Edward just joined in her humor with a smile.

Eleanor finally got her courage up to enter the ballroom. There wasn't any sense in sitting outside in the cold, catching a chill, when the story had most likely already spread throughout the room. The damage was done, and there was nothing left but to face the music. It wouldn't be nearly as bad as the first year after her brother's death. The rumors wouldn't be as thick; the whispers wouldn't be as vicious. But she was sure to hear, as she had when the title had been entailed away, that her family was somehow cursed, and that is why calamities seemed to follow them.

She slipped in through a side door, took a deep breath, and headed toward the punch once more. To her surprise, it was as it had been before. No one whispered. No one even looked at her. Perhaps the story hadn't made it back to the Marchioness yet. Perhaps there was still time to repair her reputation. She could tell Jane that some knave had set upon her in the gardens, and that is why she had hit him. Maybe Jane would side with her just this once.

Then, a tinkling laugh filtered above the crowd, and many heads and eyes turned in that direction.

"It's the Duke," one lady whispered to another. "Dancing with Lady Candace Waldrey. Don't they make a fine couple?"

Eleanor was as curious as the next person, so she turned toward the dance floor. She was familiar with Candace Waldrey, having written her an excellent review only months prior. Lady Candace had red hair, so it only took her a moment to find her on the floor, and she was dancing with... *him*. Lord Edward Dain.

Except the lady had called him the Duke. That couldn't be right... could it? Because if it were so, she had just struck the wealthiest, most powerful man in

England, other than the king. Her eyes went wide and she inhaled sharply as she watched him dance in the same way he walked and moved-- powerfully, with just a hint more aggression than society dictated. She swore he'd somehow heard her, because over the shoulder of his partner, his eyes met hers and his eyebrow lifted, as in challenge.

Eleanor had never fainted, not once. Not when her mother or father had died, not when her brother wasted away, not when she was cast out of her childhood home. But she felt she was in danger of doing so now. She took a deep breath as she swayed slightly, turned, and made her way to the front door. She'd never abandoned the Marchioness at a party, either, but she would tell the servants to alert the lady that she'd gone home ill. Eleanor had enough in her purse to hire a hack to take her home.

Edward watched her go, even as he danced with Lady Candace. Lady Eleanor wove through the crowd looking less than graceful on her feet. Despite the impossibility, he wanted to quit the dance and go assist her. Was she well? Had she damaged her hand that severely when she'd hit him? It had certainly felt as if her hand could withstand the blow when he'd been on the receiving end of it. In fact, she'd hit him surprisingly hard.

What was more perplexing than anything was that she'd completely thrown him off his hunt for Mr. Pickwick. Yes, Eleanor had been listening at the ball, but he supposed that she was still the shy girl that he'd remembered from years ago. She wasn't the type to set herself forward like this brazen Mr. Pickwick character. He'd taken one look at Lady Eleanor in the garden and all cunning, all rational *thought* had flown from his mind.

He still wasn't quite sure why he'd tried flirting with her. Of course, that was before he knew who she was. He'd never have done it if he had known it was Lady Eleanor Gilbert sitting there. But she'd cut a fine figure, and truthfully, he'd *wanted* to flirt with her. Until she'd hit him, that is. Apparently, he was a twisted individual, because her striking him just made him want to know her more. He couldn't name many women who would dare strike a man before they knew who he was, in order to protect their honor from *flirting*.

No, the women of his acquaintance were usually all too ready to set aside their scruples in order to snag a wealthy husband. He could have performed that tableau with every woman in this crowded ballroom, and only a few would have resisted his advances. And that included the married ones. Women, and men, for that matter, looked at Edward for his title and wealth. They never came to him honestly, without some sort of an agenda.

But Lady Eleanor had sussed him out. Even though she didn't know who he was, she wasn't an idiot. She could see that his clothing was of the finest make and tailoring. He didn't know one woman who couldn't spot a wealthy man by finish alone. And they had been alone. All she would have had to do was lean in when his arm was around her, and kiss him. Then screamed and waited for them to be discovered, and the irate relatives would come out of the woodwork, waving the marriage contract...

Wait. Lady Eleanor *had* no relatives, at least, none that he knew of. Edward frowned at the thought. What did a young lady with no relatives *do* when her protection and income were gone? Most situations like that resolved in the woman becoming a governess, but Eleanor was far too young and beautiful for that. He doubted any wife worth her salt would let a lady with half Eleanor's beauty reside in the family home.

So how was she here? Who brought her? Where was she living?

"Your Grace," Lady Candace said. "I believe your attention is lacking."

"I'm sorry, Candace. I was woolgathering."

"About that young lady you were watching, I gather. I wouldn't have mentioned it, only there are some speculative looks on matron's faces at the moment, and I don't want you or I to be the subject of tomorrow's gossip pages."

Edward glanced around quickly, and saw that Candace was right. An inordinate amount of the female attention was cast in their direction.

"I don't think anyone noticed exactly who you were looking at," she continued, airily. "Only that you were looking at someone else, and have been deep in thought ever since. That would have been bad enough, but then you *frowned*."

"I'm sorry, Candace."

"Smile, Your Grace," she said, then she laughed.

He managed a grin, which felt so false it would crack his face.

"That was more like a grimace," she said cheerfully, her beatific smile still in place. "But it will do at present. Now, on to the young lady. Is there anything I can do to help?"

"No, not at all." He was in danger of frowning again.

"Smile," she reminded. "Please forgive me for saying so, Your Grace, but there has been a great deal of speculation as to motive behind you throwing a last minute ball such as this. Lovely as it is, there are many who thought that you needed an opportunity to woo a certain lady. Still others thought you were further along in the process, and wished to announce an engagement in a public manner. But I see the truth of it, now."

Her teasing manner and twinkling green eyes provoked a real smile. "And that is?"

"You haven't even *started* wooing said lady. You've only begun the chase."

Chapter 10

From *Mr. Pickwick's Guide to Marriageable Young Ladies-*

Lady A.B. is lovely and cultured. Her laugh reminds one of tinkling bells. She seems as if she might make the perfect wife. Gentlemen should be advised, however, that this lady has a particular distaste for children that goes far past 'children should be seen and not heard'. This lady believes that children should not even be seen. She has expressed on numerous occasions that should she be forced to bear any of the "disgusting brats", they will be quickly squirreled away to a different estate, where they will be tended to by servants.

Eleanor's nerves were still rattled when she called at the Marchioness' house the next morning. She would have preferred to stay abed all day, until her headache subsided, but she needed to return the ball gown. Jane had it tailored to fit Eleanor, but as was her style, she hadn't officially gifted it yet. Jane never settled for one profusion of thanks, when she could quite easily have two.

Stephens led her into the dining room, where Jane had just sat down to breakfast. Eleanor didn't point out that it was noon; truth be told, the coffee, eggs, and bacon smelled incredible.

"My dear," Jane said, waving at her servants to set a place setting for Eleanor. "What on earth happened last night? Are you well?"

Eleanor was surprised to hear the genuine concern in Jane's voice, and to her mortification, her eyes began to well with tears.

"Oh dear," Jane said. "Sit! Sit and tell me. Mrs. Brooks, we need tea *and* coffee this morning."

"I'm sorry," Eleanor said, taking her seat and clearing her throat. "I'm not ill. At least, nothing more than a headache. I just felt so poorly last night, and then couldn't sleep at all."

That much was the truth. Eleanor had tossed and turned so much that she thought she would awake the downstairs neighbors with the squeaking of her brass bed.

"That is *terrible*," Jane said. "I'm sure that we will quite set you to rights. You need a hearty breakfast, tea with lots of honey, and some coffee. We will take care of you until you feel completely better."

"Thank you. I was so worried that you wouldn't... that you wouldn't care to receive me this morning, after... after I'd left in such a manner."

"You silly goose. Of course I'll always see you. You're my very closest friend."

Eleanor blinked up at her through her tears, but Jane seemed quite sincere.

"Am I, really?"

Jane looked perplexed. "Of *course* you are. And why did you tote that gown all the way over here? You know it is my gift to you."

"Thank you," Eleanor said, meaning the words with all her heart for the first time in a very long time.

Jane might be blind to the truth of Eleanor's situation, but she did seem to care, at least a little. The gravity of her Mr. Pickwick gamble was setting in, like a wine stain in fine lace. There was no taking it back, what Eleanor had done. She wondered if she'd done the wrong thing. After all, it wasn't only *her* reputation she was risking. The Marchioness regularly invited her to gatherings, and they'd been seen together on multiple occasions. What would happen to Jane if someone found out her close friend was the one publishing reviews on young ladies? A pang of guilt resounded deep within her stomach.

"In fact, I am so glad you are here. You missed a lot, you see. I don't believe I saw you in attendance after we parted ways. Is that right?"

"I had some punch, then went to the garden to get some fresh air. But I just felt worse, and that's when I had to leave."

Jane smiled as if Eleanor had given her a gift. "Then I get to tell you all about the Duke's strange behavior that evening."

Eleanor felt a swooping sensation in her stomach, but managed her expression and took a sip of heavily honeyed tea. "Oh?"

"He danced his first with Lady Candace." Jane waved the name away as if it were inconsequential. "She's a close friend of the family; almost his sister. But he wasn't attentive to her at all. In fact, he was staring at a lady in the crowd nearly the whole time."

Eleanor felt her eyes go wide. She hoped it looked like avid interest and not terror. "Who?"

"Well, the Countess Marbury swore up and down that it was none other than Lady Beverly Shaw. You know, the widow of the late Lord Shaw? And I think it is quite possible that she was right, for he danced with her on his sixth."

"My goodness, six dances?" Eleanor said.

She ignored the pit in her stomach at the thought of six different women in his arms. She was stupid to feel that way--she had no claim on him.

"He was an unusually attentive host, once he'd gotten over his momentary distraction," Jane said. "He greeted nearly everyone, and only began to dim the lights at three o'clock. It's a wonder if anyone who was there last night made it to church this morning." She punctuated the statement with a ladylike yawn.

"And what of Lady Shaw?" Eleanor couldn't help but ask. "Did she seem pleased by his attentions?"

"Who wouldn't be?" Jane scoffed. "He bowed over my hand but once, and I wished myself young and single again."

Eleanor blinked, then laughed, trying to soften Jane's statement in front of her servants. Really. Sometimes she didn't seem to think.

"At any rate, Lady Shaw became the belle of the ball. All the ladies were trying to get close to her, to see if they could spy which detail of figure, face or dress had captured His Grace's special attention. And all the gentlemen clambored to ask her for a dance, whether to steal her away for themselves or foster the goodwill of a potential duchess, it's hard to say."

"Quite," Eleanor said. "I don't know the lady. What do you know of her?"

Jane needed no further prodding, and launched into a detailed account of the woman's appearance, (blonde hair, striking blue eyes, ample bosom), her history (married in her first Season to the now-deceased Lord Shaw, two sons), and her likes and dislikes (did you know she's never worn velvet?). Eleanor nodded along, trying desperately not to dislike a woman she'd never met.

And why would she dislike her? Eleanor and the Duke had shared but a few sentences, and that had ended abruptly with her striking him in the face, and him storming off once he learned her identity. The scoundrel had begun a conversation with a strange lady by *flirting*, for heaven's sakes! He was the sort who was quality in title and holdings alone. And it wasn't her fault that she'd felt a little dizzy and warm during their interlude--she was more inexperienced than some young misses making their debut. She'd never been wooed, not once. She'd mostly been ignored, or whispered about. If she had the choice between the two, she'd choose being ignored every time.

"...and she does the promenade nearly every day, as her townhouse is just a block over from the square," Jane finished.

"But what kind of person is she? Is she kind? Smart? Funny?" Eleanor asked.

"Dear heavens. I've only spoken to the lady in passing. How should I know? The Duke seems to prefer her, and that's all that high society cares about. There's even some speculation that Lady Shaw might be the mother of the Duke's by-blow that he stores at Chatsworth manor."

Eleanor had to work very hard to keep a straight face. Jane spoke of the child as if he were a spare horse, or a carriage.

"Regardless," Jane continued, her eyes twinkling. "I fear that is the last time I will enjoy such a public spectacle for some time."

"Oh?" Eleanor said.

"Yes. I am to enter a period of time in which I will be unable to see all but the closest of friends and family."

"You don't mean..." Eleanor said, sitting up straight.

"Yes, I do. But don't tell anyone, as even the Marquess doesn't know. I've sent him a letter at Bath, and I suspect he will be home as soon as he receives it. Can you imagine? An heir!"

Eleanor nodded and smiled and effused her congratulations. She was happy for Jane, really, but she had to push down the pain that she felt in order to properly articulate the words. Eleanor did her best not to dwell on the life that she might have had, if her brother had chosen better when he married.

She tried not to measure her own existence against that of Jane's, but it was difficult to do. After all, they had debuted at the same time, and for awhile, they had done everything together. It stands to follow that Eleanor might have found someone to marry, given a chance. But after the destruction and shame that followed, no one was brave enough to have her. No one had been brave enough to hardly *speak* to her.

And now Jane was taking yet another step ahead, and Eleanor... well, Eleanor was in the same place she'd been. She tried to tally her wins, but the losses seemed so much greater, especially in the light of everyone else's successes. All the ladies of her age seemed well married, most having their second or third child. Eleanor remained and remained and remained, watching those she'd once call peers make progress and move forward and celebrate all the things that she'd once dreamed of. But perhaps she was the only one who remembered that she'd once had those dreams. Everyone else, if they thought of her at all, thought that she was content.

It felt like the smile and congratulations that she offered Jane flayed her own heart.

Chapter 11

From *Mr. Pickwick's Guide to Marriageable Young Ladies-*

On Lady J.M.- not enough can be said about this lady's kindness. She is an angel to everyone around her, whether animal, child, servant, or peer. If a gentleman were looking for a marriage that would lead to nearly guaranteed domestic harmony, this lady should be high on his list.

Edward dressed and went to his study early. He hadn't been able to slip away last night--every time he'd tried, there was another mother herding her progeny in his general direction, an overstuffed waistcoat wheezing about Parliament, a blushing miss oh-so-accidentally meeting his eye with a maidenly blush. All he'd thought of was Lady Eleanor Gilbert. What, he had wondered, did Mr. Pickwick have to say about her?

He finally was to have his answer. He reached for the booklet and flipped through the worn pages.

Lady E.G. is rarely at social events, preferring, it seems, to stay home and read religious anthologies alone. While passably attractive, this lady is not overly gifted in either intelligence or personality. It is no wonder that she is more or less a lady's companion these days, though one wonders if her friends are bored with her presence. After a disastrous first Season out, she is now a banal fixture in the

London scene-much like a piece of furniture in the corner that takes up space, but is ignored.

That's it? Edward thought, blinking. He reread the entry, convinced that he had missed some lines, and finding no more, frowned. Mr. Pickwick had missed the mark on this lady, it seemed. The Eleanor Gilbert who had cuffed his eye last night in the garden deserved more credit than she'd received. The entry struck him as odd--perhaps because it was the first one he disagreed with.

A shrill voice echoed down the hallway, and Edward tossed his well-thumbed copy of Mr. Pickwick into a smooth-sliding drawer. The door banged open.

"Have you seen this?" Lady Teresa Bunt said, flinging a copy of *Mr. Pickwick's Guide* onto Edward's desk.

"Lady Teresa Bunt to see you, Your Grace," Huntley said, most redundantly.

"Thank you, Huntley," Edward said, dryly. "Please shut the door."

The servant did as he'd asked, and he and the dreaded woman were alone. She stood there, color high on her cheeks, hands on hips that had only rounded slightly with the birth of his half-brother five years prior.

"Well?" she fairly screeched. "What do you have to say for yourself?"

"I have seen it," Edward replied, calmly, folding his hands carefully on his desk to help resist the urge to throttle her. "I'm looking into the source of the material, but I'm curious as to why you think I have to defend myself."

"Have you read my entry?"

Her blue eyes, so beguiling and soft when she had a mark, were flashing and narrowed in his direction. He noticed that she had new lines on her forehead. Her beauty was just beginning to fade; she'd better find a new sap quickly, lest she lose her ability to entrap anyone.

"I've read the entirety," he said, his voice low.

"Then you've seen the proof of your own betrayal!" she hissed.

He raised an eyebrow. "My betrayal? Whatever do you mean?"

"Read it again, then!" she said, yanking at her bonnet strings and throwing the straw contraption to the floor.

He dutifully flipped to the correct page and read.

Lady T.B. is the epitome of classical beauty with blonde hair and pale blue eyes. Do not let her ethereal appearance fool you. Underneath this pale perfection is the heart of a viper, one that has entrapped men of the highest echelon. This lady is a social climber who is not nearly as pure as she appears. Her perfidy knows no bounds.

"And?" he said, lifting his head once he was finished.

"Where did those scurrilous writers find out about Henry if not from you?" she shrieked. "We had a deal, Your Grace. I let you care for my son, and you paid for that privilege. But we both agreed to keep the deal secret. And here I find out that you've not kept your side of the bargain!"

Edward kept his face impassive, though his temper flared. "My family is not the only one that you've targeted over the years, Lady Bunt. Perhaps it was one of the others where the rumors began. Maybe the Earl of Winthrop? Or perhaps Lord Avery? Or maybe it was Baron de'Heanreux?"

Teresa's face flushed with rage. "You dare…"

"I *do* dare, madam. You forget your place with me. I paid you off once, and it won't happen again. As for my silence, I've kept my quiet. These reports haven't come from me or mine, so they've most definitely come from your other indiscretions."

"I'll go get him! He's my son, after all! You can't keep me from him if you didn't keep our arrangement!"

Edward's composure broke. He leapt up and strode towards her. She gave a little cry and tripped, falling backwards into a leather armchair.

"Madam." Edward's voice was lethal, cold. He towered over her and placed one of his large fists on each armrest, caging her in. He didn't care that he was frightening her. She *should* be scared. "This is the last conversation you or I will ever have, so listen very carefully. Should you go anywhere near my son, I will have your neck snapped and your body thrown to wild dogs."

Her eyes went wild. She'd never seen him lose his temper. She opened her mouth as if to argue.

"Don't say a word. I am deadly serious. There is nothing I wouldn't do for those I love. He is beyond your reach. He is not your son. I care not that you bore him, nor do I care that I did not sire him. He has been raised by me and my sister. If I hear that you've broken your silence on this fact, I will have you bound and gagged and shipped to the colonies in steerage. You are nothing but a scheming, conniving whore, whose greatest achievement was seducing my father before he passed. You are never to come here again, and if you do, I will deal with you severely. You will not see another farthing from me."

Her mouth opened and closed like a fish out of water. Her eyes were wide. He stood, straightened his jacket and cravat, and returned to his place behind his desk.

"Besides," he said. "I've done a very careful job of placing rumors that Henry is *my* son. And who do you think will believe you? Everyone who knows the truth is dead or on my payroll. Now get out before I lose my temper."

She burst into tears, her chest heaving as she rose, swiped her bonnet from where she'd thrown it down, and flounced away. Huntley was waiting to escort her from the house; Edward knew she wouldn't have a chance to steal anything on her way out. After the door was secured against her rantings, he sat back at his desk.

His hands were shaking, and he balled them into fists to make them stop. He'd never lost his temper with a woman before, not even her. Not even when Teresa had shown up at his father's funeral, several months pregnant and told Edward the whole sordid story. She threatened to scream it to the houseful of guests and mourners present if he didn't take her in.

Edward hadn't known what to believe. His father had been a good man, but he did enjoy women. He'd mourned for Edward's mother after she'd died, but years later, had taken up with a widowed Countess. It wasn't until his father's old valet had corroborated Teresa's story that Edward came to terms with it. She was going to bear his father's child, and she wanted a fair sum of money to do so quietly.

It had been Edward's idea to buy the child outright. He'd sent Teresa away, to one of his properties in the north of Scotland to wait out her confinement. And even then, he'd hoped that she was lying, that he was somehow paying for the care of another man's mistress. But the baby had been born, and Edward had but to look at the boy to see the truth--Henry was his father's son. Dark hair, thick eyelashes, and when he got a bit older, the eyes had confirmed it--piercing green, just like his own.

Once Teresa had more than taken advantage of his good graces--six weeks after the birth of being coddled by servants, with maids and a nanny and a wetnurse to help-- he'd informed her that she needed to leave. She'd wailed then, too; destroyed the bedroom, even going so far as to tear down the curtains and their hardware. But Edward had seen enough of her those first few weeks to know that he didn't want that woman near his half-brother. Her influence was pernicious, damning. He would raise the boy as if he were his own child, not Father's.

She'd demanded a princely sum, and he'd paid it, unblinking. But he made her sign a paper stating that he was the father, and consulted with his barrister regarding the arrangement. The staid, learned man had agreed there was nothing that Lady Teresa Bunt could do to steal dear little Henry away from him, short of getting the valet to testify. When Edward had presented the idea to the valet, the man had snorted in disgust, which was the most emotion Edward had ever witnessed from him in nigh on thirty years.

"I'd sooner put my own head into a slop bucket, Your Grace," the notoriously prim valet had stated. "I knew that woman was terrible from the start. A funny thing, that the worst ones are often the most prodigious breeders." Then he'd clamped his thin lips shut and refused to say more on the matter.

Edward wouldn't see his family torn apart or his late father's reputation ruined by that tart's accusations. Whether or not she could prove them was half the point; London society was like a great steam engine that ran on gossip. The more you fed it, the faster it went and the more fuel it wanted. One sniff of a scandal and neither he or Henry would be rid of the stench for years.

It was this reason that Edward had been searching for the infamous Mr. Pickwick. He hadn't shown it to Teresa, but the entry written about her did concern him greatly. What if someone out there knew their secret? What if there was someone else who could come forward as a witness for Lady Teresa, to help steal Henry from him? That would be the best thing for Teresa, fiscally speaking. If she could get control of Henry, get the courts to recognize her as the mother with the father of the child deceased, Edward would have to pay to keep Henry *and* Teresa in the lifestyle Henry deserved. Finances aside, for Edward could certainly afford to house, educate and feed a thousand of his father's by-blows, Edward didn't want Teresa sinking her hooks into the boy.

Henry was kind and gentle. He loved his pony and adored his 'Papa', as he called Edward. He loved his Auntie Amelia and Uncle Lucas. He was being taught everything he needed to know, being raised as a gentleman, for that is what he would be. He couldn't inherit the title--his birth was on the wrong side of the sheets--but Edward had written a generous addendum in his will. Henry could choose a career and live very well for the rest of his days. Edward now wanted to ensure that those days would be free of his grasping, conniving mother.

So he was determined to flush out this Mr. Pickwick and find out how much he (or she) knew about his family's connection to Lady Teresa Bunt.

He didn't like to admit it, but his attention was now somewhat divided by his altercation with the interesting Lady Eleanor at last night's ball. Most of his servants were still recovering from such a party. It had lasted interminably long, and some people had far too much fun at the expense of his wine cellar. His steward of house, Chester, had reported that a lady's shoe had been discovered in the shrubbery of one garden, and a discarded set of stays had been found in the gardening shed. If Mr. Pickwick had been present at the ball, he definitely got his share of gossip.

Edward sent for his secretary, Andrews.

"Yes, Your Grace?" Andrews said, at the door within five minutes.

That's one of the things Edward loved about Andrews--no matter what time of the day or night Andrews was needed, he'd show up within ten minutes, perfectly pressed, wire spectacles on the end of his nose, hair strictly parted and combed down upon his head, and a leather folio in his hands. But even above his punctuality and impeccable presentation, Edward valued Andrews' efficiency and discretion most of all.

One thing that Edward's father had drilled into him was the importance and difficulty in finding staff that were effective and loyal. Once you had such a person in your employ, his father would repeat, make them so happy they wouldn't dream of leaving. Edward strove to do so.

"Thank you for coming, Andrews. Please close the door and sit."

Andrews nodded, sat, and waited expectantly. Under Andrews' careful gaze, Edward suddenly found himself at a loss for words. How to begin? It was a strange request, at best.

He rubbed the back of his neck and grimaced. "There is a lady of my acquaintance that I wish to know more about."

Andrews expression didn't even flicker. He flipped open his folio, took out a pen, and looked up. "Very well, Your Grace. What information do you have, and what would you like to know?"

His secretary's brisk questions helped alleviate Edward's embarrassment. "The lady's name is Eleanor Gilbert. Her father and mine were friends when I was young, but the late Major Gilbert moved to the countryside, Atworth, I believe, for his wife's health. The lady passed a few years later, but the family never returned to London, until after the Major's death. Her brother was Lord Matthew Gilbert. He married an Italian woman, Maria or Margrite something or other...do you remember that scandal? It was five or six years ago now."

Andrews' pen flew across the parchment. "I believe I do remember hearing something about that. He died not long after, and the title was entailed to a distant cousin, is that correct?"

Along with his efficiency, Andrews had a mind better at retention than any vault.

"Yes. Anyways. The lady was present at the ball yesterday."

Andrews head snapped up, and his eyes showed their first hint of interest. "Oh?"

"I just realized that I had no idea what had become of her since her brother passed. The family wasn't wealthy apart from the entailment. With whom is she living, and how did she end up as a guest in my home?"

Andrews bent his head over his notebook once more. "So is there anything specific Your Grace wishes to know, or would you just like a general appraisement of the lady's situation?"

"She was acting a bit strange..."

Andrews met his gaze once more and frowned. "Are you suspecting her of thievery or other nefarious intentions, Your Grace?"

"Not at all," he said. "In fact, I have little doubt that Lady Eleanor is very *strident* when it comes to morality."

Andrews' eyebrow raised. "Strident, Your Grace? How so?"

"I witnessed the lady strike a gentleman who was sitting too close to her on one of our garden benches."

Andrews' eyes flickered down to the light bruising high on Edward's right cheek. Edward thought he saw the man's lips tremble slightly, but then it was gone. Edward decided to ignore it; he found he didn't really want to know if his secretary was laughing at him.

"How intriguing. I will be sure to make all of my inquiries as discreet as possible, Your Grace. May I ask how much detail you require, or how soon you should like a report?"

"I'd like as much detail as is possible, without raising any sort of attention toward the lady or myself. Discretion and speed are of the utmost, Andrews."

"You shall have them both, Your Grace. Is there anything else?" Andrews stood.

"No. Thank you, Andrews."

"Of course, Your Grace." Andrews bowed and took his leave.

It was evening before Eleanor extricated herself from Jane's home. Despite being fed well, Eleanor was exhausted. She'd listened to all of Jane's hopes and dreams for her future, holding a smile on her face that she did not feel inside. She adjusted the large, paper-wrapped parcel she carried against her hip. Jane had insisted that Eleanor take the aubergine gown, as well as a day dress that was getting tight through Jane's middle. Eleanor wished she could refuse; it seemed to add insult to her already injured psyche, but a quality dress was a quality dress. She was not yet financially comfortable enough to turn down expensive gifts.

Though she was tired, she walked. It was a clear night and not yet cold. There would be days ahead where she would need to hire a hack, and she best save her farthings where she could. After all, with Jane's confinement came her own. She would no longer have access to the elegant parties, balls and dinners to which Jane typically invited her. She would only have the scraps of gossip that were delivered upon the lips of Lady Anne, Lady Millie, and Lady Priscilla.

Eleanor didn't have high hopes.

She turned onto Marberry Street, and as she did, the back of her neck prickled in awareness. Eleanor had learned better than to ignore that feeling, so she stopped and turned. There was nothing behind her out of the ordinary--a couple heading into a restaurant, a small boy with a basket--nothing that would suggest any form of danger to her. Still, she quickened her step.

It was one of the things she never could have foreseen, the dangers that existed for women alone in the city. It was something she'd never considered before she'd lost her fortune. After all, there were always people about when one had money. There were maids and footmen, butlers, cooks...and all of them were there as layers to insulate the valued members of the house from the realities of life, especially the dangers that men with ill motives posed to women.

She didn't want to think about such things tonight. All Eleanor longed to do was to heat some water, brew some tea, and bathe. She didn't have access to a large copper slipper tub like in her previous existence, but she could make do with a small, circular tub that was large enough to stand in. How refreshing it would be to wash the past couple of days from her skin! She kept the thought of a warm fire and hot tea in her head as she rushed home through the thickening darkness.

She didn't see that the boy with the basket followed her all the way from Marberry Street to the front of her tenement. Eleanor didn't know that he sat himself on a pile of rubbish and studied the windows, noting that not long after Lady Eleanor entered the building, a light was lit in the attic. And she couldn't have known that he circled the building, looking for an easy way to enter.

Chapter 12

From *Mr. Pickwick's Guide to Marriageable Young Ladies-*

It would be impossible to discuss Lady V.O. without mentioning how talented she is in musical pursuits. Whether piano, violin, or flute, this lady has never met an instrument she couldn't play with absolute mastery. However, it is the other, more important qualities of said lady that are truly lovely. She is absolutely gentle, wishing to believe the best in everyone. If she has ever had a harsh word for anyone, we haven't been able to find a report of it. It would be best for her to marry a clever man, lest others take advantage of her overflowing kindness. Any man would be lucky to have such a sweet-

tempered lady as his wife--it would be impossible not to love her.

Andrews knocked on Edward's study door at ten o'clock the next morning. By the tight-lipped frown that dominated his usually stoic features, Edward knew that he wasn't going to like what Andrews had to tell him.

"Out with it," Edward said once Andrews was seated.

Andrews slid some papers across the desk and began to read notes from his ledger. "The story of Lady Eleanor Gilbert is a sad one, Your Grace. Sadder than even I knew. She was born to, by all accounts, loving parents. Her father had distinguished himself in the war and was given a barony, but you already knew that. After her mother died, when she was aged five, and her father died, when she was aged twelve, she fell under the care of her brother, the new Baron, Lord Thomas Gilbert. When she was eighteen, she was presented at court and set to have a London Season. However, her brother announced his impending marriage just weeks later, to a Marguerite Savoney, and called Lady Eleanor away to the countryside. Thomas and Marguerite were married, and from the start, the woman proceeded to run the family into financial ruin, as well as having several poorly hidden affairs. Within a year, the coffers were empty, and Thomas took ill and died. Many claim it was a broken heart. The title was given to the nearest male relative, a horse breeder out of Chauncey, a Mr--now Baron-- Desmond Fife. Lady Eleanor returned to London where she stayed for a month with the Marquess and Marchioness of Millen, at which time she had overstayed her welcome and found new lodgings with an old war friend of her father's, a Mr. Daniel McAffrey. She lives in an attic apartment in Cheapside, with twenty pounds annum and some worthless stocks to her name, and the only reason that she was at your ball is because she acts as a sort of erstwhile companion to the Marchioness of Millen when the Marquess is away, which seems to be often."

Edward's mind was swimming with information. *That* lovely woman, living in one of the roughest neighborhoods of the city? With twenty pounds a year to sustain herself? How on earth was she managing such a thing? Twenty pounds a year was abject poverty. He wasn't sure you could feed a small dog for twenty pounds a year, let alone house one and keep it warm.

And in Cheapside, she would be exposed to all kinds of degradations--whores and thieves, cutpurses and cutthroats. No wonder she'd learned to throw a proper punch! Edward shook his head at the thought. No young lady, a former friend of the family, no less, should be forced to eke out such an existence.

"And all of this is reliable information?" Edward said.

Andrews raised his eyebrows.

Edward said, "I should have asked--is there any more we can find out?"

"What more would Your Grace like to know? It will be possible to search her rooms, but not before the lady exits the establishment."

"What kind of man is this Mr. McAffrey? What happened to her sister-in-law? How is she existing on twenty pounds per annum? Is there anything else I need to know about... her character?"

"Ah," Andrews said. "I will keep digging until there is no more digging to be done. I did think that you would want to have all of the information I possessed immediately. Her sister-in-law died in a carriage accident years ago. As for this Mr. McAffrey, he is old and barely squeaking by, himself. I believe the young lady subsists mainly upon the charity of the household of the Marchioness. She takes many meals there, and the Marchioness gives her castoff clothing."

Edward winced. "This will never do."

"How so, Your Grace?"

"I don't know. I will have to think on what you've told me. Where does her twenty pounds annum stem from? Is there any way to substantially increase that number without her knowing the source?"

"I will comb her financials as soon as possible, Your Grace."

Edward sat in silence, marred only by the ticking of a clock, for long minutes after Andrews took his leave. Eleanor was living in poverty, and she wasn't doing it in the comfort of a relative or friend's home, like so many of the peerage did if they fell on hard times. She was living in an attic in Cheapside. Wasn't it only last week that three people died in a tenement fire there? His fingers drummed against the polished wood of his desk.

And why was he so concerned about her, anyways? They'd spent five minutes together in a garden, at which time she'd hit him hard enough to leave a bruise. He'd gone around telling everyone that he'd struck his face on a low-lying branch. No one, not even Percy, knew the truth of it. Andrews is the only person who might suspect that he'd spent time with the lady or spoken to her at all.

It would stay that way. He didn't need his staff gossiping within their ranks, or his sister getting her foolish hopes up. He still hadn't forgotten that he'd been looking for Mr. Pickwick when Eleanor had caught his eye. Was it possible that she was supplementing her meager income by printing salacious booklets? The idea made him scoff, but he couldn't disregard the notion. After all, people would resort to desperate measures to provide for themselves.

How could he get to know her better? He couldn't very well send an invitation around to her address. She'd know that someone had discovered her secret. And an address in that part of town was most definitely a secret. Even a dear friend couldn't overlook that amount of scandal. Edward tried to remember if he'd ever met the Marchioness. He was sure they had met, but he couldn't remember when. He had a remembered impression of blonde hair and a grating, obsequious manner, but that was all. The Marquess was older than Edward, and they knew each other from Parliament. Perhaps he could call upon the man, time it so that Eleanor was in the house at the same time?

And then what? Ask her how she was surviving on twenty pounds a year? Ask her if she was Mr. Pickwick?

Well, why not?

Edward straightened. She struck him as a plain-speaking lady. She certainly hadn't minced words in the garden. Maybe it would be a relief to confess, if she were Mr. Pickwick. Perhaps she was in over her head, and was wishing to unburden her conscience. Edward rolled his eyes at his own thoughts. Of course she wouldn't confess. Anyone who took such great pains not to be discovered; anyone who used different paper so that the source couldn't be traced... this was a person who was protecting the longevity of their business.

He couldn't blame the person. If he didn't have a vested interest in finding the person who wrote the reviews, he wouldn't have bothered. It seemed that the excerpts were written fairly, and just because some houses were in an uproar because their daughter was outed as unsuitable--that didn't bother him a whit.

Why should it? His sister was safely married, but even if she hadn't been, he knew her to be sweetness personified. Her nose was a trifle too large by society's standards, but who cared about that? Looks failed as one got older, and if he were to ever pick a bride, he would be looking for kindness and intelligence. That was the kind of thing that could be passed on, taught to their children. Looks were secondary.

Unbidden, an image of Lady Eleanor arose in his mind. Her soft-looking skin, luminous in the moonlight. Her gently curling hair, beautiful eyes and full lips. She wasn't society's standard of beauty, either. She wasn't blonde, blue-eyed, short and curvy. No, Eleanor was taller than most ladies, with a gently curved figure that he wished to sit closer to. And the way her eyes flashed when he'd been impertinent! He smiled just remembering it. That was the kind of woman who would make 'til death do us part' interesting.

Good heavens--where had *that* thought come from? Edward ran a hand through his hair and rang for tea. He needed to distract himself, keep himself busy until Andrews had acquired all of the information.

Chapter 13

From *Mr. Pickwick's Guide to Marriageable Young Ladies-*

.

Lady K.D. is on her third Season, which makes one question the intelligence of eligible gentlemen in London. Though some pernicious matrons call this lady 'quite on the shelf', nothing could be further from the truth--she is just waiting for a man of worth to woo her. While not the classic standard of beauty in this fickle age, she is highly intelligent, witty, exceedingly loyal, and perpetually pleasant. She has been running her father's large household for years with great aplomb, as her elder brother has yet to marry. It is hard to imagine one better suited to a seamless transition into wife-and-

motherhood. She is the perfect blend of responsibility and amusement--her lucky husband will never get bored speaking to her.

The next morning, bright and early, the little boy sat in the park that faced the handsome row house, and waited. He'd watched all yesterday, too, at the bequest of his employer. He didn't mind. There was nothing unpleasant about sitting on a comfortable bench amongst budding trees and greenery, watching the comings and goings of a household. They'd even been so thoughtful as to pack him a lunch of a fresh meat pie and cheese. He had but one mission--if a certain lady came walking to the front door, he was to bolt round the corner, where the man with the horse was waiting. That man would take care of the rest.

And at half past two o'clock, the boy saw a female coming down the street who fit the description of the one he was supposed to look out for--brown hair, nice figure, a lady. He scampered across the street to get closer. He needed to get a better look. There was a hedge tall enough for him to duck against without being seen.

"Lady Eleanor," the old butler said, in greeting. "I'll let the Marchioness know that you are here."

The boy sprinted down the street and around the corner.

Though Edward knew that it had been a possibility, his heart still thumped an erratic rhythm when Andrews brought the news.

"She has just arrived, Your Grace," he said, walking briskly into his study without waiting for an answer to his knock. "It will take you twenty minutes to get there by carriage."

"Have my horse saddled," Edward said, pulling on his gloves and hat. He swung his overcoat about his shoulders.

Fifteen minutes later, Edward was standing on the top stoop of the Marquess of Milton's townhome. The door was open, and he was facing an elderly butler.

"The Duke of Devonshire to see the Marquess," Edward said.

His voice and face were carefully controlled. He didn't want to give away the pounding of his heart, or the excitement of doing something even remotely scandalous. The butler too, had schooled his features into neutrality. Only the speed in which he delivered Edward's calling card on a silver tray belied his surprise that a Duke was on the doorstep.

Edward took the time alone to study the home. It was a large, comfortable looking house. The floors were polished wood overlaid with thick carpets. The hallway was wallpapered in muted tones, the better to offset the watercolor paintings hanging there. They looked as if they were all done by the same artist, and he wondered if the Marquess or the Marchioness were responsible for the pastoral scenes.

The butler returned within moments. "This way, Your Grace. The Marquess will host you in his study."

Edward followed the man to a large room lined with wooden bookshelves. A fire crackled merrily beneath a large stone mantle. The Marquess was still straightening his cravat when they entered, and Edward suppressed a smile.

"My Lord, the Duke of Devonshire." The butler gave a short bow and left, closing the door behind him.

"Your Grace." The Marquess of Millen gave a nod.

Millen was a short, stocky man. He had light brown hair that was scattered through with grey and closely cropped to his head, and a golden brown tan with freckles across his nose. Edward remembered hearing that he loved the countryside, and his horses.

"Lord Milton, thank you for seeing me on such short notice," Edward said.

The Marquess blinked. "Of course. It is nothing but an honor. Please, sit. Would you like tea or brandy?"

"Tea would be excellent, thank you." Edward sat in a chair facing the man's desk while the Marquess rang for tea.

"I must confess I'm surprised at your visit," the Marquess said. "I don't believe we've had the pleasure before."

Edward nodded. "My estate and matters of Parliament keep me from socializing as much as I'd like. I believe that I was lucky enough to see your lovely wife at the ball at Netherton Hall this past week. However, I was disappointed that you were not in attendance."

The man looked chagrined. "I am sorry, Your Grace. I was not in town."

"Of course. I was disappointed because I wished to discuss Parliament business with you."

"Oh?" The Marquess' expression had gone from embarrassed to hopeful in a second flat. This was not a man who spent much time at poker tables, but Edward found his honest manner refreshing.

"Yes. You see, there is a new bill up for debate, regarding horses..."

For the next hour, Edward drank tea and asked questions of the Marquess to which he already knew the answer. By feigning ignorance and asking for his advice, Edward hoped to endear himself to the man. It didn't seem to take much, and to his surprise, Edward found that he enjoyed the man's insight on the proposed regulation of horse importation and breeding. In fact, he was enjoying the conversation in general. The Marquess seemed to be an affable man with pleasing manners and a keen insight into the proposed legislation.

"So I am much in favor of the regulations, Your Grace," the Marquess concluded. "While inconvenient at the outset, it will protect those who are interested in preserving excellent bloodlines in stock, while making it nearly impossible for swindlers to lie about a horse's origins."

Edward found himself nodding. "Very compelling, thank you. I found that I could not clearly sort the pros and cons, as I am not a horse man, myself. I enjoy riding, but I've never been as interested in the breeding and rearing as some are."

"Quite right," the Marquess said. "I'm so glad to have been of service."

"I wonder," Edward said, looking at his pocket watch. "Would it be an imposition for me to greet your wife this afternoon? I was pulled away in the middle of a delightful conversation last Saturday, and I wished to apologize. You know how it is when one is a host."

"Of course," the Marquess said. Although it was a strange request, the man seemed delighted that Edward wished to be of greater acquaintance to them. "Let me send my man round and see if she is taking visitors."

They waited for only a moment once the message was relayed.

"This way, Your Grace," the Marquess said, heading for the door.

Edward couldn't help it; his smile turned a little feline and his heart beat faster.

Eleanor was seated on the velvet sofa furthest from Jane, a lukewarm cup of honeyed tea in hand. Lady Millie, Lady Anne, and Lady Priscilla were in chairs and seats closer. They were *still* discussing the Duke's ball on Saturday night--what people had worn, who had danced with whom and how often, the delightful array of desserts... Eleanor thought she'd scream if someone mentioned how light the puff pastry had been one more time.

A maid bustled in, approached the Marchioness' chair, and whispered in her ear.

"Oh!" Jane exclaimed, sitting up and pinching her cheeks. "Oh! Please do. Yes."

The maid bustled out again, and Jane began fluffing her dress, smoothing her hair, and adjusting her posture.

"Sit up, ladies," she hissed. "We're in for a treat."

The door opened, and it was the Marquess...and *him*. Eleanor felt it when his eyes met hers, and he gave a little smile. It wasn't a friendly smile, per se, but rather, it was the smile of the hunter sighting prey. Eleanor inhaled sharply, grateful that his eyes went next to Jane's and remained there. In fact, Eleanor doubted that anyone had seen the brief interlude. They were too busy standing and giving their very best curtsy, which Eleanor hastened to mimic, her teacup clattering in the process.

"Ladies, may I present His Grace, the Duke of Devonshire," the Marquess intoned. "Your Grace, this is my wife, the Marchioness of Milton, Lady Anne Sheffield, Lady Priscilla Downte, Lady Millie Effens, and Lady Eleanor Gilbert. My dear, His Grace wished to continue the conversation that was interrupted at the ball on Saturday."

"Oh," the Marchioness said, only looking slightly surprised. "Yes, of course."

Eleanor knew that Jane wasn't surprised that the Duke wanted to speak with her; Jane thought *everyone* wanted to speak with her. Rather,

Eleanor thought that she was wracking her brain, trying to remember a conversation that had never occurred.

Eleanor couldn't explain it, but there was something deep down inside her that whispered that the Duke was there for *her*. But that didn't make sense. She didn't even know the man. The first time she'd met him, she'd *hit* him, for goodness sakes. And anyways, there was no way that he would have known she was even here. But that little voice inside her wasn't one that listened to reason. She struggled to regain the thread of the conversation.

"...and the puff pastry was so *light*," Lady Millie said, looking enraptured.

"Thank you," the Duke said. "Although I cannot take any credit for that. My pastry chefs, Mr. and Mrs. Durand, came to me from Paris years ago. Now, I fear I cannot go a whole week without one of their croissants. They are kind enough to travel with me between houses."

As he finished this statement, his eyes lighted upon Eleanor. She thought he was looking for some sort of reaction from her, but she only raised her eyebrows in bland politeness.

"How wonderful," Lady Anne said, fluttering her eyelashes.

"Your Grace," Jane simpered. "I know that our cook is not from France, but her scones are still delightful. Would you care to stay for tea?"

The Marquess opened his mouth, as if to say something, but Edward was quicker.

"I'd love to, Lady Jane. That is, if you ladies don't mind including us boorish men into your delicate circle."

All the ladies excepting Eleanor rushed to assure the Duke of his welcome. Jane signalled her maid for tea with a slightly manic gesture. The Duke smiled at each of the ladies in turn, a slow, sensual turn of the lips that was more brandy-warm than honey-sweet. Eleanor thought that Lady Priscilla was in real danger of wetting herself from sheer excitement. Even Lady Anne looked like she might pass out from the rapture of being in his presence.

Eleanor couldn't blame them; she'd felt a faint fluttering from her stomach when he'd smiled at her, too. She took a mental stick and beat those butterflies to death before they could take up permanent residence. She had more important things to tend to than the whims of a Duke. Eleanor thought, for one horrifying moment, that the Duke could hear her thoughts. His smile seemed to change when he looked at her--it turned more towards a baring of teeth in challenge. She gave him another watered-down smile.

"Excellent," the Duke said, taking the spot next to her on the settee.

He sat so close that his knee bumped hers in the process. Eleanor subtly adjusted her posture so that they weren't touching. Even still--the heat from his knee had sent a tingle racing down her spine. What was the idiot doing? Any small impropriety, any lingering look, any physical contact--no matter how small or casual--would set the gossips to work. They'd run themselves ragged trying to suss out the minor intricacies of any relationship between

Eleanor and the Duke. And they were sitting with three of the biggest gossips in society.

Even now, Eleanor could feel Lady Anne's eyes upon her. Eleanor knew what the woman was thinking... why had the Duke chosen to sit right next to Eleanor, the only unmarried lady in the room, when there were plenty of other spots? And why had he deigned to sit so *close*? Even the Marquess had chosen a sofa upon which no one resided. Eleanor knew that the biggest part of the charade would rest on her shoulders. If she reacted to him, if she blushed or looked flustered, that would only fan the conflagration of gossip that threatened to break out.

It wasn't her reputation she was worried about; there would be little better for a young lady than to be attached--even in conversation-- to the most eligible bachelor in the peerage. But Eleanor knew how these things worked--every lady in the know would outdo each other with how much new information they could present. Eleanor had even heard of situations in which venerable gossips had paid their footmen to follow the subjects of the latest fervor. What would happen if someone were to follow *her*? Not only would they find out her true residence, but she would be in danger of exposing Mr. Pickwick, as well.

"Eleanor," the Duke began, sounding as if he had not a care in the world. "It was so good to see you and to renew our acquaintance at the ball."

Eleanor smiled at him, but it was a close-lipped, furious thing. How dare he use her Christian name, when she had given him no leave to do so! How dare he do it in front of these women! It would be all over the city by nightfall. Damn and blast this man! How could he?

"You see," Edward continued. "Eleanor and I are old family friends. Her father, the late, honorable Major Gilbert, was very close friends with my father, the late Duke. I can remember little Eleanor toddling after her brother and I as we played hide and seek in the stables. She was like a little sister to us both at the time. I was very sorry when the family moved to the country. Atworth, wasn't it?" he said, looking at her innocently.

If Eleanor hadn't known better, she would have believed the wide eyes, the sincere tone, the polite smile. But this man was showing her that he was in charge of this interaction. He was proving that he could do something as scandalous as use her first name, in company, but that he could then smooth the whole thing over, so no one would think anything of it. In short, he was toying with her. She had no memories of their families being close. But what choice did she have, but to go along with it?

"Yes, Your Grace," she said, coolly. "Although, I must admit that I don't remember you at all. I must have been too young. It was kind of you to have us reintroduced at the ball. And, in honor of our fathers' relationship and the sisterly affection you feel for me, I will try to become accustomed to the use of my Christian name. You are one of an elite circle of company who deigns to do so--these honorable ladies included."

Eleanor had learned that flattery was nearly as important as not being noticed. When in doubt, add flattery, was her motto. She couldn't help but notice that the ladies all looked gratified, even though only Jane called her Eleanor.

"I am charmed to be included in such an illustrious grouping such as this," Edward said, nodding to the ladies. "And I hope that our mutual acquaintance shall continue. I have..."

Here, he frowned and studied his teacup. The look of uncertainty made everyone lean slightly forward, even the Marquess. Eleanor's eyes narrowed. He was too good; better than she was, maybe. He had them all eating out of the palm of his hand.

"I have been looking for a group of individuals who I might be able to call friends," he finished. "It is so difficult to find an inner circle one can trust."

An inner circle! Eleanor had to call upon every ounce of self control she had so that her face didn't show her surprise. The impudence of this man! He hadn't been introduced to these ladies for more than ten minutes, and he was calling upon them to become his *inner circle*? She couldn't be the only one who found this strange...could she? But they were all nodding. Lady Anne looked like she was going to have an aneurysm brought on by happiness. And no one was paying much attention to Eleanor, which was a wonderful thing.

"We are *honored*, Your Grace," Jane said, breathlessly. "London society is a tricky thing to navigate without the right friends by one's side."

Eleanor did her best not to snort into her teacup. He was a *Duke*, for heaven's sakes! And by all accounts, he could have bought the Royal Palace twelve times over. There were some who whispered he was wealthier than the crown! Were these ladies so self-involved that they would not question *why* he suddenly wanted to make their acquaintance? It was so strange, so beyond the realms of normality, that Eleanor could barely keep from laughing.

"I thank you," Edward said, with a solemn nod. "I confess, I came here today to ask the Marquess' opinion on the new import regulations…"

Here, Jane gave her husband a glowing smile and looked as if she might swoon from pride, and the Marquess looked suitably gratified.

"...but I never thought I would have the chance to meet such an esteemed assembly of ladies such as yourselves. I can see that this is an intelligent household. The Marquess has given me wonderful advice, and the Marchioness has chosen wisely when it comes to her circle of friends."

There were flutterings, and demurring murmurs among the ladies. Eleanor took a deep breath and let it out slowly, lest she roll her eyes so hard on accident that they fell from her head.

"Eleanor," he said. "I hope you will not find it too forward of me. I've written my sister, and she and her husband are to come to London and stay for some time. I know that she will be thrilled to see you once more. She did used to dote on you so. Will you be available to join us for some celebrations during their stay?"

Every eye was upon her, she could feel it. And what else could she say? He was a Duke, after all. There was nothing about his behavior that was anything but charming and delightful. Only Eleanor knew the truth. She smelled some sort of trap, but couldn't imagine what he was getting at. Why her?

Why was he haranguing her into social engagements, and a false closeness? It made no sense. Was he *that* bored?

"I'd be delighted, Your Grace. Please send your sister my warmest regards," Eleanor said, managing another tight smile.

She could have sworn she saw the corners of his mouth waver at her expression. He was *toying* with her, the great brute! But to what end?

"Excellent," Edward said. "Now, Lady Anne. What of your husband? Is he busy as of late?"

The next half hour was pure delight to all of the ladies, excepting Eleanor. As Edward charmed the ladies, and they fawned over him in return, his knee kept creeping closer to Eleanor's skirts. He never looked at her, not once. But he had to have known that the ever-encroaching knee was tormenting her. She shifted positions several times, but by the time the tea had been served (with great flourish by Jane), his knee was touching her skirts once more.

Eleanor breathed deeply and fought the urge to blacken his other eye. Lady Millie had the temerity to bring up the mark upon his face.

"Oh, a pesky branch hit me while I was out in my gardens. Fear not, my lady, I have plans to make the branch pay..."

All of the ladies laughed, but Eleanor nearly shivered at the dark promise in his words and voice. Was that it, then? Was this torment payback for striking a Duke?

"Perhaps the branch thought you had it coming, Your Grace." The words were out of her mouth before she could stop them, the challenge clear in her voice.

Her eyes went wide. She had been doing so well not engaging his pointed remarks, as she was the only one who truly understood them. The room went silent for a moment, then the Duke laughed, and the other ladies joined in.

"You see?" Edward said, chuffing her impudently on the chin, which made Eleanor seethe. She was certain her eyes were throwing sparks, though she did her best to smile. "This is why my sister will be so delighted! She will have someone on her team at last!"

Eleanor smiled down at her teacup, but she was gripping it so that her knuckles whitened. He *was* here for her. He was going to make her life miserable on every level; she could sense it. He was a Duke, not used to being told no or not getting what he wanted, and she had defied him. She had *struck* him. He was going to make her pay.

Chapter 14

From *Mr. Pickwick's Guide to Marriageable Young Ladies-*

It is hard to imagine that Lady I.R. could be as lovely inside as she is out--but that is the case. While many of her beaux may only crave the external beauty on their arm, to see her as only pretty is a disservice. Her internal qualities of loyalty, generosity, and kindness are especially commendable in one so beautiful, as often, ladies of great beauty are told that their beauty is enough. This lady, however, didn't stop there--she is an accomplished equestrienne, well-read, and very active with several charities involving the poor. Her friends consider themselves lucky to have her counsel, and her household staff adores her. It is commendable that her father has withheld his consent to several young men--he knows his daughter's worth, and he wants to see her married to someone who sees the same.

The day couldn't have ended soon enough for Eleanor's tastes. After the Duke left, the Marquess retired to his study. The door was barely closed behind him before Lady Millie let out a very unladylike squeal.

"Can you believe it?" she said. "The *Duke of Devonshire*! My sister-in-law will just *die* when she hears this." She looked ecstatic at the thought.

"And he truly wishes to make our husbands' acquaintance, as well," Lady Anne said. "My dear Frederick is going to be so pleased. He's been trying to make headway on some issue in Parliament for *ages*."

On and on it went. The ladies tittered about their social coup, imagined grand scenarios in which the Duke offered them further social clout or priviledge, and how they could use this new 'friendship' to their best advantage. Despite how angry she was with the Duke, Eleanor couldn't help but feel disgusted at how they spoke of him. They were vultures, picking over a piece of downed prey, dividing up the choicest morsels.

"And it's all because of Eleanor," Jane said with a smile. "Dear Eleanor, why did you never tell us of your family's close friendship with the Duke?"

"I...I didn't think it was important," she said, faltering. "As you heard, ours is a friendship newly remet. I do look forward to seeing his sister, however."

Lies. All lies. Eleanor would be most gratified if she never saw the Duke, or his unknown sister, again. The Duke's attention would bring too much focus on her. Why on earth would she want that? After so many years of floundering, she had a plan for her future, and it was working. She wouldn't let the whims of a Duke, no matter how rich or handsome he was, take that away.

Edward was glad to be rid of those giggling, fawning ladies. He would have avoided such an afternoon, if possible, but he'd wanted to see how Eleanor reacted to him. It had been well worth his time. The way she'd straightened and leaned away from him, the way she had been so aware of where he was at all times--it made him laugh.

She was trying to avoid any scandal, that was certain. But it seemed like it was more than that--she was trying to escape all *notice*. Where the other ladies engaged him with their smiles and eyes and breathless questions, she was happy to sit back and let the attention fall elsewhere. When he tried to draw her into the conversation, she would answer the bare minimum and deflect attention. He'd made up his mind--a person that concerned with what society thought couldn't possibly be Mr. Pickwick.

Except for that one outburst about him deserving to be hit, she'd been the perfect lady--unruffled, cool, uninterested. But that one outburst had made all the trouble worth it. In that moment, he'd seen a bit of the fire that had nearly burned him previously. It was a delicious glimpse into who she really was, and proof that she hid the real Eleanor from nearly everyone.

He found that he couldn't wait to find out more about her--not because he suspected she may be connected to the Pickwick Guide, because he no longer thought so--but just her, as a person. He didn't think that he'd met anyone like her in his entire life. He'd had but a few short moments to study her profile during the tea. Her bone structure was fine--a small, straight nose over lips too slightly overfull to be considered perfect by societal standards. That thick mane of gently curling hair had been tamed into a chignon and tucked into a snood at the base of her neck. Her dress was blue with a darker blue trim on the bodice and neckline.

He wondered if it was one of the Marchioness' castoffs, and the thought made him frown. A woman as fiery and intelligent as Eleanor should not be beholden to others' charitable whims. She should be the head of her own household, and dressed in the finest gowns of her own choosing. Edward shook such thoughts from his head. He seemed to lose focus whenever Eleanor was in a room. She baited him without seemingly meaning to do so. The more she ignored him, the more he wanted to be noticed. It was perverse.

Now that he had ruled Eleanor out, he had to focus on his main goal--finding out the identity of Mr. Pickwick in order to secure his brother's future. Above all, Edward had to protect Henry from the clutches of the horrible Teresa Bunt. If she got her talons into the boy, there was no telling how she would use him. She didn't love Henry; she only loved herself. Those were the worst kinds of parents.

Edward looked at the clock. It was nearly five o'clock; he was expecting Andrews any moment.

The plan had been to use the time when Eleanor was away from home to do a more thorough investigation into her situation. Edward knew that however he painted it, it was breaking and entering.

He moved to the sideboard and poured himself a brandy. No matter how much he needed to find out who Mr. Pickwick was, he regretted that Eleanor had been under any sort of suspicion. He wanted to figure out who this Mr. Pickwick was, and quickly, so he could better sort his thoughts and feelings out-- Eleanor in one section, Mr. Pickwick in another. Tidy and neat, the opposite of how things were in his mind at the moment.

The clock chimed; there was a knock at the door.

"Enter," Edward said, resuming his seat behind his desk.

"Your Grace," Andrews bowed, shut the door behind him, took a seat facing Edward, and began. "I apologize, but we were not able to enter Lady Eleanor's residence today. The landlord, Mr. McAffrey, was home. The men I hired said that he is a watchful sort. I'd rather wait until he was out before we try again."

"Very well," Edward said. "Another day, then."

"I did make further inquiries into her financial situation, and I expect to hear back shortly. And...questions regarding the *character* of the young lady have all been answered positively."

"How so?" Edward said.

Andrews coughed. "It is not reported that the lady, er...has any visitors to her flat, Your Grace."

Edward raised an eyebrow.

"Male visitors," Andrews said.

"Certainly not," Edward said, setting his brandy down with enough force that some of the amber liquid sloshed onto the desk. He wasn't sure why, but he felt like thumping Andrews on the head for even entertaining such a notion.

"It is my job to make the sort of inquiries that others may find distasteful, especially when my employer is interested in a lady with such a... *unique* situation."

"I'm not *interested* in her," Edward said.

Andrews raised an eyebrow.

"Well, I *am*, but not in *that* way. I'm just curious..."

Andrews' second eyebrow joined the other.

Edward frowned into a silence that threatened to become awkward.

"Very well, Your Grace," Andrews said, standing and sketching a faint bow. "I will let you know as soon as I have any further information."

Chapter 15

From *Mr. Pickwick's Guide to Marriageable Young Ladies-*

There have been several incidents involving Lady H.G. where, after leaving a shop or a drawing room, items have been missed. Usually, it is something small, not enough to get a servant dismissed--a single silver spoon, perhaps, or a pearl button. However, recently a silver tea cup went missing from a prestigious household and sources say the lady was the thief, slipping the teacup into her reticule before hurrying away. One wonders what could possess a lady of wealth and beauty to behave in such a manner. Regardless of the motive behind the acts, this lady is bound to bring embarrassment to any man who gives her his last name.

The next morning, Eleanor met Jane to take a walk through the park. It was a lovely day--the birds were chattering to one another amidst the rustling leaves, the sky was clear and bright, as if a magnifying glass had been held against the sun. It was cold, but nothing that a warm shawl and coat couldn't insulate against, and the breeze kept the air crisp and clean, which was its own special treat, for London.

They had always preferred to walk at an unfashionably early time--the promenade in St. James park wouldn't start until early afternoon. They walked in one of the smaller parks, closer to Jane's home. It was no more than two acres, and the paths weren't wide enough for carriages-- some would barely permit two people to walk abreast. But the seclusion and privacy was part of the charm. It felt like wandering in nature, if nature were controlled by gardeners and patrolled by security.

As they made their way out to the park, they spoke of the usual things--polite chatter about the weather, Jane's new pelisse, her renovations of the nursery. But Eleanor could feel a tension with her friend, the energy not unlike that before a rainstorm broke. As soon as they entered the shaded cover of the trees, Eleanor's suspicions were confirmed.

"So," Jane started, pursing her lips. "We didn't get an opportunity to discuss the Duke's visit yesterday.."

That had been by design; Eleanor had given her excuses and exited shortly after Devonshire. She knew that the Duke's attentions to her had not gone unnoticed, that the ladies she left behind would inspect the minutiae of all that transpired more carefully than a governess with a steel comb inspecting for lice.

Eleanor gave a jerky nod, and waited for Jane to continue.

"What are your feelings on the matter?" she asked, eyebrows raised.

"What matter?" Eleanor said, knowing that she was being obtuse, but obstinately choosing to pretend she was ignorant. "The Duke knew my brother and father, and that is the whole of it."

Jane laughed, a skeptical sound, and threaded her arm through Eleanor's. "Dear Eleanor, you cannot possibly believe that. Devonshire has singled you out, markedly. I know you abhor attention, and he brings attention wherever he goes."

"Precisely," Eleanor said, nodding. She opened her mouth to continue.

"But that is not a good enough reason to ignore a man such as him!" Jane rushed on, interrupting Eleanor. "If a man such as the Duke is paying attention to you, you cannot just *ignore* him."

"And why not?" Eleanor said, her back straightening. "Why is Devonshire different from any other man? Except that he is more entitled than the others, and has more money."

Jane rolled her eyes. "He's different because he is a *duke*. And not just any duke, either. He's obscenely wealthy, has a lot of pull in Parliament, and he's *single*."

"None of that has anything to do with me," she said, exasperated. "He's just toying with me."

"You don't know that."

"I do!" Eleanor exclaimed. "When I met him at the ball, I didn't preen and bat my eyes, and now I'm being punished for it."

"Punished!" Jane said. "You have such an odd view of things. There are a thousand young ladies who would give their left arm to have Devonshire's eye."

"They're welcome to it, one-armed or not." Eleanor groused. "Bunch of sycophants. What they don't realize--what *you* don't realize--is that he is only amusing himself at my expense."

Jane shook her head, but Eleanor could still read disbelief in her eyes.

"I'm serious, Jane!" she said, stopping in the middle of the path. "For as many businesses and estates as the man is supposed to manage, it appears that he is bored. I can think of no other reason why he would bother with me."

"Are you that oblivious?" Jane said, her brow furrowed. "He certainly means to court you."

"Preposterous!" Eleanor interjected, stamping down the little thrill in her stomach she felt at Jane's assertion.

"How can you not see what the rest of us so easily recognize?" Jane gave Eleanor's arm a little shake. "You are beautiful. Intelligent. Your morality above reproach. Why wouldn't Devonshire be interested?"

Eleanor was struck dumb by several conflicting thoughts and emotions assailing her at once. First, she was humbled by Jane's assertions, and confused. Is that really how Jane saw her? Then, came shame. Would Jane still hold those high opinions of her, if she found out Eleanor was writing *Mr. Pickwick's Guide*? Next was confusion. Was it possible that the Duke was interested in her for more than his own entertainment?

Eleanor rejected that thought the instant it arose. She couldn't wonder such things, for if she entertained the thought for even a moment, hope would come yapping at its heels like an unwanted stray mongrel. And hope was insidious. It crept in like a rising tide, but when it receded, after it was gone, it left destruction in its wake.

Before she could recover enough to formulate a reply to Jane's compliments, the sound of male laughter sounded nearby. Eleanor stiffened and her heart began to race. *Him*, she thought. She had just enough time to grip Jane's forearm in silent warning before two figures emerged from around the bend in the path before them.

It was the Duke of Devonshire and a friend who looked vaguely familiar to Eleanor, but she couldn't bother placing him. She only had eyes for Edward. He was dressed in riding clothes--form-fitting trousers that encased his long, muscular legs, a dark jacket that emphasized his broad shoulders, and a crisp white shirt. The moment his green eyes met Eleanor's, she gave an inaudible inhale, and her stomach flipped. She refused to let him see how he affected her; she squeezed her hand into a fist and set her face into neutral lines.

"Your Grace," Jane exclaimed, as the men approached. "What a lovely surprise."

"Lady Millen," Edward said, nodding. "Eleanor."

The use of her Christian name rankled her, and Eleanor stood up straighter.

Edward's eyes twinkled, and he continued, "May I present the Marquess of Salisbury, Lord Percival Waldrey. Lord Salisbury, may I present the Marchioness of Millen, and Lady Eleanor Gilbert."

Eleanor performed the pleasantries with a calm countenance, though her heart was racing. She recognized the Marquess of Salisbury from the London social swirl. He was the brother to the gorgeous Lady Candace, the woman Edward had danced with at his ball. A knot formed in her gut at the memory, and Eleanor did her best to ignore the sensation. Surely the feeling couldn't be... *jealousy*. Certainly not. It was absurd to even mention the word where her emotions toward Edward were concerned.

Above that emotion came a different one. Eleanor felt in her bones that it wasn't coincidence that had brought her and Edward face to face once more. Both the Duke and the Marquess appeared to have exerted themselves recently--a light sheen of sweat illuminated their brows, and they smelled faintly of horse. But how was Edward arranging such meetings? Did he have a spy in Jane's household?

"...isn't that so, Eleanor?" Jane said.

"Mmmm," Eleanor said, hoping the entirely non-committal sound would suffice to answer whatever question Jane had posited.

She saw the corners of Edward's eyes crinkle, and the corners of her mouth turned down in response, which seemed to amuse him more. She was more annoyed at her own reaction to his smile than the fact that he got amusement from her distraction. That little uncontrollable swoop of her stomach, like a hawk diving for the ground, was too telling to ignore. But she was trying. Eleanor decided to pay closer attention to the conversation, lest he keep laughing at her.

"Oh, we wouldn't miss it," Jane said, setting her hand on Eleanor's arm. "Would we, Eleanor?"

Eleanor's head snapped toward Jane, who was obviously waiting for a response, and color rose in her cheeks. She heard Edward's deep chuckle, and her cheeks heated further.

"I'm sorry, Jane. I was distracted. What were we discussing?"

Jane shot her a look, like she knew exactly what had distracted Eleanor. "The Marquess has invited us to dine with him and his sister."

"How lovely," Eleanor said, trying to sound convincing.

Based on Edward's grin, she'd failed. Her eyes narrowed.

"So glad to hear that you will join us," Lord Salisbury said, gallantly ignoring her obvious lack of attention to the conversation. "I've heard so many wonderful things about you ladies, and I cannot wait to get to know you better. I'll ask my sister when she has a free evening, and will send a card."

Eleanor wasn't sure she trusted the way that Lord Salisbury seemed prone to smiling at a moment's notice, or the humor glinting in his eyes. Her suspicions were confirmed a moment later when he offered his arm to Jane.

"Will you walk with me awhile, Lady Millen? There are some lovely flowers up the way that I think you'd like to see."

Eleanor knew that there weren't any flowers-- this park was nothing more than ferns and forest. But Jane took his arm with alacrity, and they were off along the path through the shrubbery at a pace that was far faster than casual. Eleanor wasn't sure who was leading who, but they were definitely in cahoots. Eleanor and Edward were left in a silence--one that she felt awkward about, but which Edward seemed to be enjoying. If anything, his grin had increased.

They followed the path, albeit at a much slower pace than Jane and Lord Salisbury had. Manners dictated that the Duke set the pace, and it seemed that he was content to barely meander through the greenery.

"How is it that we keep running into each other?" Eleanor demanded.

"I wouldn't go so far as to call it fate, but if one believed in such things..."

"I don't," Eleanor snapped.

"Let's call it a happy coincidence, then," Edward said, seemingly unperturbed by Eleanor's icy demeanor. In fact, he seemed to *enjoy* her discomfort.

The realization turned her frown into an outright scowl. Edward chuckled.

"You are insufferable," she said.

"And you are unlike anyone I've ever met."

"I'm on to your games. You mean to punish me for striking you."

"Is my presence a punishment, then?" His tone was light.

"It isn't gentlemanly to fish for compliments, Your Grace." Eleanor felt as if she were the brunt of a joke shared by Jane and the two gentleman.

"I've never had to, prior. Perhaps that's what I find so fascinating."

"The novelty will wear off, I'm sure," she said.

"It hasn't yet." Edward pushed a wayward branch from her path.

"Thank you," she murmured, her manners too ingrained to be overcome by her current mood.

"Do you and the Marchioness walk here often?"

Eleanor wanted to roll her eyes at the mundane question. "When the weather permits. I'm surprised you found us here."

He didn't answer the hinted question. "Percival and I walk or ride together whenever we get the chance, although we are both busier than we used to be in years past."

"You've been friends for a long time, then?"

"Our mothers were dear friends. We shared the same tutors--we were practically raised together. We never stopped being close, even after our mothers passed."

"I'm sorry," she murmured. "I know how difficult losing a parent is. Especially if you love them."

Edward put a gentle pressure on her elbow as she stepped over a root in the path. That slight touch--there and gone-- was enough to set her heart pounding. "Yes. I was sorry to hear that your father had passed, those years ago. He was a good man."

"That part was true then? You knew my father?"

He looked at her, his brow furrowed. "You thought I made that up?"

"I was having a hard time focusing during that conversation, if I'm honest."

Edward chuckled. "I knew your father and brother when I was much younger. Our families lost touch when your family moved, although our fathers kept in touch until your father passed. And then my father passed, and I lost touch with all but the closest friends."

"How old were you?"

Eleanor clamped her mouth shut after asking--she wasn't sure what it was about Edward that made her lose all sense of social boundaries. They barely knew each other--she shouldn't ask him such personal questions. Then, Eleanor had always struggled with certain social rules. How was one supposed to get to know another person if you weren't allowed to ask personal questions?

"I was twenty-seven," Edward answered, easily. "I was at that strange time in every man's life where you run up against your own limitations. Before my father passed, I thought I knew everything. Once I inherited the title and the care of my sister, I realized how little I did know. I'm still learning--mostly from my mistakes." He chuckled.

Humility. What a strange quality to find in someone as titled and wealthy as he. The honesty of his statement flew in the face of what she thought about him. Was he a bored, entitled Duke out to torment her for his own amusement, or was he something else entirely?

Before she could think it through, they rounded a bend and saw Jane and Lord Salisbury in the distance, near a pond. Her stomach gave a little lurch, and it took her a moment to realize that she was disappointed because their time together was coming to an end. She was enjoying getting to know him. When had that happened?

"Uh oh," Edward said. "It looks like they're plotting something."

Jane and the Marquess of Salisbury stood closely, heads bent together, talking in low tones.

"It does look suspicious," Eleanor agreed. "What do you think they're up to?"

"I don't know, but I'm not concerned. I think they're on my side of things."

"*Your* side?" Eleanor said. "What does that mean?"

Edward just laughed.

He and Percy rode home at half the pace that they'd ridden to the small park. Andrews' man had come for him soon after Eleanor had arrived at the Marchioness' town home. He'd just finished breakfasting with Percy, who'd ridden over to partake of the sugared bacon that Edward hated, but which kept showing up on the sideboard every morning.

Percy was game for anything, and his presence that morning was a serendipitous turn of events. Edward hadn't told him much on the fast ride over, but Percy had quickly gotten into the spirit of things. It was about a woman, and that was all Percy had needed to hear. After all, how many times had Edward helped Percy out? Percy was a hopeless romantic who was determined to remain single--a strange combination, to be sure. He was in love with the idea of love, but wasn't keen on falling victim to it. It was a good thing that Percy's mannerisms were teasing enough that no woman had ever really taken him seriously--meaning that no woman had ever been hurt by his rejection.

That was one reason that Edward was surprised at how quiet and thoughtful Percy had become once Edward had briefly described the situation. Edward had played it off as a lark, a joke--a situation that he himself was using only for his own amusement. But Percy had gone silent, contemplative, which was rare for him. It made Edward nervous, feel as if he needed to fill the silence. So he had--with what he meant to be a short synopsis of his interactions with Eleanor Gilbert so far. He'd worked hard at making the story funny and had hoped that Percy would laugh. But he hadn't, and Edward caught Percy studying him when Percy thought he wasn't looking.

Edward wasn't surprised when Percy had gotten right into the spirit of things when it came to creating some alone time for him and Eleanor. He *had* been surprised at Percy's mannerisms after the too-brief encounter.

They'd barely mounted their horses and headed back the way they'd come when Percy said, "Is this the end of our single days then, Edward?"

"What?" Edward had said, genuinely surprised. "Whatever do you mean?"

"Lady Eleanor," he said. "Not that I disapprove of your choice. On the contrary--I like what I know of her so far. She doesn't seem overly fond of you--which means that she's either playing the coquette or she's genuinely not interested. I must admit, it would be vastly more amusing if it's the latter."

"I don't believe Eleanor has it within her to be anything but genuine. Against her own better judgement, she is all that is candid."

"Oh, it's 'Eleanor', is it?" Percy asked, his eyebrows raised. "Then things are progressing at a faster pace than I suspected."

Edward sighed. "Our families were friends a long time ago. You're getting excited over nothing, I assure you."

Even as Edward spoke the words, an internal voice challenged their truth.

Percy scoffed. "In all the years we've known each other, I've never seen you single a lady out for attention. I've certainly never seen you leave your breakfast half-eaten in order to spend a scant fifteen minutes' time with one. Nor have I seen you look so energized and excited after speaking to someone-- anyone. If I were a more jealous person, I would feel threatened."

"Don't be ridiculous, Perce."

"Good heavens, Edward. You've hired people to stand outside her friend's house and let you know when she arrives. It's downright diabolical, even if it is completely genius. I'm definitely going to use such a tactic in the future."

"It's not precisely what it looks like, Percy."

His friend's eyes went sharp. "What do you mean?"

Edward winced. He didn't want to tell Percy of his suspicions, that he'd first thought that Eleanor could possibly be the writer of the scandalous booklet reviewing ladies. And that thought made him pause. When had he kept anything from Percy? It wasn't that he didn't trust Percy, he realized. It was that he didn't want Percy thinking poorly of Eleanor. He frowned, his forehead crinkled.

Percy snorted. "Just what I thought. Perhaps you should take some time to evaluate your feelings for this lady. Figure out how you really feel, how you should proceed, before you botch the whole thing by refusing to admit the truth to yourself."

They'd parted ways soon after--Edward toward his house, Percy to his own. It was a friendly leave-taking, but Percy's warning echoed in Edward's head all the way home. What *did* he feel for Eleanor? If he were honest, she intrigued him more than anyone else had in a long time. She was different, a good kind of different. He looked forward to seeing her, and didn't want to leave when they were together. Percy was right--maybe he would spend some more time with Eleanor in order to evaluate his emotions. Maybe he *would* court her.

Edward arrived home smelling of horse. He was strangely exhilarated by his decision to keep seeing Eleanor. He wanted to see her again, as soon as possible. He wanted to be able to look into those luminous brown eyes, stand close enough to catch the faint scent from her skin. He wanted to provoke her with words until he saw the fire enter her eyes, until she dropped that carefully cultivated facade she wore like a mantle--until she was honest about who she was.

Edward was embroiled in his own thoughts until Huntley told him that Andrews was waiting for him in his study. Edward was grateful--perhaps Andrews had more information about Eleanor's financial status.

Andrews stood when Edward entered the room, and sat only when Edward was settled behind the desk.

"A thorough search of Lady Eleanor Gilbert's apartment was conducted today. The gentlemen involved said that she keeps a clean, orderly house. She has few possessions, excepting a rather large collection of fine dresses, which she stores in a large armoire." Andrews paused, consulted his notes. "There are receipts from various vendors, but nothing that would raise any alarm."

"So she isn't Mr. Pickwick," Edward interrupted. He felt relief, and... anticipation?

"Oh, no. She most certainly is, Your Grace," Andrews said, adjusting his spectacles. "I merely said the *receipts* gave no cause for alarm."

Edward felt a sense of vertigo that he hadn't experienced since his first sea voyage. He was grateful that he was sitting down. He blinked.

"What?"

"After a thorough search of Lady Eleanor's papers, which were locked in her desk, several drafts of reviews were found, matching the style and tone of Mr. Pickwick, exactly," he said. "Since the runner hadn't arrived and I felt we had time, I took the liberty of copying some of it down." He slid a paper across the desk. "It appears the young lady is preparing an addendum."

Edward scanned the parchment. Copied in Andrews' precise handwriting was a new entry, on a Lady Dianne Sheldon.

"But how is she printing them?" he asked. He could feel that his expression was stunned, but he was too shocked to care.

"Once the papers were put back into place and her apartment relocked, the gentlemen made a search of the other apartments, if they found them vacant. They were able to pick a lock to the basement, where they found an old printing press, and lines for drying papers. They found nothing to indicate that there was anyone else involved, although that cannot be ascertained from a simple search."

"Were any of your men seen on the premises?"

"No, Your Grace."

"And you trust them to maintain their silence on the matter?"

"Implicitly, Your Grace, or I should not have hired them. They have been well compensated and await further instructions."

"No further instructions, Andrews."

"I assume that you would still like me to move forward with my financial inquiry into Lady Eleanor? I have written a letter to the solicitor who distributes the funds." Andrews frowned. "I haven't been able to contact him as of yet, but I expect to hear back soon."

"Fine, fine," Edward said. "That will be all. Thank you, Andrews."

"Of course, Your Grace."

Edward sat for long hours after Andrews left, staring into the ever-diminishing fire. What would possess Eleanor to take such risks? Even though she was in dire straits, there were other, safer ways of procuring money. She could become a governess or a paid companion. The booklets couldn't be bringing in *that* much money. After paper and ink, she was perhaps making a few shillings each. If she printed a hundred, that would be no more than ten pounds.

Edward shook his head again. He was seeing things from his own point of view. He had to remember that to a lady with twenty pounds annum, ten pounds was not a sum of small consequence. He wondered how many she sold, and for the matter, how was she selling them? It's not like she could stand on the street corner and hawk her wares as so many others did. She was a lady and would be recognized as such immediately.

Street urchins, most likely. The thought of her dealing with those kinds of people made him shudder. And the question remained--what was he going to do, now that he knew that Eleanor was Mr. Pickwick?

Chapter 16

From the *Quentin Daily-*

A most curious incident occurred this past week on St. James' row. A certain gentleman of high rank visited the home of the M.M. for advice on Parliamentary matters, and then stayed for tea, with several delighted ladies in attendance. It is said that the gentleman paid very special attention to Lady E.G., as their acquaintance was renewed at the gentleman's own ball the night before. It seems that the gentleman and the lady are quite close, and one lady in attendance was heard to say that if she's any judge of character, the banns will be read before next spring. This would be a grave disappointment to every other single lady, as the gentleman is first in both title, looks and wealth. We wait with bated breath to see the outcome of this titillating situation...

For the first time in her life, Eleanor was in the scandals sheets. The paper trembled in her hands, making the words difficult to read. She spread it on her desk and slumped in her chair. Eleanor felt her heartbeat increase, until, by the time she had read the entire entry, she was gasping for breath. She set her head upon the cool hardness of her desk. After everything... after how careful she had always been not to garner any attention... after how long, *years*, it had taken before other rumors began to replace the pernicious interest that the peerage had shown to her family's scandal... All it took was for one Duke to look at her a little too long, and for a false friend to notice. He'd undone it all, all her work, all her scraping politeness, all her false smiles, all of it.

Eleanor wouldn't be able to walk down the street without someone pointing and whispering. And even worse than the pointing and whispering were the candy-coated barbs that other ladies threw her way. She could already hear the kinds of things they'd say: *So surprising that the Duke would take an interest in* your *family.* Or the things they'd whisper to each other, loud enough for her to hear: *What do you think she had to do to get his interest, do you think? Not surprising at all, if you consider what her sister-in-law was like. Bet she learned such tricks from her.*

Eleanor knew herself--she had borne such things once, because she hadn't any other choice. She had nothing and no one to protect her. But now things were a bit different. She had an income, laughable as it may be to some. She had years more of wisdom and experience to buttress herself from the bitter social winds. She wasn't trapped; she could choose whether to stay or go, whether to cower or fight back. After all, she had the most powerful weapon in all the world--

the means to put things into print. And what were whispers when compared to print?

Little by little, she galvanized herself against her own fears. If things got too bad, she could abandon her press and move to Scotland. Perhaps a wealthy family there needed a governess. She'd ask the Marchioness for a reference, if necessary. But it needn't come to that. She would keep her head down and wait for the Duke's interest to pass to another. It was bound to happen--she wasn't nearly as pretty as half the young ladies enjoying their Season. If he was in the marrying mood, or the flirting mood, or whatever the mood may be, there were ladies better suited to fulfilling it than she.

Quickly, she penned a note to Jane. She would understand Eleanor's need for privacy during this time. After all, she and her husband had fallen under the shadow of social censure, those years ago, for housing her. Eleanor pulled on her work dress, grabbed her gloves and apron, and headed to the basement. It was high time she put out this Appendix. She might want to print something completely new soon.

It had been a week since the *Quentin Daily*, London's finest gossip rag, had printed the piece on him and Eleanor. The piece had made him frown, but it was nothing new. London always had gossip and scandal, and this was barely gossip. But apparently, the lady had felt differently. She hadn't left her flat since, except for one trip Wednesday morning to the shop down the road. Andrews reported that she'd carried several paper-wrapped parcels back into the tenement, but didn't know what they were, other than that they 'looked heavy'.

Edward's guess was that it was paper. He frowned at the thought. It was a wonder that she hadn't been caught before now. Mr. Pickwick's Guide had gone through three reprintings that he knew of. Perhaps she was doing another. It hardly mattered what she was doing. As long as she wasn't visiting the Marchioness, Edward couldn't drop by and see her 'on accident'. He had to wait.

He hated waiting.

He'd written Amelia and her husband, as promised, and asked them to come to London for a few weeks. He missed them. He missed Henry, and the boy's birthday was coming up. He wasn't wild about Henry being in town so soon after Teresa's threats, but he figured that she wouldn't know. His house was the tightest run manor in London. Andrews, Huntley, and Mrs. Gardner saw to that. Edward wouldn't have it any other way--some houses were leakier than a colander in terms of gossip.

Edward had planned on inviting the Marchioness, the Marquess, and Lady Eleanor for dinner once his sister and brother-in-law arrived, but it would be deuced hard to invite her if she wasn't ever at the Marquess' house. Edward ran his hand through his hair. He felt disgruntled, reckless. He wanted to provoke her, but he didn't know why. He wanted to know how she got her information, how she'd come up with this foolhardy scheme of hers. He wanted to know it all, everything about her. She was the most interesting woman of his acquaintance, even *without* Mr. Pickwick.

A knock on the door, and Andrews ducked inside. He was wearing a deep frown, and his forehead was creased. From him, this was tantamount to a cry of alarm.

Edward stood. "Is everything alright? Is it Eleanor?"

When had he started to worry about her welfare above that of his blood relatives?

"Last I heard, about an hour ago, Lady Eleanor was quite safe, Your Grace. I believe she is still rattling around in that basement of hers. But I've disturbing news, all the same."

"Sit," Edward said, then took his own advice.

"I told Your Grace that I had sent an inquiry to the solicitor who disperses Lady Eleanor's bequeathment, a sum of twenty pounds annum."

"Yes," he said.

"I received several polite replies explaining why a meeting with me must be postponed. First, an illness. Then a *family* illness. But the report that just reached me is very disturbing. It seems that the solicitor, one Alvin Buchanan, has died."

"Oh," Edward said, his expression grave. "That is very bad news, indeed."

"Would that were all, Your Grace," Andrews said. "Mr. Buchanan was well-liked in the community, and was extolled as a trustworthy, honest sort."

"Very sad, indeed. Honest barristers are one of the pillars of our legal system."

"Quite so, Your Grace," Andrews said. "However, that is not what has me perplexed. You see, the gentleman in question died shortly after Lady Eleanor's brother. And if he died nigh on five years ago, who has been signing his correspondence to me? And even more importantly, why?"

The woman clasped her plain wool mantle tight about the neck to protect her identity and against the damp chill in equal measure. The other hand clasped a copy of the *Quentin Daily* from a week ago. With careful inquiry, she finally had a name--Lady Eleanor Gilbert. She picked her way through the puddles-- there were no cobblestones in this part of the city. At the end of the street, flanked on either side by piles of rubbish, was a door with holes that showed light through it. A sign over the door said, 'Heaven's Treasures Pub'.

Teresa Bunt rolled her eyes at the name. There was nothing heavenly or remotely close to treasure in this establishment. It was a squalid bar. The floorboards had absorbed years of vomit, piss, and dank mud--it would never be clean again, no matter how industrious the maids were. But it was a place where no one asked questions, where a woman might meet with strange men at a dark table in the back, and no one batted an eye. No one was sober enough to open an eye, most times, let alone bat one.

After the threats from the Duke of Devonshire, she didn't want to take any chances. She had seen the truth in his eyes...if she went anywhere near that brat, the Duke would follow through. She'd just be another unfortunate, nameless body dumped in the Thames or in a shallow grave. Apparently, she'd pushed him too far. She would have to be very, very careful with her next plan.

She was the first to arrive, and she ordered a cider, and read the paper clipping one more time. Teresa had grit her teeth and nearly screamed when she'd read it. After all these years of working this family, and she still was no closer to her goal. She'd received the payoff, sure, but it was nowhere close to the one she'd wanted. That old coot was going to marry her, make her a Duchess. But then he went and died before she could maneuver him into it.

Teresa'd taken one look at the son at the funeral and decided all was not lost. He was a handsome young man, rich as the father, and all she had to do was to hang around long enough after the birth for him to fall in love with her. Love, or lust-- she didn't care. But the stupid brat had ruined her figure, and the young Duke wasn't interested. All she'd gotten for her trouble was a thousand pounds and some stretch marks.

A thousand pounds was a lot of money, but it went faster than one would think, given Teresa's expensive tastes. It wasn't more than two years before she was worse off than she'd been before. She'd acquired a taste for the thrill of gambling, but she'd not enough practice to get really good at it. She owed money to some men who didn't rightly care that she was a lady. To them, her tears were no more effective or precious than that of a barmaid.

Teresa knew now that she'd never be the Duchess of Devonshire, a fact that still made her see red. She wasn't insightful enough to understand that she'd never had a chance with Edward, and that his father had treated her with carelessness. She only knew that this Eleanor Gilbert was the one who was trying to usurp her rightful throne. And, Teresa was desperate.

She needed to come up with the money by the end of the month, which was only two weeks away.

All she could hear in her mind were the words that the Duke of Devonshire had growled at her-- "There is nothing I wouldn't do for those I love." How many pounds worth, Teresa had been wondering, did he love this Eleanor Gilbert?

Cheever and Marks arrived together, as they usually did. Marks stopped at the threshold to take in the room--he was the smarter one, the one with sharp eyes. But Cheever just stomped his way over and threw his large frame onto the bench across from her. Marks joined them a moment later, jerking his head at the barmaid.

"Wut you got for us, then?" Cheever said. "Iffin it like the last time, we ain't interested. Didn't get nuffin' off that carriage, did we? Nuffin' but some trinkets. Hardly worth the effort."

Teresa sighed. "The *house* had the silver, not the carriage. I told you to *follow* the carriage until it got to the house; not to take the carriage on the side of the road."

"Well, that's not all we took on the side of that road," Cheever said, running his tobacco-stained tongue over grimy teeth. "That bird was right tasty."

Teresa tried not to shudder. She knew what these men were, and she didn't like dealing with them.

"How would you feel about picking someone up for me...holding them for a few days?" she said.

"Ah, it's a kidnapping you 'ave in mind, this time," Cheever said, a little too loudly for Teresa's comfort. "Who's the mark?"

"First, we'll discuss terms," Teresa said. "We're a team in this, so we will split the money fifty-fifty. I'll give you information on where to take the woman, and you'll keep her safe and unharmed until we are paid, at which time, you will release her, and we split the money."

That was the plan she was telling them. The real plan was for Teresa to leave town the moment the money was in her hands. She had too many bills in London, and she was acquiring somewhat of a reputation. Maybe Paris would be better, or Italy.

Teresa didn't care what happened to Lady Eleanor Gilbert, although she could guess the outcome, when Cheever and Marks found out that Teresa had crossed them.

"There are three of us," Marks said, his cold voice slithering over her like a snake. "That means we will split the money in thirds. A third for each of us."

"That's fair," Teresa said.

What did she care if they hypothetically split the money three ways? She was the one who would get her hands on it, and she'd ask for more than a thousand pounds this time. She realized that she had settled too soon for payment of the child. If Edward would pay a thousand pounds for a bastard infant, how much would he pay for the woman he meant to marry?

Marks' eyes narrowed, but he nodded. "Who is it?"

"I need you to find out everything you can about Lady Eleanor Gilbert."

Chapter 17

From *Mr. Pickwick's Guide to Marriageable Young Ladies-*

Lady A.R. has a large circle of friends, as she is young, wealthy, and beautiful. It must be noted however, that the lady has never been the recipient of a secret that she did not immediately pass along, either to other friends or the gossip rags. One wonders what kind of gentleman would want to shackle himself to such a lack of loyalty.

Eleanor stayed away from Jane's house a full two weeks. By that time, the gossip circulars had moved on to fresher meat--the story of Lord Avery's engagement had been told, and his dear, departed Countess had been hinted at. It had also been noted that Lord Avery had arrived, healthy and whole, at his future in-laws' house the day after the news about the widowed, pregnant Countess had broken, and he'd left after an hour looking disheveled and sporting a blackening eye.

One can only wonder if perhaps Lord A. tripped upon the stairs, the paper wrote.

While Eleanor felt a twinge of sympathy for Lord Avery and the other members of the peerage who had been publicly flagellated in the gossip columns during her absence, she was also grateful. If papers were printing items of such a nature about others, surely they had forgotten about her. If not forgotten, at least the fervor had died down.

She did feel badly about her long absence-- the longest she'd gone, by far, from visiting Jane-

-but the separation was necessary. It was imperative that Eleanor be able to act and speak with composure when Jane questioned her, as she certainly would. It wouldn't do to blush or act flustered when the Duke was brought up in conversation. That was the weapon of choice for any gossip worth her salt--politely bring up the subject just to see how others reacted. So Eleanor had needed time. Time to compose herself. Time to plan responses. Time for the eyes of the peerage to move elsewhere.

She arrived on Jane's doorstep with a gift--a lovely candle in Jane's favorite scent, which was rose petals. Eleanor hoped that the trifle would help Jane forgive her.

"Lady Eleanor Gilbert," Stephens announced.

And then Eleanor was ushered into the same room she'd entered a hundred times before--but found it close to standing room only. She felt the color drain from her face, even as she held her smile as she'd been taught. There were the ladies Eleanor was familiar with--Millie, Anne, and Priscilla, but there were at least half a dozen new faces in the room.

And all eyes landed on her and raked over her person as Jane greeted her.

"Oh *there* you are, darling," Jane gushed. She patted the seat right next to hers. "Come sit. I'm so glad you are feeling better, and I have several introductions to make…"

Eleanor sat dutifully, if a bit stunned. She nodded and smiled as she was introduced to Lady Susan and her mother, the Countess Charmine, Lady Hannah Brightly and her sister, Lady Thalia Brightly, the Marchioness of Winterford, and her daughter, Lady Astrid, and the Dowager Baroness, Lady Glenda. Eleanor hoped that she didn't look as pale and drawn as she felt. She was wrong to have come back so soon. She had hoped that she would find Jane alone, as she had so many countless times before. Instead, she had inadvertently swum into a social feeding frenzy.

"A gift for me?" Jane said.

"You've been so kind to me during my recent illness," Eleanor said, picking up on the excuse Jane had given for her absence.

"Don't mention it," Jane said, pulling the parcel into her lap. "You have a delicate constitution and are always ill this time of year. As your *dearest* friend, I am just delighted you are recovered. Oh, Eleanor, what a lovely candle, thank you. My favorite scent."

Eleanor smiled as Jane kissed her cheek, but she felt that the longer she held the expression, the more brittle it became. She knew what was coming--the whispers, the glares, the barbed comments.

"Lady Eleanor," the Countess Charmine said. "How lovely to meet you at last. Although, from all of the glowing things that the Marchioness has told us, I feel as if I know you already."

"How kind of you to say so," Eleanor said. "I'm delighted to make your acquaintance."

"The Marchioness and I have known each other for years," Lady Glenda, the Dowager Baroness said, her eyebrow raised. "It's a wonder we haven't met before."

"Despite her beauty, Eleanor has always been quite shy," Jane said, interceding. "You are more likely to find her quietly reading or painting than socializing."

Eleanor focused on keeping her perfect smile in place, but she wanted to laugh. She hadn't painted a day in her life, not even when she'd had the time and means to do so.

"Fine qualities in a young lady," Lady Glenda said with an approving nod. "Fine qualities in a *wife*."

Oh, so that's what this was, then--not a torches and pitchforks affair, but more of an interview. These, Eleanor thought, were the most curious ladies of society. These were the ones who had been visiting Jane---probably daily--for two weeks, waiting to catch a glimpse of Eleanor.

And all because some gossip rag had proclaimed that the Duke of Devonshire was interested in her, maybe as a wife. If only these ladies knew the truth--that Edward wished to pay her back--nothing more. That she had struck his beautiful face! She was in no more danger of marrying the Duke of Devonshire than Stephens, Jane's elderly butler, was.

"Easter is fast-approaching," the Marchioness of Winterford said. "I've heard the

Duchess of Melfast will be hosting the event of the Season. A ball the evening before Lent begins! She's having the invitations engraved, and the envelopes are said to be lined in gold."

"How charming!" Jane said, pouring Eleanor a cup of tea and adding a spoonful of honey.

"She did ask me," the Marchioness continued. "Where she might send *your* invitation, Lady Eleanor."

"Oh," Jane laughed, waving her hand. "Send it here. That's where all the invitations are sent."

"Yes," Eleanor said with a bland smile, though her heart beat erratically at the question. "My cousin has been kind enough to take me in, but he is reclusive in nature, and prefers for all social interaction to occur *outside* his home. That is why I am so grateful that the Marchioness and her husband have taken me under their wing." She patted Jane's hand. "They have treated me so well that I quite feel that this is my second home."

It was clear that Jane was enjoying Eleanor's sudden fame far more than Eleanor was. She blushed prettily.

"Speaking of social engagements, I've heard that Lord and Lady Wilcott arrived in town two days ago," Lady Hannah said, a sly glance toward Eleanor. "Certainly Devonshire is busy with family obligations."

Eleanor took a sip of her tea without tasting it. If Lady Hannah thought that she would be baited into responding to that non-question, she was sorely mistaken.

"Though," Lady Thalia said, picking up her sister's thread of conversation, "Perhaps the family is only inviting *close* friends of the family to visit."

Ah, Eleanor thought. *The sharks are circling.* The only question became--how many sharks were in the room?

Eleanor was spared having to answer by Stephens announcing, "Lady Amelia Wilcott." He bowed and quit the room, leaving a lovely woman in his stead.

Eleanor caught the pure shock on Lady Thalia and Lady Hannah's faces. It would have been comical, had her own heart not felt as if it were going to pound out of her chest. *Why was Edward's sister here?*

Lady Amelia Wilcott gave a graceful curtsy, the ribbons on her dress fluttering artfully as she dipped and rose. She was tall, for a lady, but had a pleasantly curved figure that was set off to perfection in her light green taffeta dress. Her hair was as dark as her brother's, and her eyes looked intelligent. In her kind expression and elegant bearing, it was plain to see that this was a lady of quality.

"How kind of you to receive me," she said, after introductions were made, her voice musical. "My dear Lady Eleanor, how wonderful it is to see you again."

She stepped forward and kissed Eleanor's cheek; a whisper of contact that left behind the perfume of lavender. Somehow, when they sat again, Eleanor was sandwiched between Jane and Amelia. Eleanor knew that she ought to be gratified, that she was flanked by the two ladies in the room who seemed to care for her, but she felt more scrutinized than ever. All eyes were on the settee where they sat.

Eleanor was unsettled at being the center of attention. But more than that, she was confused. She understood why Edward took perverse pleasure in making her uncomfortable--to him, it was all one big joke, and he wanted to get back at her for their interlude in the garden. At least, that was the explanation she had given herself.

But that didn't explain Lady Wilcott's presence here. Was the entire family in on the joke? Or was Amelia here for a different reason? She didn't seem to be teasing Eleanor; instead, she had immediately partnered with Jane to answer the group's questions on Eleanor's behalf. Eleanor took a deep breath and tried to regain an understanding of the conversation taking place around her.

"And what of you, Lady Eleanor?" Lady Thalia said. She seemed to have recovered from her shock at Lady Amelia's presence. "Do you have plans for Easter festivities?"

"Actually," Lady Amelia said, kindly. "She is to spend the day with our family, at Netherton Hall. Isn't that right, Eleanor?"

Eleanor smiled and nodded, though her insides were a riot of confusion. Really, this pretense was getting confusing. Why were the Duke and his sister taking an interest in her, someone they hadn't seen in years, a young lady of no means and little beauty, from a family that was plagued with scandal? Could it be that Lady Amelia was in earnest, and really wanted to make her acquaintance? Or was the whole family so bored with their wealth that they toyed with strangers as sport?

"And," Lady Amelia added, patting Eleanor's hand. "We are sure to see you at the Duchess of Melfast's ball."

Again, Eleanor nodded. She hadn't planned on attending; she wasn't even sure that she was to be invited, but it was best not to argue in front of the other ladies. They had assembled in hope of catching some tidbit of gossip, a morsel of delicious news that they could share with their friends. Eleanor would do her best to give them nothing.

She fortified herself and tried to participate in the conversation as the afternoon wore on, but it was all she could do to keep the polite smile in place. As she internally roiled with confusion, it became clear that there was a war of attrition taking place in the beautiful, pastel-pink drawing room. The ladies that Eleanor did not know well would not go away until they had extricated every bit of gossip from the situation, or until they threatened to float away from all the tea they sipped.

But finally, finally--the other women left, and it was only Jane, Eleanor, and Lady Amelia.

"Thank the heavens above," Jane hissed, as the rustle of silk faded down the stairs. "I've had to use the privy this last hour. Please excuse me."

She rushed from the room, and Eleanor and Lady Amelia were alone.

"I'm sorry for that," Amelia said.

Eleanor frowned in confusion. "Sorry for what?"

"My brother is very concerned about the social...inconvenience that his attention may have caused you."

Eleanor raised an eyebrow. "Forgive me, Lady Wilcott, but I find that very hard to believe."

"Please, call me Amelia," she said. "And why do you doubt it? He told me so, himself. Why else would he have sent me?"

"He sent you?" Eleanor twisted her hands together.

"Of course. How else could I have found you here? And now that we are alone, I would like to invite you, the Marchioness and the Marquess to dinner tomorrow evening. It will be a small, family affair, the better for us all to get to know each other."

"I don't understand," Eleanor said, shaking her head. In her confusion, the truth tumbled out. "I thought he disliked me. I...I hit him, the first time we met."

Amelia laughed, a tinkling, silvery sound. "No wonder he's enchanted. You're not anything like anyone else. Well, I cannot speak for my brother, of course, but his desire to be better known to you is very real. That I can say. And I would be honored to know you, too."

This statement flustered Eleanor more than anything else that had happened. It had never occurred to Eleanor that the Duke's interest might be *real.* She thought that he'd been entertaining himself, that she was just a unique diversion, a side-show that had caught his momentary attention. To hear that it could be something *more...* she was flummoxed.

Amelia laid a hand on Eleanor's arm. "I can see you have lots to think about, and I must get back. I didn't think it would take so long for the others to leave. But then, there was blood in the water, was there not?" She winked.

Eleanor laughed. "At least I will be unavailable for tea tomorrow, as I have a dinner to prepare for."

Amelia's smile was dazzling. "Then you will come?"

Eleanor nodded, even as her nerves screamed at her to fake an illness or injury or prior engagement. She told herself that it was because Amelia was so kind, and that Jane would be apoplectic if Eleanor turned down the invitation. But the truth was, the temptation to see *him* again was too strong. She'd tried not to think of him, or to feel nothing but irritation towards him, but she had failed.

"How wonderful! Lucas and Henry will be delighted to hear it. And Edward, too, of course. We will see you at six o'clock. Please give the Marchioness my regards." Amelia kissed each of Eleanor's cheeks and saw herself out.

Jane bustled in not three minutes later. "Drat. I was afraid of that--I missed her."

Eleanor had succumbed to the exhaustion that had been swirling in her mind ever since she'd walked through the door and saw the crowd of ladies that were assembled--assembled to watch her perform. It was tiring to hold a pleasant expression for hours on end, when one felt anything but pleasant. It was difficult to maintain a facade of politeness when the ladies poked and prodded in turn with efforts ranging from vague inquiry to downright rude questions.

"Eleanor, you need a brandy." Jane didn't wait for an answer, and Eleanor found herself holding a nearly full snifter two moments later.

"Drink," Jane prodded. "Drink, then explain. I must confess that I am surprised. The Duke of Devonshire?"

She flopped onto the settee next to Eleanor and kicked off her satin slippers. Eleanor blinked; she couldn't remember ever seeing Jane in any state of relaxation or dishabille.

"You play your cards very close to your chest," Jane continued. "But then, you always have. I thought he was just curious, you know. But today proves that he is very serious about you."

"What?" Eleanor had taken several sips of brandy. The warmth in her stomach had restored her enough to speak.

"You know that he will look into your...situation," Jane said, cautiously. "You may need to be careful that you aren't followed."

"What do you mean?" Eleanor said, her voice an octave too high.

"I know, Eleanor." Jane sighed. "I've known all along." She paused. "It isn't always easy, being married. As a wife, I have to abide by my husband's wishes, whether that be regarding which kind of carriage we purchase, or how long our houseguests stay." She swallowed deeply. "No matter how dear that houseguest is to me, or how dire her situation may be."

Eleanor's face crumpled, and she began to cry. It was too much--she'd been hiding this secret from Jane for so long--to find out that Jane already knew--that she had always known, was painful. She curled in on herself, over her brandy.

"Oh, dear," Jane said, scooting over to her and putting an arm around her shoulders. "I'm sorry. Please don't cry. I have a hard enough time not weeping these days, without you adding to my struggle. We need to talk about the Duke."

"He's invited us to dinner tomorrow night," Eleanor managed, through hiccups. "Amelia said it's to be a small, family dinner."

"Ah, 'Amelia' is it?" Jane asked with a knowing smile. "How is it that you have succeeded where so many other women have failed?"

"I hit him. I hit him in the face when he tried to fl..flirt with me." She dissolved into hiccuping tears once more.

Jane laughed and kissed the side of her head. "You will have to tell me that story someday. But you've caught his eye. He's the first one to be interested who I believe is worthy; and about time, too. So tell me--is the story about his family knowing yours a complete fabrication?"

"I don't know," Eleanor said. "I was too young to remember, but it seems an odd thing to make up. Perhaps my brother mentioned a Devonshire, but I didn't pay much attention back then, when he spoke. I wish I had." She sniffled. "If I could go back, I'd do so many things differently."

"We all would, darling," Jane said, sounding a bit jaded. She stroked Eleanor's hair. "We all would."

Chapter 18

From the *Quentin Daily-*

Lady A.W. is the sister of a certain noble gentleman who has been mentioned numerous times in this column as of late. This lady, recent to London from her brother's country estate, sought out Lady E.G. at a well-attended afternoon tea reception at the home of M.M. It was there that Lady A.W. announced that Lady E.G. had plans to spend Christmas Day with said gentleman and their family. The intent of such an invitation remains to be seen, but speculation is rampant...

At promptly six o'clock the next evening, the Marquess and Marchioness of Millen, along with Lady Eleanor Gilbert, pulled up in an elegant landau to the front of Netherton Hall. The three passengers of the vehicle had spent their polite chatter, and now were sunk into silence, looking forward to the evening ahead. One passenger was especially nervous.

Eleanor felt as if the butterflies she'd beaten to death had risen from the grave and brought friends. She was alternately filled with dread and strangely giddy--she felt she was equally in danger of running screaming from the place or giggling to herself--neither of which would make a good impression. And she still wasn't sure of what this really was about. She felt like she was missing something. Why would a man of the Duke's wealth and stature be interested in her? What was his purpose?

When she had asked Jane that question as they got ready, Jane had laughed.

"Surely you cannot be that thick, Eleanor. The man means to court and marry you."

The words had swam around in Eleanor's head like the fish she'd once seen in a pond. Around and around the words went- 'court and marry you' 'court and marry you' 'court and marry you', until they were all she could think of, until the words had no meaning at all. But regardless of the Duke's intentions, she meant to conduct herself in such a fashion that her father would be proud of her, were he still alive.

Netherton Hall seemed to loom larger without the crowds in front of it. As the footman helped her out of the carriage, the huge front doors were opened, spilling light onto the steps. Eleanor took a deep breath, pulled the satin-lined velvet cloak closer around her form and turned to face the house. Jane had tried to hen-peck her into wearing light blue, but Eleanor had refused. In the end, they'd settled on a midnight blue silk with a simple, jeweled neckline that showed her shoulders, but no decolletage, even though Jane moaned that a *little* exposure was acceptable. Eleanor had conceded to borrowing a pair of Jane's sapphire earrings and letting Hattie, Jane's maid, pull her hair up into a complicated confection of curls and braids.

Their wraps taken, the butler led them into a sitting room with a cheerful fire crackling behind an ornate brass safety screen. The reason for the precaution, Eleanor saw, was sprawled in the middle of the floor with a set of painted metal toy soldiers--a little boy wearing trousers and a newly-rumpled white shirt.

But there was Edward, drawing her eyes, and her heartbeat sped up. He was dressed impeccably in a black suit with a bottle green waistcoat that matched his eyes. His crisp white cravat was stuck through with an emerald pin.

Eleanor tried not to let her eyes linger on his imposing form as the butler announced their party, but it was difficult. She made her eyes go to the other people in the room. Lady Amelia Wilcott looked radiant in a rose-colored gown. Her smile crinkled the corners of her eyes as she greeted the newcomers--she looked genuinely happy that Eleanor was there. Lord Wilcott was tall and quiet, but his eyes softened whenever he looked at his wife.

"Hullo, Eleanor," Percy said, impudently leaning in to kiss her cheek.

Eleanor thought she saw Edward roll his eyes.

Eleanor pursed her lips against a smile. "Lord Waldrey, it's nice to see you again."

"I wouldn't have missed this evening for the world," he said with a smile. "Dinner and a show-- what more could a gent hope for on a fine evening?"

"Oh, stop it, Percy," Lady Candace said, wedging herself firmly between him and Eleanor. "Very sorry that my brother is being his usual self," she said to Eleanor. "I'm Lady Candace. I've heard nothing but wonderful things about you."

Candace looked ethereal in a gauzy gown of light pink that accented her flawless skin and bright cheeks. If Eleanor didn't know her to be sweet and kind, she would have been tempted to give in to knee-jerk jealousy and dislike her.

"It is lovely to meet you," Eleanor said.

"Oh, yes," Jane said, grasping Eleanor's elbow. "Lady Candace, it's so lovely to meet you."

Lady Candace was gracious enough to turn her smile upon Jane. "Lady Millen, I hear that your parlor is the pinnacle of style..."

All this time, Eleanor could feel Edward watching her carefully. He said nothing, but Eleanor could feel his eyes.

Finally, she turned to him and offered a small curtsy. "Your Grace."

"We are well past that, Eleanor," he said, a mocking look in his eye. "Please, call me Edward."

Eleanor couldn't come up with any words, let alone the appropriate ones, so she settled for nodding. She was too aware of being watched, of everyone's eyes not so subtly tracking their interactions.

"Lord Millen," Candace said, "I've heard that you are an excellent horseman. Lord Wilcott just purchased a Percheron, and he and Lord Waldrey have been discussing its care. I am well out of my depth with the conversation, but it seems they need a tie-breaker."

"Lady Millen," Amelia said. "Would you care for a glass of punch or champagne? My brother has an excellent wine cellar, and it is too rarely enjoyed."

Candace led the Marquess and the other gentlemen to one side of the room, while Amelia led the Marchioness to the other, effectively leaving Edward and Eleanor alone.

"Perhaps the birthday present I bought for my sister is insufficient. I purchased her rubies; now I am thinking diamonds may have been called for."

Eleanor laughed. "You will never hear me argue that point. Anyone who could so easily capture Jane's attention is a rare creature indeed."

Edward smiled down at her, and Eleanor became aware of the fluttering in her stomach once more. The longer he looked, the hotter her face became, until she could bear it no longer and turned away. The little boy on the floor was staring up at them curiously. He had the same dark hair and deep green eyes as the man standing next to her did.

"Henry," Edward said. "This is my dear friend Eleanor Gilbert. Eleanor, this is Henry. Henry, how do we greet ladies?"

Henry stood up and gave a formal bow. His face was very serious.

"How do you do, Lady Eleanor?" he said, then looked to Edward for approval.

Edward nodded.

"Very well, thank you, sir." Eleanor curtsied, and the boy smiled. "Are you planning a great offensive?" She pointed toward the mass of brightly painted tin soldiers.

"It's the battle of Waterloo," the boy said. "Napoleon's on the march, and we must stop him."

Eleanor settled to the floor in front of the soldiers, and the boy blinked in surprise.

"Which side is the French?" she asked.

Henry looked at Edward for permission, and with another nod, he had it. Henry came to his knees and his face lit up with a smile.

"These here are the French," the boy said, pointing towards the blue-painted soldiers. "And here are the British in red. But I don't have any different colors to show the Dutch or Prussians."

"Hmmm," Eleanor said, tapping her chin. "Do you suppose it matters? After all, even if there were different armies, there were only two *sides* in the battle."

"You're right," Henry said, scooting forward and straightening some calvary who'd tipped over. "This was Napoleon's last fight."

"Indeed it was."

"The British stopped him. The Duke of Wellington led the charge."

Henry stated this so firmly, that Eleanor's lips twitched. She didn't have the heart to tell him that his great military heroes didn't lead charges; they simply commanded them done.

"Well, which one is he?" Eleanor said.

Henry pointed to a cavalry soldier that was out in front.

"And do you see any potential problems with the Duke's military strategy?" Eleanor asked, her eyebrow raised.

Henry studied the array of metal toys, and then frowned. "No. Britain won, didn't we?"

"We did." Eleanor smiled. "But the Duke of Wellington said later that it was a very close battle. We could not have beaten the French without very good friends that we could trust, and that is a lesson in of itself--good friends you can trust are exceedingly important."

The little boy studied her intently, then turned back to his toys.

"Do you see I've got a cannon?"

Eleanor stifled a laugh and smiled instead. "No, where?"

He handed it to her, and she turned to show Edward. When she turned, the Duke was sitting on the edge of a nearby chair. She couldn't read the look he was giving her, but the intensity of his gaze was nearly more than she could bear. But she couldn't look away, either. It was like looking at a dancing flame. They were locked there, for long moments, deep green eyes meeting large brown ones.

"Dinner is served, Your Grace," the butler announced, from the doorway.

Edward's eyes flickered away toward the door, then back to Eleanor, and the spell was broken. She put down the toy cannon, and smiled at Henry.

"Will you do me the honor of walking into dinner?" Edward asked, his voice low.

He offered her his hand to help her up. She took it. They went.

The dining room was down the large hall, through an entryway. The room was big enough that it easily fit the dining table large enough to seat seventy. Two large fireplaces warmed the space, and Eleanor was grateful to see that a smaller table had been set in front of one of them. A low bowl of white roses and ivy rested in the center, between two lit silver candelabra. The polished silver, gold-edged china and cut crystal glimmered in the flickering light.

"I hope this is acceptable," Edward said to the group. "We don't usually dine at the main table if it is family and friends."

"Lovely," Jane said. Her cheeks looked pleasantly flushed, and she smiled.

Eleanor was glad that Jane looked happy. Even the Marquess seemed to be enjoying his conversation with Lord Wilcott and Percy. It didn't escape her notice that she and Edward sat at one end of the table with Henry beside Edward. Lord and Lady Wilcott sat in the center, Percy and Lady Candace beside them, and the Marquess and Marchioness were seated at the other end.

Amelia said grace, and a bevy of servants placed a bowl of soup before each of them.

"Thank you," Eleanor said to the footman when he set the low bowl before her.

She caught the Duke looking at her with one of his unreadable expressions, and though her cheeks grew hot, she lifted her chin.

"Yes, Your Grace?" she murmured, in challenge.

It was not the fashionable thing to do, acknowledging servants. Most of high society treated them as one would treat a gas lamp--

inanimate and not worth acknowledging until you had specific need of it. Many of the peerage thought it degrading to thank those beneath them in station. Eleanor had once thought so, herself. Then she had been forced to live among them, forced to shop with them, dine with them, haggle alongside them in the market. If there was one thing she wouldn't change about her experiences over the past years, it was realizing that people are people, no matter the rank.

Edward shook his head and began to eat his soup. Eleanor's eyes narrowed, then she caught herself. She couldn't make a scene, though she longed to demand to know what he was thinking, or kick him under the table so that he dropped his indiscernible expression. The whole evening, he had been nothing but stoic, watchful. If he truly wanted to get to know her, shouldn't they *speak*?

"How is your soup, Eleanor?" he asked, taking another bite of his own.

Eleanor realized that she'd been staring at him with a clenched jaw and hadn't tasted her soup. She lifted the spoon to her mouth and only with effort kept an unreadable facade. It was hot, creamy, rich and flavorful.

"So, how is it?" he prompted.

"I'm not sure," Eleanor said. "I feel that I need to spend more time with it. At worst, it is incorrigible; at best, silent."

The corners of his mouth twitched. At last, a reaction.

"The soup?" he said.

"Yes," she said. "It flummoxes me. I can't decide if it is bored and therefore toying with me, or if it has other motives."

"It's cream soup," little Henry supplied, from her other side. His eyes were big. "Don't you like it?"

"I do like it, Henry," Eleanor conceded. "It's very good."

"Delighted to hear it," Edward said, smiling. "It's all settled then, between you and the *soup*."

The desire to kick him under the table increased. And what was worse, she could have sworn that the blackguard knew it, for he continued in the same vein of conversation. Not that she could protest, as she had begun the bizarre analogy.

"Have you tried many soups, Eleanor?" he asked politely.

"Yes, Your Grace, I have."

"It's Edward, if you please," he said. "Tell me about some of them."

"The soups?" she repeated, eyes wide.

"Yes, the soups. What kinds have you had, what kinds did you like, dislike?"

It was a question posed so mildly that anyone who overheard it would think that they were having a very ordinary, if very boring, conversation. But Eleanor had become attune to the shape of his lips, the way they moved or tried not to curl when he was teasing someone--teasing her. And he knew, as well as she did, that the soup was a euphemism, for him. Therefore, other flavors would be...other men?

Eleanor straightened. "I fear I must change my answer, Your Grace."

"It's Edward."

"I myself have not tried many kinds of soups, you see," she continued without acknowledging him. "But

I have been in proximity when *others* have tried soups. Being a keen observer, I believe I can tell you which kinds of soup would suit me, and which would not."

He was smiling openly now. "Pray, do continue."

"There are some ladies, for instance, who seem to enjoy a rustic soup, flavored liberally with beer. This soup is most commonly served at the docks, and sometimes can be fought over by two or more ladies. I can tell you that I have no desire to try that kind of soup, as it is dissolute and prone to late afternoon napping."

Edward chuckled, his eyes twinkling.

"Then there are the kinds of soup that are too rich," Eleanor continued. "It matters not to *that* kind of soup who eats it. Those kinds of soup care only that they have one who is young, beautiful, and easily fooled. Those kinds of soup need lots of attention, but again they are *shared*."

"So what you are really saying is that you dislike sharing your soup," Edward said.

"Was a soup that was shared ever mine to begin with? But that is not the only point of contention," she said. "Every kind of soup is different. Some are dull, some unintelligent, some foolhardy with finances, others have damaging vices."

"Are you sure that you even *like* soup?" Edward said, grinning.

"It depends completely on the soup," Eleanor argued.

"I say," the Marquess said, from the other end of the table. "What are you two discussing so avidly down there?"

"Soup," Edward replied.

"Quite right. Nothing better than a hearty stew on a cold evening," the Marquess said.

"Carrot soup is my favorite," little Henry added, solemnly.

He looked to Edward for approval of his statement, and Edward nodded at him, his lips twitching with humor. Even Eleanor had to smile.

"This is why the man doesn't enjoy socializing," Percy said, rolling his eyes. "Beautiful ladies at his table, and all he can think to speak about is *soup*."

"So, what about reformed soup?" Edward said, in a low voice, once the other end of the table took up a conversation about livestock once more.

Eleanor frowned. "I don't know that I'm familiar with that kind."

"You know, soup that has seen the error of its former ways."

Eleanor thought, then spoke slowly. "If I could be absolutely convinced that a soup were mine and mine alone, and that it was moral, responsible, intelligent, and all the things a soup should be, I may be persuaded to eat it."

"You have high standards," he said, smiling once more.

"No higher than any young lady's should be," she said, her eyes flashing. "But so many of my counterparts seem to think that the richness of a soup absolves it from all other requirements. I've seen that road travelled many a time, Your Grace, and it ends in misery."

"You mean a stomachache?" he said, lightly. "And please call me Edward."

"A stomachache, a broken heart, disillusionment...whatever you wish to call it."

He nodded.

"What kind of soup do *you* like, Papa?" Henry asked, innocently.

"I like a soup with a lot of personality. You know, something that really smacks you in the face with its flavor."

He cast his green eyes upon her, and she could feel the heat crawling up her neck. At that moment, the servants moved to clear their soup course.

"Let's see what we'll be discussing next," Edward said, as a maid set a dish before him. "Look at that. Sausage."

She took a deep breath and seemed to steady herself.

"Before we move on to discussing, er...sausage," Eleanor said. "Though I think more highly of maids than most, I wouldn't deign to share my soup with one."

She looked at Henry, then at Edward. The meaning of her statement and her glance hit him as squarely as her fist had upon their first meeting. She didn't know. *She didn't know.* Eleanor believed the stories, that Henry was Edward's son, born on the wrong side of the sheets by an unnamed servant at his country house. Which means that his secret was safe. Henry was safe.

And Eleanor was trying to keep him at arm's length because she thought him the kind of man who would do such a thing. Edward felt excitement bubbling up inside him like a glass of champagne. He wanted to laugh. She, the lady who spent each night in a drafty attic garrett, held her morals and values of higher importance than all the wealth of Netherton Hall spread out before her. She was kind to Henry, but standoffish to Edward, which showed that she placed the imaginary blame on the correct person. He wanted to yank her out of her chair and kiss her senseless. He wanted to tell everyone how wonderful she was. He wanted...

He wanted to court and marry her.

He leaned back in his chair and grinned. Eleanor's frown deepened.

"Do you understand what I meant, about the soup?" she demanded.

"I understand perfectly, Eleanor. I quite respect the sentiment. The thing about soup is...it's not always what people say it is. Why, once I thought I was about to enjoy a bowl of carrot soup, but it was pumpkin. Appearances can be deceiving."

"Are you two still talking about soup?" Percy said, his lip curling.

"As if that's any worse than you and Wilcott speaking of nothing but horses for the past half-hour," Amelia said.

"Hear-hear," Jane added with a smile, toasting with her glass. "Do save us, Eleanor, Your Grace. This end of the table is dreadfully dull."

It was inevitable, Edward knew. He couldn't expect to have Eleanor's undivided attention through the entire meal. But even when he spoke to others and engaged in the conversation, his attention was on her. He noticed how she spoke to Henry, how she reached over and helped cut up his slice of cold ham, how her smiles and laughs did not come cheaply. The more she spoke, the more he watched her, the more he wanted to know her.

Henry began to fall asleep during the third course, so Edward had a maid come and take the boy to bed. He no longer slept in the nursery, but in a bedroom close to Edward's own. Eleanor waved goodbye to the sleepy boy as he gave a yawning bow, and Edward thought his heart might burst with the emotion of it. No one except Amelia and Lucas had ever treated Henry in such a manner. Most people flat-out ignored him, like the boy was some kind of mess that a pet had made on the carpet. Even the Marquess and Marchioness had avoided looking at him.

Edward understood, to an extent. There were many peers who had sired bastards, but they were kept secret, away from eyes. Not many men trotted out their illegitimate children in front of guests, or dared to name them 'family'. But Eleanor seemed to be in the same frame of mind as he was--it was not the *child's* fault. A child had no control over the circumstances of their own birth, and did a child born out of wedlock not deserve love?

"I wonder," Edward murmured to Eleanor, once the others were engrossed in their own conversation once more. "Are you attending the Duchess of Melfast's ball?"

A blush tinted Eleanor's cheeks, and Edward couldn't help but notice that it made her look even more fetching.

"Yes, Your Grace. At least, my invitation arrived this morning."

"I hope you'll do me the honor of saving me the first dance?"

Edward's fingers were clenched in his lap. He couldn't remember the last time he'd been nervous asking that question, but then, he'd never cared about the answer quite so much.

"Yes, Your Grace," she said.

Her blush was in full effect now, a becoming pink that flushed her from collarbone to forehead. Edward felt gratified--perhaps he wasn't the only one who was feeling high emotions.

"Wonderful. I look forward to it."

Chapter 19

From the *Quentin Daily-*

Sources say that an intimate gathering happened at a gentleman's estate yesterday evening. Lady E.G. was present, as were other esteemed guests. It is clear that the gentleman of high rank wished to know the lady better. The outcome of this gathering is as of yet unclear. Be assured, dearest reader, that the Quentin Daily will be following this story. Perhaps there will be another installment after a certain ball in the coming days...

Eleanor was doing her best to ignore the numerous entries in the gossip sheets, but she found it more difficult than she would have liked. For one thing, the gossip reports fueled her own, deep-down secret hope--that Edward *was* courting her, that he *did* look at her that way.

But hope could be painful. Hope was like being lifted to an enormous height--exhilarating, but always fearing that terrible drop. And Eleanor had experienced that fall before. She wasn't sure that she would survive another. So she did her best to ignore the hope that she felt, to starve it and lock it away into a dark corner of herself, until it became so emaciated it didn't have the power to hurt her.

It was an understatement to say that she was nervous the evening of Duchess of Melfast's ball. Adding to her consternation was the fact that, although she was getting ready at Jane's house, Jane would not be accompanying her.

"I'm too big for my ball gowns," Jane complained, her feet propped upon a padded stool. "I feel enormous, and this process has just begun."

Despite her complaints, Jane looked happy and radiant, a smug smile on her face as she reclined in her rooms.

"Anyways," Jane said, waving her hand toward her dressing room. "All my gowns are at your disposal. I took a guess and had Hattie take in the lilac and the peach. You may borrow my ermine cloak."

So nighttime found Eleanor bundled in furs, ensconced in the Marquess' carriage. Hattie, the chaperone, sat next to her, and the Marquess was on the bench seat opposite. He looked out the window and took periodic sips from the flask tucked into his breast pocket. Far from being offended at his taciturn nature, Eleanor was grateful for the quiet. It gave her time to collect herself and figure out how she was feeling.

There was a small crowd in front of the grand townhome when they arrived, but it was cold, and people quickly moved into the warm foyer. Eleanor handed Jane's ermine cloak to an attendant, and surveyed the ballroom.

"Shall we?" the Marquess said, offering Eleanor his arm.

Eleanor smiled politely and allowed him to escort her into the crowd of people, though she wasn't sure if she was ready. Above the lilting strains of music and the decadent rustle of silk dresses, the sound of whispers followed as they walked. But they hadn't made it very far before Lord and Lady Wilcott approached.

"Eleanor," Amelia said, kissing her cheek. "You look divine."

Eleanor smoothed the lilac silk of her skirt. Of all the dresses Jane had ever given her, this was her favorite--just off the shoulder with intricate folds as the only ornament, it was simple from afar, and only interesting when you looked closely. Hattie had pulled her hair up into a complicated arrangement of curls, accented by grey pearls that matched the earrings she wore.

A warm hand cupped her bare elbow, and a shiver of awareness slinked down her spine.

"I believe I have the first dance?" Edward said.

Eleanor nodded, trying furiously to fight the blush rising in her cheeks. It wasn't her fault, she thought. He looked too handsome in his crisp black jacket and waistcoat. A white cravat stuck through with a ruby pin was the only bit of color on his person. He looked dark, dangerous. It didn't help that Eleanor was aware that everyone was watching them. She was flustered by his appearance, but trying not to show it.

Edward led her to the dance floor, and took her in his arms. The warmth of his hands seeped through the silk where he held her waist and hand. It was difficult to look him in the eye--he was too close, his eyes too sharp--she felt like he could see every emotion racing through her mind.

"Have you changed your mind?" he said.

The abrupt question jerked Eleanor from her private reverie.

"What?" she said.

"About the dance? Have you changed your mind? You're very quiet."

For the first time, Eleanor noticed the grave expression on his face. Was it possible that he was just as uncertain as she was?

"No," she said. "It is just difficult to speak with you when you're so close, and when everyone's watching."

"They are all very interested, aren't they?" he asked, with a smile. "It's a wonder they don't have anything else to do. I take it you've seen the *Quentin Daily*?"

Eleanor did her best to look unaffected. "Yes. I'm not used to being under public scrutiny, just because some individuals are making suppositions."

"Is it worth it?" Edward asked.

"Is what worth it?"

"Is being the subject of gossip worth spending time with me?" he asked, his eyes intent on hers.

"That's a very forward question," she said, blustering.

"I've been told that I'm too forward," he said, smiling. "By you, if I'm not mistaken."

"There aren't many young ladies who wouldn't trade a few lines in the gossip sheets for the opportunity to spend time with a Duke."

Gone was the smile, the genial manner. In its place was the cold mask he showed society at large. Eleanor realized she'd upset him.

"A Duke?" he said.

Several awkward, choking moments passed.

"Or you," she finally murmured, looking at his ear. His ear was far safer than his eyes, she'd realized.

"Thank you," he said. "It can be difficult, having such an esteemed title."

"Oh, I can only imagine, Your Grace," she teased. "Servants and money and deference wherever you go-- a hard life, indeed."

"It *is* a difficult thing, when you are trying to suss out who is a true friend... or who might make a good wife."

Eleanor couldn't help it--her eyes dropped to his earlobe again. (Finely formed, that earlobe.) She couldn't pretend to ignore the meaning of his words. She could feel her face being painted in a heated blush--she thought between her purple dress and her pink face, she must look like a countryside sunset.

"What are you doing tomorrow evening?" he said.

"Tomorrow evening?" Eleanor repeated, blinking at the rapid change of topic.

"Yes."

"I'm to dine with my cousin that evening."

"Ah," he said, then frowned. "What about lunch the next day? Would you join us? Henry has taken a liking to you, and it's his birthday."

She glanced down the ballroom at Amelia and Lucas. "I wouldn't want to intrude upon your family gathering."

"Nonsense. You will be a delightful addition. Two o'clock? I will send the carriage."

"No," she said, quickly. "I will find my own transportation, but thank you."

"Wonderful," he said. "I'll be sure that Mrs. Gardner makes soup."

She smiled, but shook her head.

"Your cousin is welcome, you know," he said.

"Thank you, Your Grace, but he is nearly reclusive. He never accepts social invitations."

"It's Edward," he said, then quickly added, "Please bring a friend, if you so desire. Or if your cousin changes his mind. I would like to get to know him."

"Thank you."

"Now let's give those gossips their money's worth," he said, and swept her across the ballroom floor in grand style.

The problem with dancing with Edward, Eleanor thought, was that there wasn't any time to privately recover. Her heart was pounding, she felt that her breaths were coming too short for the small amount of exertion that a simple waltz should be, and her cheeks were thoroughly heated. But she had to act as demurely as any other lady at the ball-- more so, because so many eyes were on her. She could feel them, like a flock of pigeons sitting all-too-casually near a picnic, waiting for a crumb to fall.

Eleanor was determined not to give them their crumb of gossip--they could watch all they wanted. Instead, she calmly claimed a crystal cup of punch and stood near the edge of the room. It was funny--she'd stood to the side of many a ballroom without being noticed. But now she felt that she could slip around one of the mammoth pillars in this ghastly, overdone ballroom, and still, eyes would be upon her. She wasn't under the safe, comforting cloak of anonymity anymore.

"Eleanor, there you are," a feminine voice trilled near her elbow.

Eleanor turned to meet the kind eyes of Lady Candace Waldrey. Her brother Percy, the Marquess was right behind her.

"Damned difficult to get over here," he said, dusting off his velvet jacket as if he'd just been in a scuffle. "The hounds sure are thick in here tonight."

Candace rolled her eyes. "Stop calling them hounds. They are unmarried ladies, not dogs."

"Of course *you* feel that way," he said. "You've never been an eligible bachelor surrounded by them."

Eleanor smiled. "So in this scenario, you are a fox?"

"Being hunted," Percy said, gravely. "Yes."

"That's a clever way of looking at things," Eleanor said.

"Please do not encourage my brother," Candace said, laughing. "He thinks he is witty enough, without you complimenting his insults."

"It's gotten worse, you know," Percy said, ignoring his sister. "Now that the biggest fox has all but been bagged, the hounds are setting their eyes on lesser prey."

"The biggest fox?" Eleanor said.

Percy seemed not to hear her question. He yanked at his starched collar. "That blasted Mr. Pickwick hasn't helped matters, either. The mood has turned desperate among some of the hounds. One wonders if they'll start biting at each other at any moment. Of course, some of them have fared well in the reviews, which means there are fewer foxes to hunt."

"Oh, do shut up or go away," Candace said, her cheeks pink. "We unmarried women are *not* hounds. And if you're so dismayed by the current social paradigm that pushes all of the unwed nobility together for a few months a year, please feel free to do something about it. We *hounds* are at the mercy of the foxes, after all. Perhaps you should think about how it feels, to know that your entire life's security depends upon securing the attention of a man wealthy enough to support you and future offspring, intelligent and discreet enough not to lose his fortune at the gaming tables, and pleasant enough to spend countless hours with! If you consider the parameters, there are very few *foxes* worthy of chase, indeed!"

"Well said." Eleanor would have clapped, but one hand was occupied by punch.

"Hmmph," Percy said.

"And furthermore," Candace said, "Mr. Pickwick should be commended for not being blinded by the silly things men usually are attracted to in a lady. Do you know that I had a dancing instructor who spent *hours* trying to teach me the best way to maneuver my fan, so that I might attract suitors? Thank heavens Mama found out and fired her. But can you imagine that line of reasoning--that by a certain tempo of fan movement, I might capture a husband? Mr. Pickwick at least values women for their core values, for how they treat others. Not how they look, or how much fortune they have, or whether they wave their fans alluringly."

"Oh, do stuff it, Candace," Percy drawled. "As if you are *above* all the social games. Don't forget--I know how much money you spent on dresses this year."

"Of course, I spent money on dresses," Candace whisper-hissed, through a smile. "Just because I don't *agree* with the status quo, doesn't mean I'm absolved from participating in it. I'll not play coy with you--I do want to get married, and to marry well, and part of that involves getting gentlemen to glance at me more than once."

"Well, then," Percy said, with a satisfied nod, as if Candace had just admitted to perfidy. "You admit that you care about looking pretty, about having all the latest frippery." He waved his hand in the direction of her person. "Right there, you say that even *you* care about the silly things men are attracted to."

"I have to be, to some extent," she fairly growled. "If I'm to find a husband."

"See?" Percy said, victorious. "A hound, just like the rest of them."

"My, my," the Duchess of Melfast said, approaching Eleanor's elbow. She was a well-dressed, portly woman with a keen nose for gossip. "This seems to be a wonderful discussion. Pray tell, what are you speaking of?"

"Fox hunts, Your Grace," Eleanor replied, cooly. "We are in a heated debate over the morality of such sport. Please lend us your wisdom on the subject."

The Duchess of Melfast couldn't care less for horses or sporting, Eleanor well knew. The lady was city-bred and raised, and had as little opinion on fox hunting as she had the composition of the stars.

"My viewpoint is that neither the foxes nor the hounds should be blamed for the circumstances in which they meet," Eleanor continued. "After all, a fox will be a fox, and a hound, a hound. There isn't any sense trying to change their nature with reason."

Candace's chin went up in challenge, as Percy smiled.

"That being said, certainly some hounds are far crueler than others, by nature, and some foxes aren't worth catching at all," she said.

Candace smirked, and Percy frowned.

"Er...well, I wouldn't know about that," the Duchess said.

"But how do you think the hounds feel?" Candace said. "After all, they all do the chasing, but there is only one fox. Surely that is demoralizing at best."

"It's the fox you should feel sorry for," Percy argued. "They are the one being chased."

"How do you know they don't like it?" Candace asked, her eyes wide and innocent.

"Cause it ends in their brutal demise!" Percy all but yelled.

"My friends are calling me," the Duchess said.

"Lovely punch!" Percy called to the woman's back as she hurried away.

"Poor dear," Candace said, shaking her head. "She's never been in the middle of a Waldrey family argument before."

"So you do that often?" Eleanor asked, with raised eyebrows. "Argue with each other?"

"Our parents were disgustingly in love with each other," Percy said. "But they taught us the importance of verbal discourse, and how to express differing points of view."

"Sometimes at loud volume," Candace said, sarcastically.

"Our home was often loud, growing up. Not for the faint of heart."

"But full of love." Candace was quick to add. "Being part of our family growing up made me excited to have a husband and children of my own, someday."

"So the disagreements never bother you?" Eleanor asked.

"Bother her?" Percy made a rude noise of disbelief with his mouth. "If she had been born male, she would have become the most fearsome barrister the country has ever known, she likes to argue so much!"

Candace elbowed her brother sharply, but subtly, in the side.

Percy continued, "Regardless of what I say about foxes and hounds, I really do feel bad for the chap she catches one day. He'll be so henpecked, he'll wish for death."

"He will not!" Candace said, looking scandalized. "I daresay that I have enough good qualities to make any husband happy."

"My mistake," Percy said. "He will be *happily* henpecked."

"What are you all talking about?" Edward said, appearing at Eleanor's side. "Anything interesting?"

"Animals, mostly," Eleanor said. "We've covered foxes and hounds, and now we're on to hens."

Edward frowned at Percy. "And you mocked me for talking about soup."

"Lady Candace," said an approaching young man dressed in a bright yellow waistcoat with a matching flower in his lapel. "I believe I have this dance."

"Go away, Lord Philips," Percy growled. "Or do you forget I was at The Black Crow last weekend, too?"

The young man's eyes went wide, and he did an about-face that would have made a soldier proud and walked away. If he had been going any faster, people would have worried about a fire.

"Oh dear," Candace said. "Now I'm curious. What happened at that fancy gaming club of yours?"

"It's not *mine*," Percy said.

"With all the money you spend there, you should own at least a percentage by now," Candace chided. "Really, Edward. Can't you accompany him once in awhile and keep him sober?"

"You know I don't go to those places. I like a return on *my* money," Edward said, smiling. "Besides, Percy's just bored. He's always bored when he's in the city. It's like the collar he keeps yanking at- -too tight, too constricting. He's happiest in the country with his horses and properties."

Percy cocked his head. "You're right. The city's so--"

"Dirty," Edward said.

"Crowded," Candace offered.

"Dangerous," Eleanor supplied.

"Exactly," Percy said.

Chapter 20

From the *Quentin Daily-*

A ball took place in a grand London home last evening. The uppermost echelon of the peerage was invited, and our readers will be delighted to hear that Lady E.G. and a certain gentleman shared not one, but two dances--the first and the last. Sources say the gentleman was at the lady's elbow nearly the entire evening. It appears that the rumors of this gentleman's preference haven't been exaggerated. Sources say that the Lady will even be spending Easter with him and his family. With this kind of marked behavior, can wedding bells be far off?

The day before little Henry's birthday party dawned cold and clear. Eleanor pulled on her sturdiest boots and her warmest shawl, and trudged out into the crisp wind. She did her best to ignore how the cold stung the tip of her nose and crept up her skirts. She was on a mission. She trudged up Monroe Street, basket in hand, and ducked into a toy store. Row after row of brightly colored toys assaulted the senses, but Eleanor knew what she wanted. Transaction completed, she went to the bookstore.

Every little boy should have lots of books. Perhaps it was the influence of her father, who would pull her up on his lap on the great leather chair before the fire and read to her, but many of her best, earliest memories were of children's books. She found two of her long-ago favorites in the Children's section. She hoped that nostalgia hadn't colored her memory, that the books were as good as she remembered. She wandered into the surrounding rows, just browsing. When she saw one spine, she laughed and thought of Edward. Her hand reached out to snatch it from the shelf, to buy it, but she caught herself.

Would it be appropriate to give him a gift? Was it safe? She bit her lip. The Eleanor of three months ago wouldn't have even considered it. That Eleanor would have declined the invitation to the birthday party, or made up a sudden illness or sprain to get out of it. But she was different now. It wasn't just that the Duke of Devonshire was, by all appearances, courting her. Even that thought made her flush. It was more than that. Last night, at the ball, Eleanor had felt something that she hadn't felt in years--*belonging*.

When she was with Edward, Percy, and Candace, they didn't look at her and see her brother's disastrous marriage. They didn't see the scandal of her family. They didn't see a ruined, penniless woman. They saw Eleanor, and treated her as an equal, as someone they wanted to know. It was intoxicating, that feeling. She still was drunk on it-- the warmth of it was still in her belly, like a good whiskey. So on a whim, she pulled the book from the shelf and added it to her stack. Maybe she would give it to him, maybe not.

She had been calling him Edward in her head for awhile now, since that first night in the garden. But she hadn't yet brought herself to calling him that out loud. It was just another layer of protection that she had on, one of the last, if she were being honest with herself. How had she found herself here--in a bookshop, buying a present for a *Duke*? She could pretend that he wasn't interested in her, but her instincts told her differently.

She knew it was all a house of cards. If Edward knew where she lived, if he knew how she made money--it would all fall down. She wouldn't just have ruined Jane's reputation, Edward would be affected, too. She shook her head. What was she doing? If she had any sense, any kind of self-preservation, she would write a polite cancellation and never see him again.

But his attention was like the warmth of a fire when she hadn't even realized how cold she was.

He was like sunlight on her skin--yes, she could live without it, but now that she knew what it *felt* like... Eleanor shook her head once more and tried to focus on the task at hand. A book for the Duke--no, a book for *Edward*.

They'd been following her all morning, and Cheever was getting restless.

"Walking all over bloody London, she is," he hissed, stamping his damp feet and shoving his gloveless fingers into his fragrant armpits. "We could have taken her six times already."

"You know what she said," Marks said, puffing on a cheroot. "We don't take her until she says so. We just watch and report."

"And why do we always have to do exactly what she says, eh? You and I are smart enough fellows. We could run our own gambit, just cut the lady out of it altogether."

Marks shrugged. "We could try, but we don't have the connections she does. You think that either of us could get out of this alive without her? Once we take the lady, if that Duke is attached to her--welp, it will get right messy with the coppers. They don't take kindly to our kind laying a finger on the posh set."

"We could just snap her neck and have done with it."

Marks scowled at him. "And how would we get paid then?"

"Dunno." The large man shrugged. "That part ain't my job, now is it?"

"*Thinking* ain't your job, Cheever. Don't forget it. It ain't time now, anyways. She'll send us a letter when she wants it done. We don't move until then. We just watch."

And watch they did, all the way back to the ramshackle tenement in Cheapside.

"So... a Duke, eh, my girl?" Mr. McAffrey said later.

They were seated in front of his warm grate, a supper of roast chicken, bread and potatoes on the table between them. Mr. McAffrey topped off Eleanor's wine glass.

"I don't know what it is between us," Eleanor answered.

Over the years, she'd learned that Mr. McAffrey was the best kind of confidant--he remembered all, judged little, and didn't bring things up in conversation unless she did.

"Well, that's all right, then," he said with a smile. "If you were proclaiming your undying love after so short a time, I'd know you were just interested in his fortune."

Eleanor balked. "Certainly not. I hope you know me better than that."

"It's a rare woman who would be interested in who that man really is. Goodness knows even *I* would marry him for his fortune." He winked.

An image of the grizzled Mr. McAffrey dressed in an elaborate wedding gown, complete with veil, popped into her mind. Eleanor laughed.

"I don't doubt that's half of why he's interested," he continued. "It must be a novelty for him for someone not to care a whit for his wealth."

"I didn't say I didn't care," she admitted, somewhat ashamed. "Even visiting such a house is a pleasure. It's delightful to sit in a warm room with delicious food, having your wine glass filled by someone else before you even have to ask..."

"I knew you liked my company for a reason," he said, snapping his fingers.

She smiled. "I had forgotten what that was like. I hadn't let myself imagine that I might experience it again. But it certainly isn't worth marriage, as so many think. I couldn't marry a man without being sure as to the kind of man he really was. I've seen so many ladies be desperately unhappy after getting married to wealthy gentlemen."

"Unhappiness is a common enough problem, in marriage," he said. "No matter what the rank of the people. It is rare for true affection, even love, to survive the windstorms of life. I've seen couples get married at the height of passion, then not be speaking within the month. But I've seen people marry out of practical necessity, and then it turns into lasting friendship and love."

"Are you suggesting I marry out of practical necessity?" she said, her eyebrow raised. "I hadn't thought I was in straits as dire as that."

"You joke, Eleanor, but what will happen to you after I am gone? I am paying for this building with my army pension. I won't be around forever. Where will you go in ten years? Where will you be in life then?"

These were the questions that threatened to choke her with panic late at night when she lay alone in the dark.

She forced a smile and patted his hand, still strong despite the wrinkles present there. "I will be fine. I am in excellent health, and if things get too dire, I can take a position as a governess or teacher. Don't concern yourself about me."

"But I do," Mr. McAffrey said. "You think I don't know what you've been up to in that basement? You forget that I have the spare key. And I can read."

"It never occurred to me that you didn't know," Eleanor said, honestly. "You of all people should understand why I'm doing it."

"Oh, I understand, girlie. I do. And I'm not condemning it. But I am concerned about your future. If you are discovered, then your possibility of becoming a governess or a teacher will be gone like that." He snapped for emphasis.

The truth of his words chilled her. "I know. But I couldn't *not* do it, once the idea entered my mind."

"I understand," he said, his words gentle. "But if I could choose between a future of you as a grand Duchess or printing that blasted booklet and living alone... well, I bet you can guess which one I'd rather see."

"He might not even be interested in me in that way." Her hands fluttered helplessly on the table.

He laughed. "It's all in the papers, him inviting you to dinner, singling you out for his special attention."

"Mr. McAffrey," she said with mock sternness. "Do you mean to tell me that you read the gossip sheets?"

"When my very favorite person is featured, yes, I do." He smiled and looked ten years younger for it. "Besides, a young man would have to be deaf, blind and stupid not to think you're wonderful. Beautiful, smart girl like you."

Eleanor ducked her head. "You are not the least bit biased."

"And humble, too!" he said. "It's a wonder no one's beat the Duke to it by now."

"You hardly have to remind me of my impending spinsterhood," she said, dryly.

"Oh, psh. Your beauty hasn't even peaked yet."

"We should eat together every evening. I forget how wonderful you are for my self-esteem. But for the other matter, I'm not the type of woman to aspire to being a Duchess. I just want to live a normal, comfortable life, and I can do that here," she said, straightening her spine.

"I daresay you could do it in greater comfort at Netherton Hall," he said, his eyebrows raised.

"It's pointless to think about. Men like that don't marry ladies like me."

His brow furrowed. "What on earth are you on about? What do you mean, men like him?"

"Great men. Men of great wealth, from a titled family line. Men of financial and personal *quality*." She flopped her hand through the air, as if to encompass her thoughts of the man, as if to fill in the holes in her description.

"Oh, you think he is of *personal quality*, do you?"

"It doesn't matter what I think. That's the point. He would never be interested in me if he knew who I really was. The truth of my brother's death, the truth about *me*. That I am penniless, that I live..." She caught herself, but it was too late.

"Here. That you live here."

"I'm so sorry, Mr. McAffrey."

"You have no reason for it, my dear. I know that you are grateful, just like I know that your current address has to be kept a secret if you hope to maintain any social standing."

"I'm sorry," she said again. "And I *am* grateful. I don't know what I would have done without your kindness."

"Pfft." He shooed her gratitude away like a pesky fly. "I'm happy to have you. But back to the real issue here. If that man has any brains in his head, he will see that you are of personal quality, too. Anyway, I will accept the invitation tomorrow. I want to see what this Duke is all about before he whisks you out of my life forever."

"Never," she said, firmly. "That will never happen."

Chapter 21

From *Mr. Pickwick's Guide to Marriageable Young Ladies-*

Regarding H.H., lately of Phillips Street--this lady is a shining star. While her beauty, excellent personality, and myriad of talents have already brought streams of hopeful beaux to her door, it is of note that she has not committed herself as of yet. Flighty? No, but she does require someone of strength and gentleness to temper her delicate feelings and help guide her through life. Though she is one of the most popular with the younger gentlemen of the Season, this lady would be a better match to someone of great strength, dignity, and dare I say it--wealth. She would be vastly unhappy if made to retire to the country. This lady would be an excellent match for someone looking for a great hostess and social maven, as well as a delightful companion.

They were in the front parlor, the one with the excellent view of the long drive. Edward tried to act as if he wasn't waiting for her, looking out the window every couple of minutes. He caught Amelia with a private smile upon her lips, but she could think what she wanted.

Eleanor was late. Fifteen minutes, to be precise. What if she had decided not to come? What if she *had* decided to come, but there had been a carriage accident? Hired hacks weren't known for safe driving practices or timely maintenance. He should have sent the carriage right up to her door. It was all he could do to keep from pacing, but his sister was amused enough. Even Lucas looked in danger of smirking.

Finally, a cheerful clatter sounded from the cobblestones of the drive. A small, hired hackney meandered up to the portico, and two figures alighted, carrying a pile of parcels between them. The first was an old man, dressed in crisp military dress, and the second, he'd recognize from a great distance, through a blizzard. She was wearing a deep green dress, topped with a grey cloak and gloves.

"Get away from the window," Amelia said, with a giggle. "You don't want to frighten her off before she's crossed the threshold."

Edward whirled to face his meddling sister, and saw Lucas turn away with a cough that sounded a lot like a laugh.

"I thought Lucas was bad," she continued, shaking her head. "But even he had the sense to hide it a little. I'll tell you this--you better marry her quick, or people will be calling you the next Baron Humphries."

"That sap?" Edward said, indignant.

"Lady Eleanor Gilbert, and retired Captain Daniel McAffrey, Your Grace," Huntley announced.

Edward barely had time to school his face into something other than a scowl. Eleanor looked even more beautiful than before. She wore a deep green velvet gown that contrasted sharply with her fresh-poured cream skin. Her shining brown curls were swept up onto her head in a simple arrangement, with a few wisps curling down to frame her lovely face.

Introductions were made. Mr. McAffrey was wrinkled, but still had a full head of hair. His uniform was a little loose, but his eyes reminded Edward of one of Percy's hawks--they were intelligent, fierce, and taking in every detail at once. It was but a moment until Amelia and Lucas had somehow whisked Mr. McAffrey to the far side of the room, over near the sideboard.

His sister definitely deserved diamonds, Edward decided. He'd buy them the next time he set foot into a jewelry store.

"Did you bring me a present?" Henry said, at Eleanor's knee.

"I did." She smiled down at the boy, and the sight did a strange, twisting thing to Edward's insides. "Mr. McAffrey was good enough to carry them in for me." She presented Henry with three wrapped parcels-- two square and smaller, and one tall, wide, and very thin.

Henry unwrapped the smallest one first, revealing several children's books.

"Thank you, Lady Eleanor," Henry said.

He tore into the next package, the brown paper tearing beneath his eager fingers. Inside were two sets of tin soldiers, each painted in different colors.

"The Dutch and the Prussians, as requested," Eleanor said, smiling at Henry's enraptured expression. "Don't forget the other parcel."

He scrambled to unwrap it, revealing two thin boards with hinges in the middle. When he folded it open, it was a map of a battlefield, complete with arrows that showed the movement of the different armies.

"It's the battle of Waterloo," Eleanor explained. "And if you have any questions, I've brought you a real, live Captain, who was present at the time."

Henry's eyes went wider as he looked from the board to Mr. McAffrey's uniform. Then he rushed at Eleanor, hugging her tightly around the middle, his eyes squeezed shut. Edward opened his mouth to rebuke Henry for his exuberant display, or to apologize to Eleanor, but she caught his eye and shook her head, hugging the child back.

It was only a moment until Henry caught himself, and stood straight. "Thank you, Lady Eleanor."

"You are very welcome, Henry," she said, gently. "What else did you get for your birthday?"

His eyes lit up once more. "Uncle Lucas and Aunt Amelia got me a slide whistle and picture books and a hobby horse. Papa says that if I treat that horse very well, then next year I might have a pony and learn to ride."

"That is wonderful," she said. "And what did your Papa give you?"

Edward's heart clenched at the word. He never knew that he needed to hear it from her own lips, that she acknowledged that Edward was Henry's father, and that she wouldn't be too proud to call him such, in public or private. Edward was aware that as he watched Eleanor and Henry, nearly everyone was watching him from across the room. He found he didn't care. Let everyone call him a lovesick fool--he was no longer certain he wasn't.

"Papa got me an 'elescope."

"A telescope, Henry. A telescope," Edward corrected, smiling. "I'm sure you'll grow into it."

"Perhaps later you will show me your telescope, Henry," Eleanor said. "But until then, would you like to show your new soldiers to your aunt and uncle?"

Henry scrambled to do her bidding, and Edward wondered if he were as wrapped around her little finger as Edward suddenly felt.

She turned to Edward with a smile that he couldn't read. "I found something for you in the bookstore as well, Edward."

His heart seemed to flop at the sound of his name on her soft lips. He could barely focus on the wrapped parcel she handed him. He tore a corner of the paper and unwrapped it by rote. When he saw what book he held, he laughed out loud.

"*A Gentleman's Guide to Self-Defense*?" he said.

She arched an eyebrow. "It seemed appropriate."

He shook his head, then rubbed the back of his neck. "I actually have a present for you, as well, but I'd rather give it to you at a later time. Would you consent to a drive through the park tomorrow morning?"

Edward didn't know why *he* felt so nervous. She couldn't possibly know what he was to ask her, could she?

She colored slightly. "Of course."

He took a deep breath. If he was going to ask her that all-important question, perhaps it was time they started to be honest with one another?

"I'll pick you up at your residence at ten?"

"My cousin..." she began, twisting her fingers into her skirts.

"Does not exist," he murmured, glancing over to the others, to make sure no one could hear.

Her face drained of color, and she swayed where she sat. For a moment, it appeared she was in very real danger of swooning. Then she drew a deep, ragged breath, and tears welled in her eyes.

"Your Grace..." she began.

"I thought we were past that," he said, interrupting. "For the last time, it's Edward. And I will pick you up at your residence at ten."

There was no more time for conversation, as the grouping by the sideboard was moving their way.

"Shall we sit for luncheon, brother?" Amelia asked.

"Of course," he said. "Please lead the way."

He stood and offered Eleanor his hand. She looked at it dumbly, for a moment, then took it and rose from the settee.

"I apologize, Eleanor," he said, his voice low. "I did not mean to upset you. But there are things that I wish to discuss with you--delicate matters that require discretion. I would like us to be able to entrust each other with such things. I thought that...I thought that I would start as I mean for us to go on."

She had no response. She just looked at him, and blinked, and then they were at the small table that had been set for them near the fireplace. He winced, even as he held her chair for her to sit. Had he bungled the whole thing, then? He wanted to assure her; she had nothing to fear from him--not recrimination or threat of exposure, nothing. He wanted them to be able to trust each other, but perhaps the timing of his words had been poor. In fact, with even the smallest amount of retrospect, he should have done it when they had a private audience, not on Henry's birthday with friends and family surrounding them.

He was a blasted idiot.

"He knows," Eleanor said to Mr. McAffrey, once they were settled into the bench seats of a barouche.

Edward had offered one of his carriages to take them home, and Eleanor hadn't seen the point of declining. At least he'd had the sense to choose a carriage without the ducal crest emblazoned upon the side. At least he somewhat understood the situation. They hadn't had another moment alone to speak alone the entire afternoon. Eleanor had done her best to enjoy what was a very pleasant gathering, but her mind had been racing the entire time.

"Ah," Mr. McAffrey said. "I wondered if he did. He doesn't strike me as an idiot, and a man like that has to have sources. I'd be rather disturbed if he were to court you without knowing nearly more about you than you did."

Eleanor's mouth opened, then closed. She shook her head. "But why *would* he court me, if he knows?

Mr. McAffrey's brow wrinkled. "He's in love with you. Anyone with half a brain can see it."

"That's not it at all," she said. There was a sinking sensation in her stomach. "He must suspect I'm Mr.

Pickwick. He doesn't mean to court me. He just wants to *question* me. This was all a ruse."

Mr. McAffrey rolled his eyes. "I knew that there would be a day that you acted like a typical lady of your age. My goodness. He wishes to question you? I don't doubt it. I think he has at least one question he wishes to know the answer to, very much."

Eleanor's mind was racing too quickly to catch the implications of what he'd said.

"But why would he care so much about Mr. Pickwick?" she said. "After all, his sister is already married. It makes no sense."

"Oh, look!" he said, pointing. "The neighbor children are building a fort. It's very small. They might have waited until they collected more sticks."

"Are you not listening to me?" Eleanor said.

"I'm giving you the same quality of attention you're giving me, my dear." He patted her gloved hand. "Now, do be quiet and look at the flowers. It's springtime, after all."

Chapter 22

From *Mr. Pickwick's Guide to Marriageable Young Ladies*-

Lady C.B. is exceedingly shy, having grown up in the countryside with her five brothers. So far, she has been greatly overlooked in her debut Season, as gentlemen mistake shy for boring. The opposite is true, here. When coaxed from her shell, this lady reveals that she is obviously witty, intelligent, and kind. It is the crowded ballrooms that don't agree with her--she does well in more intimate groupings. This lady will be the first to admit that while she does wish for a happy marriage and children of her own, more than anything, she longs to return to the more sedate pace of a country estate.

At nine-thirty the next morning, Eleanor paced her bedroom, barefoot. Dresses were laid across her bed, hung over the open doors of her armoire--it looked as if the cedar closet had been violently ill. Her brown curls hung in disarray down her back. But it was her mind that was the biggest problem.

She hadn't slept well the night before. She kept trying to figure out what Edward's motivations could be. Eleanor felt as though her different factions of thought were fighting a battle much like the one depicted on the board she'd given to Henry. On one side was the hopeful part, which wanted to believe that Edward cared for her, that his intentions were as they seemed. On the other side were all the doubts and insecurities she had--those that came from being a lady, and those that came from having a Mr. Pickwick-sized secret.

What if he proposed and then he found out she was Mr. Pickwick? Would he be content to break their engagement privately, or would he tell everyone, leaving her an outcast? What if she never told him? *Should* she tell him? After all, husbands and wives should have few secrets between them. But Mr. Pickwick--that was a huge secret. Could a relationship thrive if she kept that secret from him?

And what if he wasn't privately interested in her at all? What if she had it all wrong? Edward hadn't declared any intentions. What if she had misread all those lingering glances and murmured conversations? What if he hadn't felt what she had felt when they'd danced together--his hand at her waist, their fingers commingling in a delightful way that made her feel breathless, reckless... What if he hadn't felt *anything*? What if he had only been trying to get to know her out of morbid curiosity?

She was running out of time. He'd be there soon. Eleanor yanked a bristle brush through her unruly strands and pinned her hair into a simple, low bun.

She'd sorted her dresses based on her thoughts--several would be appropriate if she were going to suffer through a formal courtroom inquisition, while others were more appropriate for meeting a lover.

Eleanor erred on the side of caution and chose a demure navy blue walking dress that buttoned up all the way to the neck. If she were about to have her private hopes and dreams dragged through the mud in a very public fashion, at least she wouldn't add to the awkwardness of the situation by showing any clavicle.

She was sitting on a low stool wrestling with the tiny leather buttons on her boots when a knock sounded on the door.

"Go away, Mr. McAffrey! I don't have time to tie your cravat today. I'm going for a drive, remember? You may want to get a bottle of out of your stash that I'm not supposed to know about. This might go poorly."

A low chuckle sounded on the other side of the thin door, a chuckle that definitely didn't belong to Mr. McAffrey. The sound sent Eleanor's heart pounding. She yanked her skirts down over her boots and threw the door open.

"Why are you here?" she said, flustered.

His smile was one of a little boy who'd gotten away with something. He leaned in the doorway; he seemed to fill the frame, his shoulders nearly spanning the width.

"Am I not allowed to come to your door?"

"I was going to meet you outside."

"If you had, I wouldn't have been able to see where you live." He peered over her shoulder.

She turned and surveyed the space with dismay. Her two rooms were littered with dresses and boots, hosiery, and to her mortification, undergarments. Eleanor started to close the door, but he reached out and pressed it open. She stared at his hand spread against the painted wood. It was uncommonly attractive, that hand--far more attractive than any hand had the right to be. She was staring, and barely heard him speak.

"So can I see your home?" he said.

Eleanor wished that she could think of a reason not to let him, but she was so distracted by that *hand*.

"Er...alright," she said, turning to the side to let him pass.

She caught a whiff of sandalwood as he passed, and did her best not to inhale deeply. If he was going to question her, if this were nothing but a pretense, then she needed to stop noticing details about him--enticing details that distracted her and muddled her mind.

"You have a lot of dresses," he said.

She couldn't read his tone.

"It's not usually this bad," she said, picking up a book from the floor. "I'm sorry."

"Eleanor," he said, his voice deep.

She could sense his eyes upon her, feel him silently demanding that she meet his gaze. But it was too heavy. She was afraid of the judgement she would see there. She felt like she was seeing her apartment through his eyes--the shabby floors, the peeling paint, the brass bed with rust at the edges.

"Eleanor," he repeated, taking her bare hand.

She shivered at the contact and looked up. Smiling green eyes met hers. She couldn't help but smile back, albeit tremulously.

"I wanted to see your home," he said, chuckling as he toed a lone boot. "It's a bit messier than I expected, but otherwise, is just like its owner..."

"Inexpensive and quirky?" she interrupted.

"Warm and beautiful," he said.

He slid his arm around her waist. Heat bloomed from the spots they touched, and she found herself turning towards him, like a flower to the sun. He was close, too close, and yet she craved more and feared it, all at once. Her breath was shallow and quick, her heartbeat was pounding. He slid his fingers along her jawline and his gaze was nearly unbearable, so she closed her eyes. She didn't see him lean in, but she felt his breath against her lips, felt the rasp of his cheek against hers.

Then he was kissing her, and she was kissing him back. It was everything she had always wanted. She sunk into him, his hands pulling her close and running along her back. Eleanor had never understood before, how some ladies were led astray--but she understood now. The kiss was like being pulled beneath a rushing, powerful undertow. This--this kiss, these emotions--she would gladly drown in them forever.

"Marry me, Eleanor," he said, his voice husky. "I love you, dearly."

His words were like a bucket of cold water, dousing her. How could he love her and want to marry her if he didn't truly know who she was?

"Er...well..." she said.

He raised an eyebrow and smiled. He tucked her hand into the crook of his elbow.

"I believe you promised me a drive. The carriage is waiting," he said.

"But..."

"No 'buts' about it, Eleanor. Let's be on our way."

He gave a gentle tug toward the door. Eleanor's mind was a muddle as she followed him down the stairs, jamming her hands into her gloves as she went. Had that just happened? Had the Duke of Devonshire just proposed to her? Or had the kiss muddled her mind and made her dream up the sound of those words from his lips? It felt like she was walking through some sort of fugue dream state as she followed his broad shoulders down the stairs and out the front door, and allowed him to help her into the sleek black curricle.

It was only when Edward picked up the reins and clicked at the pair of horses that she shook her head slightly. Her mind was racing.

"Did you just..." she began.

"Ask you to marry me?" he said, chuckling. "Yes, I did. And I'm waiting for an answer."

"But you don't know me all that well." She realized that she was wringing her hands, and promptly stopped.

They were off her street now, the matched pair of glossy black horses tossing their heads merrily as they headed towards the park.

"I know that you are gentle and kind to my son, that you are fierce and intelligent. I know that you have maintained grace and elegance under dire circumstances. I know that you have high moral standards, that you don't care about my wealth, that you get along with my closest friends and family. I know that I think of you more than anyone else, that your company is more enjoyable to me than anyone else, that you are the person I want by my side for always."

His words caused a panic to rise in her gut. They weren't true. How could she live up to such a view of herself? He didn't know who she was, what she'd done. He didn't know that if they married, he became in grave danger of a scandal of her making. Her hands were sweating within her gloves. She barely saw the scenery passing by, barely heard the click and clack of the cobblestones or the cries of the sellers from their corner carts. Her heart pounded.

What would he do if he found out? She realized that she did love him, then. She couldn't marry him under false pretenses. She wouldn't, couldn't put her needs above his. It didn't matter that she was poor, that he was offering her a life of luxury and security. Who was she to marry him, when she would bring shame upon him, upon Henry? If she truly did love him, she had to end this. He had to know.

Her heart pounded, and nausea twisted her gut.

"I'm Mr. Pickwick!" she blurted, gripping the side of the carriage. *"Mr. Pickwick's Guide to Marriageable Young Ladies.* That's me."

"I'm well aware," Edward said, expertly maneuvering the horses through the park gate.

"Aware?" Eleanor parroted, sounding shrill even to her own ears. "You're *aware*?"

"Certainly," he said. "And we can discuss the future of that illustrious publication later. But right now, I'd like..."

"The *future* of the publication?" she said. "The *future*?"

"Breathe, Eleanor. Breathe."

Did he sound...*amused*? She scowled at him.

"Ah, *that's* better," he said, not sounding the least bit ruffled. "If you are angry with me, then you cannot possibly be having an apoplexy as I feared a moment ago. In fact, I feel that I'm beginning to become accustomed to you being upset with me. Hopefully, that will not be the baseline for our marital relationship."

"You forget yourself, sir," she said, stiffly. "You have proposed, but I have not yet given you an answer."

"Must I kiss you again?" he said, his voice as sumptuous and dark as the silk of his waistcoat. "I warn you, if you provoke me too far, I shall do so in full view of all the gossips. Then you would have to marry me."

"You...you knave! You wouldn't!"

"Is marrying me such a chore, then? Will I have to bully you into it?"

His tone was laughing, but in the words she heard an undercurrent... of concern? Vulnerability? Could it be that he wasn't as sure of himself as he seemed?

"No, of course not," she said, losing most of her bluster. "But it would be nice to feel as if I weren't being maneuvered into a lifelong commitment."

"I wouldn't dream of it."

She could hear the seriousness in his tone and expression.

"Thank you," she murmured. "Are you angry?"

"About our dear Mr. Pickwick?" he said.

It was strange to hear the words so casually from someone's lips, from *his* lips. The truth seeped into her then. He knew. All her secret maneuvering and careful planning had been for naught. He knew. And he wasn't yelling. He hadn't opened the door, pushed her out of his carriage without stopping. He hadn't blackmailed her--except for pressing her into a wildly advantageous marriage to a man she loved, that is. She suddenly felt like laughing.

"No, I'm not angry," he said, his eyes twinkling with mirth. "After all, it was Mr. Pickwick who brought us together."

"How so?" Eleanor frowned.

Edward pulled the curricle to the side of a shaded lane. "Before I tell you this story, may I have your word that you will not repeat a word of it, to anyone? Someone I love very dearly would be put in danger should this information be known."

His face was very serious, his posture rigid. Eleanor at once felt the gravity of what he was about to tell her, and a following rush of gratitude that he felt he could trust her.

"I swear that no one will hear it from me, Edward," she said, placing her hand over his.

"My son is not my son," he began. "He is my half-brother."

Eleanor sat, stunned, as he related the whole, sordid tale. At the end, when he lapsed into silence, she found tears running down her cheeks and hastily wiped them away. What kind of man would so unselfishly preserve his half-brother's future, at the expense of his own reputation? What kind of man would have the maturity at such a young age, to sacrificially give of his time, finances, and protection? It must be an amazing thing to be loved by such a man. It must be beyond imagining to be a valued member of his family.

"Yes," she finally said, turning to him. "I would be honored to be your wife. I would be honored for Henry to call me mother."

His face lit up like the dawn. Before she knew what was happening, strong hands pulled her ever so gently to him. He cradled her face and deposited a lingering kiss on her lips. His breath upon her cheek further muddled her senses.

"I love you, Eleanor. I will do my best to make you the happiest of women."

"I love you, too, Edward." She meant it. She'd never met anyone like him--caring, selfless. He knew her deepest, darkest secrets, and those of her family, and he hadn't flinched once.

Then his lips were upon hers once more, and she felt like she was soaring, breathless. It was as if everything she could ever want was found beneath the palms that were pressed against his chest. She didn't know if the kiss lasted moments or hours--she was spinning and delirious with happiness.

But he pulled away, and Eleanor became aware of the distant clatter of carriage wheels and hooves against cobblestones. How he had the presence of mind to preserve her reputation during a moment like that, she didn't know. But she was grateful all the same.

He withdrew a small velvet box from his coat pocket, and opened it. Inside was a stunning engagement ring. The center stone was a massive emerald, cut in the traditional style, flanked on either side by slender diamond baguettes, on a gold band. Edward plucked the ring from the box, removed her left-hand glove, and slid the ring onto her finger.

"There," he said. "Now we are properly engaged."

Eleanor turned her hand this way and that, letting the morning light play off the stones.

"It's beautiful," she said, her voice thick. "Thank you."

"It was my mother's. It's been in the family for generations." He flicked the reigns, and the horses started again.

Such a casual statement, and yet, so much meaning. It sunk in then, even deeper than before, that Edward was offering her the protection and prestige of his name and title, a name and title that had been carried on for ages. He was the eighth Duke of Devonshire, and each

Duke before him had sacrificed to increase the holdings of the estate, and to protect the family name from scandal or besmirchment.

"I'll have to give it up," she murmured. "Won't I?"

"Mr. Pickwick, you mean? I don't know. I understand why you started it, and frankly, I've heard it's been very helpful for several titled gentlemen who wanted to find brides of inner quality. Let's think on it for awhile. There's no need to make a decision quite yet."

They rode for a moment in silence.

"I'll have the papers drawn up. You will need to sign. I'll procure a special license. Have you given any thought to where you would like to get married?"

"Anywhere but Heatherton Chapel," she said.

It was where her brother had married Marguerite. Eleanor couldn't imagine being happy in such a place, with bitter memories hanging about like shrouds.

"I was thinking more like St. Paul's Cathedral, myself."

"That's fine, but can we please keep the crowd to a minimum? I don't like a lot of attention." Eleanor adjusted her skirts.

He laughed and dropped a kiss on her forehead. "You really *aren't* like most ladies, are you?" Then he frowned. "One more thing--I will write to the Marquess of Millen and ask that he hosts you in his home until we are married. With news of our engagement will come a lot of scrutiny, but it's more than me being concerned about people finding out where you live. It's a matter of security--you will need footmen or grooms around when you venture out."

Eleanor frowned. "Is that really necessary?"

"Unfortunately, yes." He grimaced. "Someone tried to take my sister, once."

"What?" Eleanor gasped.

"She was newly in London. Her first Season. There was a carriage accident on one of the main thoroughfares, so hers was diverted into a side street. It was a mistake. Three men tried to pull her and her maid from the carriage--they rendered her coachman unconscious. But Lucas happened to be walking that street because he was lost. That's how they met."

"That's a terribly romantic story," she said.

"It wasn't at the time," he said sardonically. "I can assure you that she was in no mood to be wooed at that moment. From that point on, she didn't go anywhere without a maid, a coachman and four grooms."

"That seems like a lot," she said, frowning.

Eleanor was used to going wherever she pleased, within reason. She stuck to well-lit, well-populated areas, and didn't go out alone at night, at least not often.

"I agree," he said. "It *sounds* like a lot. But she never argued. I think that during the attack, she would have given her left arm to have more protection than a slip of a maid and an embroidered parasol. I was foolish to agree to anything less, considering that she was driving all the way across town that day."

"And what about for me?" she asked. "Will I still be allowed to go and do as I please?"

"Of course," he said, looking affronted that she would have to ask. "But you will do so with protection. If you don't like the visibility of four groomsmen, I'll hire some gentlemen to follow you more discreetly. But there is value in heading off an attack by appearing well protected."

She looked out over the greenery of the park, trying to let the gently rustling leaves and bright flowers calm her. Her head felt light. Everything was moving so quickly. Sure, she was still aglow with happiness. She was engaged to Edward, after all, and nothing could drown out that warmth. But her life was changing, too. She was moving away from Mr. McAffrey, into Jane's house, and from there, Netherton Hall. She would be guarded, protected. Eleanor instinctively knew that Edward would not *try* to stifle her, but things would have to change, nonetheless.

"I'm sorry, Eleanor," he said, gently. "I wish that my family name would only give you more opportunities, but to some it will make you a target. I know it will be a change for you, but in time, you will grow used to having servants about. Perhaps it won't be as bad as you think."

"I do understand. I'm not naive to the thought processes of the criminal sort, unfortunately. I'm sure that the groomsmen will be as unobtrusive as possible. It's just everything. I'm concerned about leaving Mr. McAffrey, for one thing. And how long will I be living with the Marquess and Marchioness, do you think?"

"Ah," he said, smiling. "We will try to limit that visit to two weeks. If we hurry the preparations, you should be the Duchess of Devonshire by the middle of the month. As for Mr. McAffrey, he mentioned yesterday that he enjoyed gardening. I was wondering if he would be interested in taking one of the cottages on Chatsworth. That is where I have historically spent most of the year. I'm sure that my groundskeeper could use extra help, and that way, you would be able to see him whenever you wished."

Eleanor blinked up at him. "You would do that?"

"It's nothing, really."

Eleanor didn't care that they were in view of others; she hugged him soundly, her cheek pressed to his chest, her head tucked beneath his chin. "Thank you."

He chuckled and kissed the top of her head indulgently. "You are most welcome."

The woman watched the brazen interlude in the open-top curricle and gritted her teeth. The ten carat emerald and diamond ring winked on the hand that was clasping the Duke's neck. That little serpent had managed to succeed where all the other ladies of the peerage had failed--all the ladies, including herself. She pressed her lips into a thin line and watched as the Duke flicked the reigns and put his horses into a trot. As the barouche and its happy occupants disappeared around a far corner in the lane, Teresa mentally composed the message that she would send to Marks and Cheever.

Perhaps it was the conversation she'd had with Edward, or the many emotions of the day, but as Eleanor walked home from Jane's house that evening, her feelings were unsettled. She felt uneasy, and kept throwing glances back over her shoulder. It was silly, of course--no doubt an effect of her emotions running high all day.

They had returned to Netherton Hall to find Lucas, Amelia and little Henry waiting for them. Once Amelia saw the ring on Eleanor's finger, she'd pressed her hand to her chest and smiled broadly, tears glistening in her eyes.

"I never thought I'd see this day," she said, hugging Eleanor tightly. "I am so glad for you both."

Congratulations and well wishes were shared, and Amelia insisted that they would begin ordering Eleanor's trousseau the very next day.

"If you are to be wed within weeks, the modiste will have to work long hours to get your gown finished. We must start immediately."

While Eleanor didn't care much for what she wore, she did smile in remembrance of Amelia's solemn attitude towards the matter. She was like a little general faced with a military challenge-her head high, shoulders squared. Eleanor was happy to let her deal with the preparations.

From Netherton Hall, Eleanor had requested that Edward's carriage take her directly to Jane's house. Jane would never forgive her if she had to read of Eleanor's engagement in the gossip sheets like everyone else. Besides, telling Jane was one of the fastest ways to spread information. Jane had squealed and exclaimed, congratulating Eleanor and launching into unsolicited advice on everything from Eleanor's wedding clothes, to whether she should fire all the staff at Netherton Hall and start, as Jane put it, 'with her own regime'.

At least Jane couldn't spread the gossip tonight. She had insisted that Eleanor stay for dinner, and it was now later than Eleanor would have liked. But it was one last walk through the city that she loved--one last, unchaperoned waltz with the sights, sounds, and smells of a part of the city she would never see again once she was married. No, that was untrue--she would see them again, but her perspective would be markedly different. She would be greeted everywhere; there would be no more anonymity for her.

A fresh prickle ran up her spine, and she glanced over her shoulder once more. Nothing. Perhaps the day's conversation about Amelia's narrow escape had affected her more than she liked. The thought of strange men manhandling the gentle lady was shocking. Of course Eleanor knew that such things happened--she'd seen and heard more than her fair share of violence in Cheapside, but Amelia was a lady, and someone she knew.

It happened before she could take in a breath to scream--heavy footsteps on the cobblestones behind her, a large hand with fingers the size of sausages clamped down upon her mouth. She gave a high-pitched *mmph* and was yanked off her feet. She smelled body odor and had the impression of two large shapes beside her.

"She's got a plan for you, sweeting," a Cockney accent breathed in her ear.

Who? Eleanor thought, panicked.

A sharp pain to the back of her head, and her world went black.

Chapter 23

From *Mr. Pickwick's Guide to Marriageable Young Ladies-*

Lady T.N. is lovely enough, but the soft, sweet voice she uses in social settings changes to shrill demands once she is safely at home. Her father and brothers have sent her to London with not one, but two chaperones, making one wonder if they believe she cannot be trusted. Rumors about her time at her family's country house abound, but this is verifiable fact--all the male servants at the London home in which she is ensconced are elderly or married, and they are expressly forbidden from entering the house, while the lady in question is not allowed outdoors without her two chaperones.

Eleanor woke with a sack over her head. From the foul smell of it, it had recently been used to haul rotten potatoes. Her hands were tied tightly behind her back and well on their way to numb. She was leaned over on her side, her face pressed to the ground, her legs out before her at an angle. Wherever she was, it was dank and foul, and smelled of vomit, urine, and a hundred other things she couldn't name. With her head near the wet ground, the air felt too thick and malodorous to breathe.

Her head was pounding. Pain radiated from a spot at the base of her skull all the way to her temples and eyes. She felt like she was going to be sick. She did her best to breathe deeply through her mouth. Eleanor swallowed the bile that rose in the back of her throat along with the panic that threatened to swallow her whole. She had to be calm, smart, but terror pulled at her like an undertow, threatened to drown her.

She'd always feared it would come to this, ever since she started *Mr. Pickwick*. It was only natural-- after all, she had been writing about the nobility, and despite their many faults, the nobility protected their own. Who had found out, she wondered? Was it Lady Anabella's father, or perhaps Lady Clarissa's brother?

It didn't really matter. What shocked her was that they had decided to just do away with her altogether, instead of taking her to trial. But perhaps that wasn't so surprising--the nobility liked to make problems disappear in a tidy manner, and public trials were anything but tidy. No, they just wanted her and Mr. Pickwick to go away--to fade into obscurity. There was nothing for it--she would be dead soon. Why had they waited long enough to transport her elsewhere?

Maybe they wanted to dispose of her body so that she was never found. She thought of Edward, of Mr. McAffrey, of Jane. They would never know what had happened to her. Tears dribbled down her face, adding to the foul humidity contained within the sack hood. They would live the rest of their lives wondering about her. She hoped that Edward didn't think the worst of her. She hoped he knew that she hadn't taken her engagement ring, worth a small fortune on its own, and fled. She hoped that someone would discover her body, if only to put it to rest in a churchyard.

"You hit her too hard, you imbecile," a man said. "A chit like that needs barely a tap. What iffin' she never wakes up?"

"You tole me to hit 'er, I hit 'er," another one said. This voice was deeper than the first.

"She'll wake up," a lady said. Her voice was cultured and cold. "We ladies are tougher than we look."

"It don't matter, nohow," the second voice said. "She aint gonna..."

"Quiet, you idiot," the woman said.

Eleanor heard rustling, and could see light change. Then the sack was pulled off her head, roughly, several pieces of hair going with it. Eleanor winced and blinked, trying to adjust her fuzzy eyesight. She couldn't see much, but the room appeared to have a dirt floor, rough wood walls, and dim lighting.

"See?" the lady said. "She's up already. No harm done."

The lady was surprisingly beautiful, considering she had thrown her lot in with the grubby men behind her. Her gown was of fine make. She was a bit older than Eleanor, at that time in a woman's life where they traded a soft, youthful loveliness for a more intelligent, harder-won beauty. She was thin, with dark brown hair that curled about her temples. Her lips were shaped like a rosebud. Her eyes were large and deep brown--expressive eyes, and right now they were cunning and cruel. She looked vaguely familiar to Eleanor, but she couldn't place the woman.

"You poor dear," she whispered to Eleanor. "You thought you'd won, didn't you? Thought you'd tricked him into marriage, pulled yourself up from the bottom rung right into the palace." The woman nodded. "I can respect that. I know what it takes to get a noble man's attention. And to keep it long enough for a Duke to want to marry you? That takes talent. But my respect only goes so far. Unluckily for you, I'm on the bottom rung, too. And I've had my hooks into this family long before you came around."

It clicked into place. "You're Henry's mother."

"Who's 'Enry?" the larger of the two men demanded.

"It doesn't matter," the woman whispered, ignoring the man. "You understand, right? That I don't care that you've seen my face?"

Terror gripped Eleanor in it's sharp talons. This woman was planning on killing her. Or having someone else do it. She didn't expect that Eleanor would be around long enough to tell the authorities who it was who had kidnapped her. Eleanor opened her mouth--to scream, to argue--but the instant she did, the woman thrust the cloth sack into her mouth.

"Sorry, dear. I don't really want to hear it. And we do have neighbors." She patted Eleanor's cheek roughly. That's when Eleanor noticed her engagement ring on the woman's finger. "Ah yes," Teresa said, holding her hand out to catch the light. "Thank you for the beautiful ring. I'll treasure it always."

Teresa stood and turned her back on Eleanor, and spoke in low voices to the men. She flung a shawl around her shoulders.

"I'll be back in the morning," she said, opening the door. "Keep watch, and keep her safe until then."

The door snapped shut behind her, and Eleanor was left in the room with the two men. She closed her eyes tightly, but tears leaked from them, anyways. She was not missish--she knew what kind of men would agree to kidnap, and perhaps murder, a lady of noble birth. Eleanor couldn't help it--she was frightened. There was no greater chasm than between the emotions she'd felt in that sun-lit curricle this morning to the ones she experienced now, lying on the foul, muddy floor of what looked to be an abandoned warehouse of some kind.

The two men sat on chairs that looked too decrepit to hold them, a low-burning lantern on the barrel that they used as a table between them. As she watched from beneath her eyelashes, one of them produced a pack of cards, and they began to play.

Eleanor didn't fail to notice that the larger of the two men glanced her way more often than she was comfortable with.

When would someone notice she was gone? And what would happen in the morning?

It was late in the evening, and Edward couldn't sleep. He'd had his dinner and a nightcap, but in truth, he was too excited to rest. So instead of heading towards his chamber and his bed, he lit the lamps in his study and rang for tea. He had many letters to write-- to his solicitor, instructing him to draft the wedding contract, to his banker, instructing him to have notes of writ completed, extending Eleanor all the credit she could wish at the best shops in London, to the stewards of his estates, informing them of his impending nuptials, to his great aunts... on and on it went.

Only the crackling of the fire, the faint hiss of the gas lamps, and the muted scratching of his pen marred the silence. So when he heard the distant echo of a commotion coming from the direction of the entrance hall, his pen paused. The voices--male, he could now hear--approached rapidly, until the door to his study banged open, and Andrews strode in.

Andrews' crisp white shirt was half untucked, his cravat limp around his sweaty neck. The tails of his jacket were rumpled, and he was missing his hat. For Andrews, a man of impeccable appearance, this was tantamount to a yell. Edward came to his feet.

"What is it?" he demanded. "What's wrong?"

"Lady Eleanor," Andrews gasped. "She's been taken. Rode here as fast as I could once the boy found me."

Horror. The room seemed to spin, and Edward had the impression of there not being enough air in the room--or, at least, he couldn't get enough into his lungs. His pen snapped in his hand and he absently tossed the pieces on his desk.

"Taken by whom?" Edward said. "What boy?"

"I know where they have her, Your Grace," Andrews said. "Huntley is having the horses saddled, is arming some of the men."

"Is she hurt?" Edward strode toward the door.

"I don't know, Your Grace," Andrews said, nearly jogging to keep up. "The boy saw them take her, but he said it was two men, both very large. He didn't have a hope of stopping them, but he followed them to a boarded up storefront on Chauncery, near the docks."

Edward was repulsed by the thought of Eleanor in such a place. He knew what the docks were like--damp, smelling of rotten fish and human waste--it was a place where trash washed up, especially of the human variety.

"Has there been a demand of ransom?" he asked.

"Not yet," said Andrews. "But forgive me, Your Grace. I was going to tell you what I'd discovered first thing in the morning. The ransom demand may not come to you."

"What?" Edward said, taking the stairs two at a time.

"She's an heiress, Your Grace," Andrews wheezed.

Edward jerked to a stop on the landing.

Andrews continued. "The lawyer, the one who died--his son took over, and promptly lost all the clients, except for those with the meagerest payoffs. But he retained the stocks that Lady Eleanor had inherited from her father. Apparently, before he died, Major Gilbert had won a large stake in Stockton and Darlington Railway Company in a game of cards. Of course, back then, that stock wasn't worth the paper it was printed on. People thought they were destined for bedlam, with all their ideas."

"But now..." Edward began.

"Exactly, Your Grace. And she owns five hundred shares, a considerable stake. The young lawyer was trying to draw up paperwork to effectively declare her dead and transfer ownership rights to himself. I have no idea if he approached Lady Eleanor about the situation, or not."

"Then it could be his doing--the lawyer's," Edward said, his voice grim. "Maybe he decided that fraudulent paperwork wasn't enough, and decided to hire someone to do the deed."

"I couldn't say. I only heard just before Tristan found me."

"Who's Tristan?" Edward said, once more in motion.

"The boy. The boy I had following Lady Eleanor."

"Why did you have a boy following Eleanor?" Edward demanded. They'd reached the front hall. Edward swung on his great coat and accepted a pair of pistols from Huntley. "Loaded?"

"Yes, Your Grace," Huntley said, his eyes tight. "Would that I could go with you."

"Keep the house safe, and prepare a bedroom for Lady Eleanor for when we return. Also, call for the doctor, but tell him nothing, and sequester him in one of the rooms in the east wing until we arrive. Lady Eleanor may need medical attention, but I'd rather not tell the whole sordid story unless the doctor needs to know."

Huntley nodded. "Yes, Your Grace."

"Now, why were you having my betrothed followed, Andrews?"

"You told me to do so, Your Grace," Andrews said, sounding exasperated.

"That was before! No matter. Thank goodness for miscommunication." Edward mounted his horse; Andrews did the same. "Lead the way, and be quick about it."

If something happened to Eleanor--but no, he couldn't think of that, or terror and anger would swamp him, render him useless. He had to focus on the one thing, the one plan that gave him hope--he had to get her back. Everything else was details that they could sort out later.

It took too long--everything--the frenzied saddling of the horses, the slapping of his boots to his horse's side. Edward was vaguely aware of the eight men saddling their horses alongside him--footmen and groomsmen, all armed, all starkly silent except to calm the horses as they stamped and shook their heads. Even the horses could feel the grim desperation of the mission.

They mounted and were off. Edward followed Andrews, the frantic pace of the horses leaving no doubt to anyone who heard that this was not a pleasure ride; it was the gravest emergency. Above the pounding of horse hooves against cobblestones, the thrumming tempo of his own heart and lungs, the great, heaving bellows of his horse beneath him--all Edward could hear were his own frantic thoughts.

Why had he let her go home alone? He should have had men watching her since he showed any affection for her, since he *felt* any affection for her. It was unforgivable, that mistake. What would he do if the worst happened? What if they harmed her, or killed her, or worse yet--what if Eleanor simply vanished and he went to his grave never knowing what had happened? His thoughts pulled him deeper into an emotional vortex with no bottom, no end.

He loved her, and in that moment, he would have sacrificed it all--his money, his estates, his body and life itself--just to know that she was safe. What would he do without her? How cruel for something like this to befall her after he had seen her joy in the park this afternoon. Faster than the tempo of the feverish ride, he murmured desperate prayers--for her safety, for her well-being, for her very life.

They stopped at the corner of a fetid dockside lane that merged into an even more pungent one. The air here was thick and squalid with the sharp smell of rotting fish and the heavy stench of stagnant water. Edward sat ramrod on his horse, his mouth pinched into a thin line of barely suppressed worry and anger. He was livid that anyone had dared take his dear Eleanor here, to this horrifying corner of London.

Andrews and the head groomsman were discussing something in low tones ahead of him, their heads close together. Edward watched the steam from the horses' mouths rise in the air, watched their tails swish tersely. He knew he was in no position to be part of the planning stage, but his fingers clenched the reigns in impatience. Finally, finally--though it had been only moments, they jerked their heads in a request for the men to follow, and stirred their horses forward. Their target was a darkened, dilapidated warehouse.

Chapter 24

From *Mr. Pickwick's Guide to Marriageable Young Ladies-*

As of late, Lady G.T. has had difficulty in concealing her horrific temper, even in public. Numerous people have noticed her stamping feet or balled fists when a favorite beau dances with another lady. What the public might not know is that at the familial estate, the lady's tantrums are legendary. It is claimed that the family recently switched to silver serveware not because of style, but because the lady had thrown too many china plates at dinner. Any intelligent gentleman will steer clear, as this lady's kind of excitement quickly grows old.

It felt as if it had been hours upon hours, but Eleanor knew that couldn't be the truth. The oil lamp was still burning, and the men were only on their second game of cards. She had been frozen in the same place since Teresa had left. Her back ached, her head pounded from where they'd hit her. Her wrists and ankles were raw from the biting rope wound tightly on them. Eleanor had tried stretching--once. The large man's eyes had tracked the movement too close for her liking.

She'd seen that same attentiveness once, in the eyes of a hunting dog. The situation now was clear--he was the predator, Eleanor the prey. So she acted like prey should, in order to avoid attention--she stayed silent, motionless, praying that he couldn't hear the ceaseless pounding of her heart from where he sat. But her lower leg was falling asleep right along with her hands. The needle sensation was nearly overwhelming. Maybe she could just--

Her foot bumped a piece of timber, and the large man turned toward her and made to rise from his chair.

Eleanor's heart began to thump so hard she could feel the beat in her temples, in her teeth, in the wound on the back of her head. Her breathing became a desperate wheeze in and out through her nose, as she couldn't breathe around the ball of fetid burlap shoved in her mouth. She thought she might vomit, but if she did, she would choke on it. She was utterly helpless; her hands and feet were bound, her mouth constricted. She was at their mercy, and that mercy did not exist.

"Cheever," the other man barked. "Leave her 'lone."

"You aren't my boss," Cheever said.

"You're right," he said, calmly dealing another hand. "But *she* is. And *she* told us to leave the lady alone until morning. Once we get paid, you can do whatever you want."

Cheever slid a tongue over his teeth. "What's it matter if we wait? What's a few hours matter? She doesn't need to know."

"And yet she will," the man said. "Don't mess this up. Wait until morning. I'm not giving up a fortune because you couldn't keep your trousers up."

"Pfft," Cheever said, but he turned back to the card game.

Eleanor thought that her heartbeat would never slow, but after long minutes, it did. She focused on breathing. In. Out. In. Out. But her mind wouldn't slow, no matter what she did. Her thoughts raced. That woman wanted something from her--ransom, most likely, but the cold, hateful expression on the woman's face made Eleanor think it could just be cold-blooded murder. That woman *hated* her, and Eleanor had never met her before today.

Eleanor tried not to think about Edward--how he'd react when he found her missing, whether he would think that she had just run away--lest it make her break down into sobs. She couldn't afford to make any noise or draw any attention. Her only hope of making it through the night unmolested was in staying still and silent. Even that might not be enough. But what about the morning? Would anyone miss her before her time was up? What was to happen at dawn?

That woman seemed to have a plan, and it seemed like they were all expecting money. Ransom, then. Edward would know that she hadn't abandoned him. Even if they never found her body, he would know her fate. That provided her only a little comfort. Eleanor realized now how dangerous it was for her to walk alone. But who could have imagined that on her last night of freedom, this would happen?

She thought of Jane, with the baby on the way, who had been a truer friend than she'd known. Of Amelia and Lucas, who she'd just met, but were to be her family. Of Henry, who was sweet and tried so hard to make Edward proud. Of Mr. McAffrey, who had taken her in and loved her, when no one else would. But most of all, she thought of Edward. His confidence, his love, the joy on his face when he'd slipped that ring on her finger.

Eleanor never thought that she could hate anyone the way that she hated Marguerite, but she had been proven wrong. When she'd seen her engagement ring on Teresa's finger, she'd wanted to scream and pummel the lady with a blunt object, something stronger than her fists. Anger was clearer, sharper than the grief and fear that threatened to drown her like a rising tide. It was easier to contain. What she would do to have their situations reversed, to see her attackers bound and gagged and lying in oozing mud, while she sat in relative comfort, laughing at them.

She'd kick them in the stomach, maybe, starting with that Cheever over there. Then she'd get something heavy and bash them over the head. Then she'd scream at them, tell them to go to the devil. It was all balderdash--she'd be too terrified to do any of that. But she *would* hand them over to the authorities and watch them hang! Well, she wouldn't care to *watch*. But she'd hear that it had been done, at least.

Something in her expression must have shown her thoughts, because the next time Cheever looked over, his eyes narrowed.

"Don't you be getting any ideas, 'luv," he sneered. "Ain't no one coming fer ya. You and I are going to get to know each other in due time, luv. In due time." He punctuated this statement by adjusting himself lewdly.

"Your turn, Cheever," the other man said, spitting to the side. "You gonna call or what?"

In the space of a heartbeat, the door banged open so hard it hit the wall and splintered. Eleanor gave a reflexive shriek that was dampened by the filthy burlap in her mouth. Cheever and the other man were up instantly, knocking over the barrel and the oil lamp, pulling weapons from their pockets--one gun, one knife.

It didn't matter.

The gunshots nearly deafened Eleanor--she couldn't tell how many shots had gone off, but her head was ringing, her eyes screwed shut. There was silence, and she couldn't tell if it was real, or if she had gone momentarily deaf. When she got the courage to open them again, she screamed into the burlap. Cheever was laying facing her, one hand outstretched so that it nearly touched her face. His eyes were open and sightless; a bullet hole oozed blood from his forehead.

Then strong hands were pulling her upright. Edward was there, removing the burlap from her mouth, cutting the bonds at her wrists and feet. The blood rushed into her hands and she flexed them, feeling the sharp ache with a wince.

"Eleanor," his low voice said. He looked over his shoulder.

She smelled smoke.

"We have to move, love."

He lifted her gently, but she couldn't suppress a groan. Her head ached, and her body felt as if she'd been run over by a carriage while she was unconscious. Edward stepped carefully over the two fallen men. Dead--she checked the other, and he had a hole in his chest. But the fire from the tipped gas lamp was spreading. She hated fire. She buried her head into Edward's broad chest.

"Get me out of here," she begged.

A moment later, she was breathing different air. It couldn't be called *fresh*--there was no such thing this close to the docks. But it wasn't stifling and tainted with her own fear.

"Fire's spreading," a man said. "Best get her out of here before people start gathering."

She was transferred to someone else--she couldn't say who--then lifted in front of Edward on his massive horse. He clicked his mouth, and the horse moved forward, away from the smoke, away from the muck and squalor of the docks, all the way onto a cobblestoned street.

Teresa watched. From a third-floor room across the street, she saw the ten horsemen carefully picking their way down the street.

"Damn," she whispered. "Damn."

She recognized the tall form of the Duke of Devonshire easily, and wondered that he would ride down into this muck himself to save his bride. She didn't attempt to warn Marks and Cheever; such an action would have been pointless and self-sacrificial, and nothing she ever did was either. They were grown men; they knew what they'd gotten themselves into.

She didn't move, hardly breathed as the men surrounded the building. There was only one way in, one way out. No one could sneak in, but no one could get out, either. She didn't blink as she heard the shouting, didn't wince at the gunshots that followed. Only when the large frame of the Duke emerged, holding a wrapped bundle, did she frown.

Teresa wondered if Marks had been able to keep Cheever from her, or if the girl was ruined. She wondered if the Duke would still have her, were that the case. From the way he took her gently up onto his horse, it appeared he cared for her. Deeply. A pang of some long-forgotten emotion struck her heart, but she ignored it.

Ignored everything, save for the curls of smoke that were chasing the men from the building. All the riders mounted and rode off.

There was no sign of Marks and Cheever, but Teresa could see the flames licking at the doorway of the abandoned shop. That answered that, then. No witnesses, save for the lady. Teresa would have to flee. She glanced down at her hand and saw the emerald and diamonds glint in the low light. It hadn't been for nothing--a ring this valuable would see her settled far from London. A new life.

So Teresa watched as people sounded the alarm, as they put the blaze out with buckets filled from the pump down the street. She was still watching as the sooty crowd began to disperse. Then she made her way down the rickety staircase with her valise, slipped into the crowd, and disappeared.

Chapter 25

From *Mr. Pickwick's Guide to Marriageable Young Ladies-*

It is difficult to imagine a lady less qualified to run an estate than Lady P.Y. She is much like a vase of flowers--stunningly beautiful but nigh on impossible to speak to. Any gentleman not thoroughly dazzled by her eyes and smile will quickly notice that she has no substantial response to his questions. Unfortunately, this general lack of wit has not tempered the lady's opinion of herself-- on the contrary, she has decided she is highly intelligent, which is the most dangerous kind of stupid.

Eleanor must have passed out, for the next thing she knew, they were at Netherton Hall. She was being carried up the carpeted staircase while Edward and another man spoke in low voices.

"We have the Duchess suite prepared, Your Grace," the man murmured. "The doctor is standing by. We were lucky--Dr. Havelston hadn't quit the city yet, and he was willing to come. He is extremely discreet."

"Send him," Edward said. "She has a head injury."

Eleanor heard a sharp intake of breath, then footsteps hurrying away. Edward carried her down the hall and into a grand apartment. She was able to get a glimpse of rose wallpaper and sumptuous furnishings in the sitting room, but he hurried through and set her on the bed.

"Oh, no, Edward," Eleanor croaked. "I'm filthy. Please, the bedding."

From her position on the bed, she could finally see his face. It was drawn in stark lines, the cords of his neck were prominent, the corners of his mouth drawn down into a harsh frown.

"Eleanor, my love, I don't give a damn about the bedding. Are...where do you hurt?" his hands fluttered over her like nervous birds that weren't sure where to land, then curled into fists at his side.

"My hands," she admitted. "And I've got a splitting headache."

"All due respect, Your Grace," said the smartly dressed, grey-haired man striding into the bedroom. He inserted his person between Eleanor and Edward deftly. "Step back. Now, my dear. What is injured?"

"They hit me over the head, I think," she said. She gingerly touched the base of her head and grimaced.

"Your Grace, help her sit up. And I need better light."

"Huntley!" Edward roared. "Light!"

Eleanor winced.

"Your Grace," the doctor hissed. "She may have a concussion. Loud noises are to be avoided at all costs."

Edward looked stunned, he turned to the flurry of servants who were lighting lamps and candles.

"Did you hear what the doctor said?" Edward stage-whispered. "Be quiet!"

The doctor rolled his eyes. "It doesn't matter how high the rank or how educated a man is, he turns into a feral beast when the woman he loves is injured."

Eleanor managed a weak smile. Edward helped her sit forward, one warm hand behind her back, and the doctor examined the back of her head, probing gently at the lump at the base of her head. When the doctor was finished, Edward let her recline back against the sumptuous bedding and pillows. The doctor held a candle up to her eyes.

"Any nausea or vomiting?" he asked.

"Nausea, but I was not ill," she said. From the corner of her eye, she saw Edward's hands clench into fists.

"What else hurts?" the doctor was crisp, professional, and that helped put Eleanor at ease.

"My hands are sore. They tied my wrists." She held them up for inspection.

"Anything else?" The doctor asked, after examining her wrists.

"No."

"Forgive me, my lady. Did anyone take liberties with you?" he asked.

"No." She shook her head, and instantly stopped when the movement made her dizzy. "One was going to, but the other kept him from it long enough."

Edward kicked a chair, and Eleanor started at the noise.

"Your Grace, please leave the room. Have a brandy. Go kick a chair elsewhere. *You* are the one who is preventing her healing at this moment."

Edward looked properly chastened. "I won't make another noise. I'm sorry. But I'll not leave her, either."

"One more outburst, and I'll have your men remove you," the doctor snapped. "This is not about you or your feelings."

Edward nodded and ran his hand through his hair, and the doctor turned back to Eleanor. "I will bandage your wrists after you bathe. These ladies will no doubt assist you in that endeavor." He nodded toward two maids who were still lighting candelabras. "Take special care with the lump on the back of your head, but get as clean as you can. Come away, Your Grace. Your evening is just beginning."

Edward looked loathe to leave her, but he saw the necessity of it. She had the dock's muck the length of her body, and in her hair. He pressed a gentle kiss to her forehead and ducked out.

Eleanor allowed herself to be undressed and helped over to sit in the large copper tub that was filled nearly to the brim with hot water and close to the fire. Before tonight, she'd never let another person bathe her, but tonight she didn't have the energy. All she wanted to do was sleep. So she accepted the gentle ministrations of the kind maids, and wanted to weep at the stark contrast of treatment she'd received, all in one night.

They seemed to understand her need for silence, too. She didn't want to talk about it tonight, or maybe ever. Through the now-murky bathwater, she could see the bruises beginning to bloom along her side where they'd tossed her to the ground. It could have been worse, she realized, starting to shake. It could have been so, so much worse. They were planning on killing her. The big one wanted to rape her. There's no doubt that the other would have, too. His only qualm was about waiting for the appointed time to do so.

"I'm going to be sick," she gasped, leaning over the side of the tub.

Water splashed onto the parquet floor with her movement. A metal basin appeared beneath her, and Eleanor clutched at it, emptying her stomach. When she stopped retching, the basin was withdrawn. She saw one of the maids cover it with a cloth and carry it into the water closet. She felt wrung out, too exhausted to move.

"I'm sorry," she said.

"Don't mention it, my lady," the other maid said. "Let's get you dried and into warm clothes. You're shaking like a leaf."

"She's sustained a head injury," Dr. Havelston said.

Edward was pacing the length of the feminine sitting room, darting glances every few moments at the door to the bedroom.

Dr. Havelston continued. "I would advise letting her rest, but waking her every hour. If you cannot wake her, wake me. I'll take a bedroom in the guest wing."

"Very well," Edward said, waving his hand. His eyes were still on her bedroom door; his ears strained for sounds of help needed.

"Your Grace," he said. "I do not expect that her physical injuries will be much cause for concern. The protocol I have suggested is one of precaution."

"Good," Edward said, nodding.

"But I must caution you that in cases such as these, there may be more serious emotional injury that needs to be dealt with."

Edward's head whipped around. "Meaning what?"

"Meaning that she may not know the full extent of her own mental distress for some time. You should pay special attention to her emotions. Listen, without trying to solve the problem. And do not force her into any social situations that she doesn't wish to attend. Sometimes, a change of scenery can go a long way in the healing. If the weather holds, you may consider relocating to the countryside."

"Thank you, doctor. That is very helpful information to have."

"Don't thank me," he said breezily, patting Edward's elbow. "I'll be sure to bill you soundly."

Edward lifted the corners of his mouth in the approximation of a smile.

"And keep the lights burning, so that she can see where she is whenever she wakes," he added, his face grim. "Sometimes that helps."

Though she was exhausted, Eleanor could barely sleep. She drifted into shallow, dreamless sleep, only to jerk awake for no reason at all. In that dark, foul-smelling room, she had kept her fear tightly leashed. Eleanor thought that it would recede fully once she was safe, but that didn't seem to be the case. Just when she thought she felt safe and warm enough to rest, just when she relaxed into the crisp sheets covering the down mattress, she woke gasping for air past a wad of burlap that was no longer in her mouth.

Every time she woke, Edward was there. He was as constant as the ticking of the ornate enameled clock on the stone mantel, or the crackling of the fire. He wasn't sleeping either, that was certain. He'd fussed over her the first few times she'd woken, but now just met her eyes and nodded when she checked whether he was still there. He'd moved a small writing desk to face the bed, and he'd sat all night writing. What--she wondered, as she drifted back to sleep.

Chapter 26

From the *Quentin Daily*-

A certain gentleman of esteemed peerage and a Lady E.G. were seen driving through the park in an open curricle yesterday. All who witnessed their interaction can have no doubt as to the gentleman's intentions. It was said that at one point, the vehicle nearly hit a tree, but that the driver barely noticed! It was also noted that the lady in question is now in possession of a spectacular ring, which she is wearing on the fourth finger of her left hand...

Despite Dr. Havelston's warning, Edward hadn't needed to wake Eleanor once. She kept shuddering awake with a cry or a gasp, and when she did sleep, she shifted and moaned. He doubted she'd strung more than an hour's sleep together at one time. He'd sat at that frilly desk, the one that his mother had used, and written letters--one to Mr. McAffrey, asking him to visit, one to a Mr. Rotherton, jeweler, one to a Mr. Thornton, and the last to the Marchioness Millen, stating that Eleanor would be *his* houseguest for the coming weeks, not hers.

But mostly, he just watched Eleanor-- watched her and blamed himself. If only he had demanded that she take several footmen with her. If only he had accompanied her himself. She'd given a basic story of what had happened; Edward had confirmed who the woman in the warehouse was. When the sky turned grey, Edward handed the letters off to Huntley, instructing that they be delivered immediately, and that the messengers should wait for responses.

Dr. Havelston was in promptly at daybreak. He checked on Eleanor, and nodded. "She's got good color, and her breathing is solid. If there was any danger, it's passed."

Edward nodded.

"Get out, and get some sleep," Dr. Havelston added. "You look terrible."

Edward took one last look at Eleanor--she looked peaceful for the first time all night. He didn't want to leave her, but he had things that needed doing.

Back in his own chambers, he shucked his clothes, washed his face, and donned a fresh outfit. His jawline was shadowed with the hair he hadn't shaved, but it was the best he was willing to do for the time being. Andrews was waiting for him in his study, a tea tray in place on the desk. Edward had never been more grateful for the efficiency of his household staff as he was in the past twelve hours. He settled into his leather desk chair and poured himself a strong cup of tea.

"Your messages were delivered, and a response was received from Mr. Thornton, who will be here at seven o'clock, as requested," Andrews said.

Edward glanced at the clock. It was still only six thirty. He nodded.

"The messenger from Mr. McAffrey stated that the old man nearly struck him when he refused to give a specific accounting as to why Lady Eleanor Gilbert had not arrived home yesterday, and was only slightly mollified when he was informed that she was safe and resting comfortably here. I'm sure that you will be receiving him as a caller within the next few hours."

Edward smiled and sipped his tea. He had no doubt that he would be hearing from Mr. McAffrey, most likely loudly.

"The messenger from the Marchioness has not returned, so it is my estimation that the Lady is not yet awake," Andrews said. "Mr. Rotherton will be arriving at ten o'clock, although the messenger stated that he was a bit perplexed with regards to your open request to 'bring the best'. He gratefully accepted the offer of accompaniment, so I've sent four footmen to assist him."

"Thank you, Andrews. I'd like you to sit in on the meeting with Mr. Thornton. As soon as Lady Eleanor and I are wed, we will be relocating back to Chatsworth. Please notify the house and make any preparations. We will also need to hire the future Duchess' lady's maids, although Eleanor may wish to be involved in that process."

It was only a short wait until Huntley was announcing Mr. Thornton at the door. Mr. Thornton was no one that would capture attention-- he was shorter than Edward, medium build, medium brown hair, muddy brown eyes. His suit was in the middle, too--not too fine, not too cheap, and it fit like it was off the rack. His posture was neither too confident or too schlumpy. His entire persona was carefully managed, precisely assembled to allow him to blend--into expensive houses, dirty slums...into the woodwork, if necessary.

Edward nodded at the chair next to Andrews. "Thank you for coming. It's a time sensitive issue."

Thornton nodded. "If I'm called, it usually is."

Edward steepled his fingers. Now that he had the man here, he didn't quite know how to begin.

Finally, he said, "There is a woman..."

Mr. Rotherton's case was a trove. There were finely wrought necklaces next to heavily ornamented ones, citrines the color of the sun, emeralds as dark as forest glades, and sapphires as deep as reflecting pools. The man had followed instructions, as ambiguous as they had been-- he'd brought only the finest examples.

"Forgive me, Your Grace," he said, twisting his gloved hands together over his paunch. "I wasn't sure exactly what you were looking for.'

"Diamond earrings, for my sister, " Edward replied. He touched a dangling pear diamond and set it swinging gently from the radiant above it. "These will do nicely."

"Very good, Your Grace," the man said, a beaming smile on his face. "Anything else?"

"Some baubles for my betrothed, of course," Edward said.

He was a bit melancholy about the ring that Teresa had stolen--it had been his mother's after all, and his grandmother's before that. But the emotion was a small island of regret in a sea of thankfulness for Eleanor's safety. Jewels were easily replaceable, while his intended bride was undoubtedly one of a kind. His hand lingered over a ring. The center stone was a ruby as large as his thumbnail and as red as pigeon's blood. It was flanked on either side by sparkling diamonds.

"An excellent choice, Your Grace," Mr. Rotherton said. "The ruby is twenty carats, from Burma. It once belonged to the Maharaja of Kolhapur's wife, who named it 'Angarika', which means 'flame of the forest'."

Edward remembered what he'd thought of Eleanor the night they'd first met--that he had never met a woman with a more fiery spirit.

"I will take it," he said. "And that little crown thing, too."

"Ah, the diamond diadem," Mr. Rotherton crooned. "Twenty carats of the finest diamonds, set in a starburst pattern with grey pearls. Your bride will love it."

And you will love the bill, Edward thought. But he smiled and thanked the man all the same.

"Where is she?" a male voice boomed in the hall. "Don't you stand in my way, you little pea-hen! I'll fight you all if I have to. Where is my Eleanor?"

Edward hurried out into the hall, where Mr. McAffrey was squared off with Huntley and two of the footmen.

McAffrey's eyes narrowed when he saw Edward. "You! Where is she? If you've harmed one hair on her head, I'll run you through with my saber. Title be damned! Where is she?"

Edward held his hands up and approached the man as one might a growling, snapping dog. "I will tell you everything, but not in the hallway, and please lower your voice. There are those in the house I'd rather not hear this story."

As to prove his point, Mr. Rotherton appeared in the doorway behind him.

"Mmph," McAffrey said, jerking the hem of his jacket back in place. "Alright, then. Lead the way. Just don't think you can pull the wool over my eyes. I might be old, but I'm sharp as anything."

Huntley ushered them into Edward's study and closed the door, leaving them alone. Edward took his place behind the desk and gestured at the fresh tray that had magically appeared in his brief absence.

"Coffee? Tea?"

"Now, get to the point. Don't try and distract me with beverages." McAffrey thumped a stubby finger on the polished mahogany desk. "Where is Eleanor? She always tells me if she won't be home, and then your man came around this morning saying that she's safe and *here*? I've never received such an ominous assurance in all my life!"

"I apologize. It's been a long night."

Edward poured himself a cup of coffee, added two sugars and cream. Then he launched into an explanation of what had occurred the night before, beginning with the engagement, all the way to the letter that morning.

Mr. McAffrey's frown only deepened.

"So she'll be alright, then?" he finally said. "She...are you *sure* of it?"

"The doctor assures me that there will be no lasting physical trauma, but he is concerned about her mental well-being. He suggested that we relocate to the country as soon as possible."

"Hmmpf," McAffrey said. He stared down at his twisted together fingers.

"Which brings me to my next point," Edward said. He chose his words carefully. "I have need of a hard worker on my property in the country. The pay isn't excellent, but it includes a small cottage. Would you consider the position?"

McAffrey's head jerked up. "I don't want charity."

"It's not. I know that it would weigh heavy on Eleanor's mind to leave you. It would be a great favor to me if you would consider relocating with us."

"Well, we'll see," he said, frowning. "I'm not sure if she's really accepted you. You can't expect me to take your word for it. I'll see her myself."

Edward nodded. "You're welcome to wait until she's ready to accept visitors, but I'll not wake her just to soothe your worry."

McAffrey gave a jerk of a nod. "I'll find my way to the kitchens, then. I suppose you won't begrudge me a cup of tea and a biscuit?"

"Of course not. Make yourself at home."

Chapter 27

From *Mr. Pickwick's Guide to Marriageable Young Ladies*-

Lady P.A. is exceedingly forthright in her words and has an unladylike laugh--qualities that may scare off young or weaker men. She is in her fourth Season, and there are many unkind ladies who titter at her. Gentlemen, be advised! This lady is a delight when one gets to know her. She is witty and charming to converse with, as well as being fiercely loyal to her friends and family. She would be an excellent match for a man who prefers to listen rather than talk--that man will always have his wife on his side, and he will always be amused.

When Eleanor finally woke for the day, the ornate clock on the mantel showed that it was past noon. Two maids occupied the settee near the fire, their heads bent over mending. Eleanor must have made some small noise, for their heads jerked up and they stood.

"How are you feeling, my Lady?" a young lady with red hair asked.

The other ducked out the door quickly. Eleanor wondered who she was reporting to. She remembered there had been a doctor, and Edward had stayed long into the night writing letters at the desk that was back in its place against the far wall. It had been a comfort, to have him close. Every time she'd woken, he was there.

"Would you like some tea? A breakfast tray?" The maid was wringing her hands, and Eleanor realized she hadn't answered her.

"I would like coffee, if you have it," she said. "With cream and sugar? And anything to eat would be lovely, but don't put the cook to extra trouble. Whatever is available for lunch is fine."

"Very good, my lady."

"And is there a dressing gown available? Or a comb? I'd feel a lot better if I were presentable."

The fresh-faced redhead nodded her understanding. "Yes, of course. Lady Wilcott sent some of her items up for you."

It was difficult for Eleanor to get out of the massive bed--it felt as if her entire body was bruised. But she set her teeth and pressed her lips into a line, and except a slight hiss, managed the business without letting on that she was in pain. Still, it felt like she'd run a mile once she finally got the dressing gown on and dropped into the chair before the dressing mirror.

If the maid noticed her exhaustion and pain, she didn't mention it, but she was singularly gentle when combing out the tangles in Eleanor's hair. Eleanor had guessed that she would look terrible--anyone who went through an ordeal such as hers wouldn't look their best--but she was still shocked to see the bruise upon her cheek, and the dark blue hollows beneath her eyes that proclaimed her poor night of sleep.

It was a companionable silence, though. Eleanor thought about the events that had transpired yesterday. She knew now that she would never argue against adequate protection again. She had been scared for herself--terrified, even--but above that was her concern for how guilty Edward would feel. And Mr. McAffrey! How would he feel, knowing that she had died in such a way? Regardless of the fact that an entourage might be stifling at times--she would be grateful for it in the future.

A knock on the door preceded a parade of people entering the room. There was the doctor, whom Eleanor remembered from the previous night, a maid with a tray, and two more maids, each holding the end of a trunk. Eleanor wondered vaguely how many maids were employed, and whether they were all in her room at the moment.

The doctor, a stern looking man in his fifties, surprised her by chuckling. "It is good to see you out of bed, Lady Eleanor. How are you feeling?"

"Just fine, thank you," she lied.

He smiled, studied her, then nodded. "Alright, then. I'm leaving something in case you need a good night's rest and cannot get it. Take things slow and rest as needed. If you need anything else, please send someone, day or night."

Eleanor nodded gratefully. She was thankful that he wasn't going to demand that she get back into bed, even though she was sure that he knew she still wasn't feeling well.

Thirty minutes later, she was feeling far more human. Her hair was combed and pinned into a low chignon, and she was dressed in a loose-fitting velvet day dress. She'd eaten lunch, had two cups of coffee, and was relaxing, her feet upon a stool in front of the fire. The maids had left, at her gentle request.

A low knock on the door, and Edward entered.

"I heard that you were up and about," he said. "I'm sorry I couldn't get away to see you until now. It has been a busy morning."

Eleanor smiled as she took in his rumpled hair and the shadow of hair along his jawline. "Did you sleep at all last night?"

He shrugged. "It doesn't matter. I brought you something."

Eleanor opened the small box he handed her. A pigeons-blood ruby ring glinted in the light. She held trembling fingers to her lips and was surprised to feel the pinch of tears in her eyes.

"It's lovely. Thank you."

"I'm not sure if we'll see the other one I gave you again, so this one will have to suffice." He shoved his hands into his pockets, an unreadable look on his face.

"It's perfect. I love it." Eleanor slipped the ring onto her finger and held it up to the light.

"I'm so sorry, Eleanor," he said, his face bleak. "I don't know what I was thinking, letting you go home unaccompanied."

Eleanor scoffed. "You drove me to Jane's. It was my fault that I left there and walked alone. It is I who should be apologizing, not you."

"I should have known that Teresa wouldn't just go away. I should have known it." He ran a hand through his hair distractedly.

"There is no fault on either of our sides," she said, firmly. "Not really. And while I will gladly accept chaperones in the future, can we just put this behind us and go on as before?"

He shook his head. "I don't think I'll ever be able to forget seeing you like that."

"If I can overcome it, you certainly should be able to," she said, tartly. "The people involved have been punished..."

"They will be," he interrupted.

Eleanor flapped her hand. "No matter. She can't hurt me anymore, Edward. Those awful men are dead. I will have nightmares, maybe. Maybe not. And we will both be more careful going forward. But this is still the happiest time in my life. You...you have not rethought our relationship?"

"What?"

"You still love me?" she pressed.

"Of course I do." He looked affronted that she'd ask such a question.

"And you still wish to marry me?"

"Yes. Of course."

Eleanor beamed, ignoring the pain in her cheek as she did so. "Then I am radiant with joy, and no kidnapping plot will change that."

"It's not as simple as that, Eleanor. You've been through an ordeal."

"You forget, Edward, that I have not been sheltered like other ladies. This is painful, but it isn't the hardest thing I've gone through. Besides," she said, briskly. "Things worked out for the best. If nothing else, you will never hear me complain about being trailed around London by six footmen as if I were the mother duck and they the ducklings. I understand the need for it now. We will call this whole thing an object lesson."

"A lesson for both of us," he said, his face grave. "I'm not sure I will ever forgive myself."

"Do stop being so self-involved," she said, smiling. "Not everything revolves around you."

"My loving fiancee," Edward said, sarcastically. "Is this the treatment I have to look forward to when we are married?"

"That and worse!" she teased.

Edward laughed. "I hope it is alright, but Mr. McAffrey is here to see you. You weren't up when he first called, but he insisted on waiting until you felt up to it."

"Oh!" she said. "He shouldn't have bothered."

"Rest assured that Mrs. Gardner has seen to his every comfort," he said, sarcastically. "I daresay the King wouldn't have been fed half as well and fawned over as much, were he to grace us with his presence."

"You could have woken me."

"Absolutely not. You needed your rest. And he can wait a little longer." Edward paused, and shifted, running his hand through his hair once more. "The doctor says that it might be best for us to relocate, at least for awhile, to let you recover. He suggested the countryside might be a welcome change."

Eleanor frowned, waiting for the part that Edward seemed nervous about, but he just looked at her.

Her eyebrows raised. "Is that it?"

"I know that the countryside will be a change for you, but I assure you that the house is spacious--larger than this one--and there are many things to do to keep oneself occupied. Percy's familial seat is less than two hours away by carriage. He and his sisters come to the house often to visit, and there are several in the village who make for good company. You won't be *too* bored, I hope."

She wanted to laugh. Edward was afraid that she didn't want to move to the country? What would she be leaving behind, after all, but the ballrooms and drawing rooms that she never felt a part of, anyways? *Mr. Pickwick,* a voice whispered inside her. She frowned. What would become of *Mr. Pickwick,* once she married? Just because she had secured her own happy future didn't mean that she believed in *Mr. Pickwick's Guide* any less. If anything, the past few months had proved that the guide was a valuable resource to many.

"Of course we will go. I can't wait to see Chatsworth for myself. But I would like to marry in London, if possible. So that Jane may come?"

He smiled, relieved.

"Very well. Now that you've agreed to marry me, yet again, maybe it is safe to tell you that you're an heiress?"

"What?" Eleanor said, leaning back in her chair.

"My secretary Andrews has been trying to speak with the barrister in charge of executing the accounts your father left to you, ever since we met at the ball."

"Whatever for?" Eleanor frowned and tilted her head.

"Er... I asked him to look into your situation..." Edward flushed at the admission.

Eleanor opened her mouth, then closed it again. "Very well."

"He recently found out that the son of the lawyer had taken over the accounts, and was trying to bilk you out of your fortune."

"What fortune?" Eleanor shook her head. "There wasn't a fortune."

"Well, you are right, in that there *wasn't* a fortune. But now there is. The stocks that your father gave you were to a small company that was focused on creating propulsion methods from combustion. They were mostly unsuccessful....until they weren't. Have you heard that they just approved a railroad project, that will connect Shildon to Darlington?"

Eleanor shook her head.

"Well, the Stockton and Darlington Railway Company that just secured that approval is the one you own stock in. You are rich, and I would advise you to hold those stocks. I think they will appreciate even more."

Eleanor sat in stunned silence for many moments, then said, "They were right. You really *do* have Midas' touch."

Edward laughed. "You always were valuable, Eleanor. The fortune has nothing to do with it."

"Thank goodness no one knew, especially me," she said, thoughtfully. "Things might have turned out so differently."

"Do you think so?" he said, cocking his head.

"Mr. Pickwick wouldn't exist, for one," she said.

"Maybe, maybe not." He shrugged, then grinned. "I'm sure you would have found a way to throw all of London into a tumult, even without your booklets."

"Hmph," she said. "Wait until I let it slip that you married me for my secret fortune!"

He smiled at her, and placed a warm hand gently on her unmarked cheek. She felt a faint blush rise at his touch, at the weight of his eyes on hers. It was almost too much, this love she felt for him. Last night had put things into perspective. What would her future look like without the people she loved? Without him?

"Will you marry me as soon as possible?" he asked, his voice low.

"As soon as my bruises fade," she said, primly. "I'm not *very* vain, but I am a *little* vain."

He chuckled. "Very well."

There was a knock on the door.

"Eleanor, dear?" Mr. McAffrey said, gently.

"Come in," she said, smoothing her skirts and shaking off the shock of the last few moments.

"I had better go, lest Mr. McAffrey think I'm somehow coercing your answers with my presence," Edward said. He smiled and dropped a kiss at her temple.

"Hmmpf," Mr. McAffrey said, opening the door. "I thought you said you'd let me know the moment she woke up."

Edward rolled his eyes and went for the door.

"And stay out!" Mr. McAffrey called, once Edward had closed the door.

"Mr. McAffrey, do you mean to tell me that you don't care for my choice? After all your encouragement, I had the opposite impression."

"Oh, no," Mr. McAffrey said, amiably, waving his hand at the door. "I think he's a fine fellow. But as your father and brother are absent, someone must keep the chap on his toes."

Eleanor shook her head, smiling. "Don't be too hard on him. I've already been quite the bothersome fiancee. I don't want him to start rethinking our arrangement."

"Pfft. That fellow? He's a goner. I knew it from the moment I met him. He's head over heels for you, my dear. And I like him all the more for it. It shows his good sense, that he realizes what a treasure you are."

Eleanor rolled her eyes. "Of course, *you* aren't biased."

He sniffed. "Just because I love you doesn't mean that my opinion isn't completely valid."

"So you approve of the match, then?" she said.

Although she had phrased the question casually, his answer meant a great deal to her. As he had already pointed out, he was the closest thing to family she had.

"Wholeheartedly. He is a fine man, both in title and character. I've done some asking. He doesn't hold to vices like some men do, and he pays his bills on time with no credits taken. Everyone agrees he is wealthy, but all his servants seem happy to be here and well-fed. That Mrs. Gardner is a wonder. If a fine woman like that has worked for him nigh on fifteen years without complaint, that is all the recommendation I need."

Eleanor raised her eyebrow. "I've yet to meet this Mrs. Gardner, but I've had her cooking."

"A fine woman," he repeated.

Eleanor thought she saw a dusting of pink along his cheekbones, and she pressed her lips together to contain a smile.

"Have you heard we are to leave, to the country?" she asked. "After we're married."

"He mentioned that," Mr. McAffrey said, rubbing the back of his neck. "He offered me a job there, one that comes with a little hut on the grounds."

Eleanor had heard many things about Chatsworth, and from all descriptions, there was nothing on the grounds that could accurately be described as a 'hut'.

She smiled. "I didn't ask him to do that, if that's what you're wondering."

"I did wonder that." His eyes were sharp upon her face. "You didn't put him up to it, then?"

"This is the first I've heard of it," she said, honestly. "He knows how much you mean to me, but if he says there's a position available, I don't doubt that there is."

He chewed his lip a little, a habit that Eleanor recognized as meaning he was carefully considering something.

"I've always wondered what it would be like to move back to the country. I was born in Dentdale, you know, but my family moved when I was but a boy."

Eleanor *did* know. She waited.

"I think I will," he said, confidently. "I think I'll come keep an eye on this Duke, make sure he treats you with all the deference you deserve."

She smiled widely, even though it hurt her cheek to do so. "I'm so glad! It would have been the only sadness I had about leaving London."

"Is that so? What about your friend, the Marchioness?"

Eleanor waved a hand. "Mark my words, she'll be my houseguest at Chatsworth so often I won't have a chance to miss her. And I'm sure we will be back in London often. But with you at Chatsworth, I will lack for nothing. My happiness will be complete."

"Then of course I will come, my dear. I would like to be where you are, as well. Now let me see that trinket on your finger. Have you bit the stone yet? Is it real? I wouldn't want him to give you paste."

Chapter 28

From the *Quentin Daily-*

On the sixth of May, the Duke of Devonshire, Edward Dain Montclief, married Lady Eleanor Winthrope Gilbert in St. Paul's cathedral. The bride wore a beaded dress of white peau de soie, with a lace veil nearly ten feet long. The bride was given away by Captain Daniel McAffrey, a war hero who served with the bride's father, the late Major Matthew Gilbert. In attendance were the couple's closest family and friends, including the Lord and Lady Lucas Wilcott, the Marquess and Marchioness of Millen, the Marquess Salisbury, his sister the Lady Candace Waldrey, and her betrothed, the Marquess of Shelbourne.

The wedding breakfast sparkled merrily--the long table was set with white linens, china and crystal. Arrangements of white roses and trailing ivy in low silver bowls lined the center of the table, sprinkled through with the flickering light of tealights. But Eleanor thought the most beautiful sight of all was all the people that she loved at the same table.

Jane had come, though her high-waisted dress could barely hide her condition. Henry was in an animated conversation with Percy about horses, and Candace beamed up at her fiance, the Marquess of Shelbourne, a handsome young man with soft eyes.

"To Mr. Pickwick!" Edward said, lifting his glass.

Eleanor nearly choked on her champagne.

"For bringing us together," Edward said.

444

The wedding guests glanced at one another. There were many raised eyebrows and curious looks, but they raised their glasses and a murmured chorus of "to Mr. Pickwick" was repeated amongst them.

"And to wonderful beginnings."

From the *Quentin Daily-*

A most curious toast was given at a wedding recently. It seems that our infamous Mr. Pickwick is credited--by the illustrious groom, no less--as being responsible for the match of the Season. With such eminent patronage, Mr. Pickwick will certainly become a household name, if he isn't already.

Epilogue

People didn't remember a gently aging woman with brown hair, until he mentioned the large emerald ring. It seemed as if she couldn't help but wear it-- he didn't know whether it was vanity, or her playing out the fantasy that she'd held too close for years--being the Duchess of Devonshire. She never saw him, so he let her lead the way--from the slushy roads outside of London all the way to the squalid docks of Liverpool. It was far easier to follow someone who was going willingly than it was to transport a human bundle. It wasn't that she was foolhardy--he couldn't remember when he'd followed a lady who possessed the level of street smarts and caginess. It was just that he was very good at blending into the background--he could switch from derelict to a member of the peerage with the change of a coat and the straightening of his shoulders.

It was only once they had reached Liverpool proper, in the common room of an innhouse that reeked of ale, turned fish, and unwashed bodies, did Mr. Thornton make his move. It was the simplest thing in the world. He supposed that the lady had chosen this inn because it was cheap-- but cheap prices bought no loyalty from the staff. A few coppers and a tilted head in her direction was all it took for the barmaid to slip the contents of the vial into a tankard before it was delivered.

He saw her head droop, saw her stand and make her way unsteadily up the staircase to her rented room. He followed.

"Let me help you, madam," he said, at her elbow.

Then they were in her room together, with the door shut firmly behind.

"Who 're you?" she slurred, stumbling toward the bed.

"No one worth remembering," he said, briskly.

"Drugged me," she remarked, before falling headfirst against the mattress.

"Very astute of you," he said.

In a trice, the ring was removed. He tucked it into his pocket, and headed back downstairs to find those he'd hired to assist.

An hour later, Mr. Thornton stood on the dock, one foot up on a mooring post and watched the *Lady Rowena* break free of the harbor and hit open water. The off-white sails of the ship unfurled against the twilight sky--huge flags of surrender. Along with twelve other female criminals, Lady Teresa Bunt was bound for New South Wales. The others would be free to return after seven years, but Lady Bunt's paperwork showed a life sentence.

It had all been done discreetly--some of it legal, some of it not. It didn't matter--the sentencing paperwork had been convincing enough for the Captain, and it would be recorded by the authorities at the port of call, as it was here. Lady Bunt would never be free to return. The Duke of Devonshire, his new bride, and their son, Henry, were safe from her. Mr. Thornton stood and watched the ship get smaller until it was no more than a smudge on the sea in the night.

The sound the machine made was soothing. The momentary press of the metal against the parchment, the slightly slick hiss of the fresh-printed page being pulled, the rustling as the hung pages dried. Eleanor would never tire of it, even though she wasn't the one operating the machine anymore. Edward was adamant--she would do the writing and proofing only.

He'd relocated her press from the tenement basement to a long-forgotten basement room in Chatsworth, and found her two helpers, both exceedingly trustworthy--Mr. McAffrey and one Peter Brumlee, a young man injured in the last war. He was intelligent and quick, but heavily scarred and extremely shy. Far from feeling confined in the secretive, underground room, young Peter Brumlee thrived there. He had the cottage next to Mr. McAffrey, and he lived a quiet, solitary life full of books that seemed to suit him.

And in this way, Mr. Pickwick lived on. The Duchess of Devonshire was, by society's standards, the most unlikely of suspects. After all, no husband would allow his wife to pursue such a foolhardy scheme, and no lady of her wealth and stature would dare risk her reputation in such a manner. Her sources changed over the years--Beatrice married that Vicar's son and moved to Bath. She sent a few verifiable tidbits through her letters, but soon became too busy with her children and soap shop to write much at all. Ida married, too, but stayed in the employ of the Duchess of Interwile.

Emily remained unmarried, and she and Eleanor still met whenever possible in the back of that pub. Eleanor found that with the right outfit and discreet security, she could enjoy some of the freedoms of her former life. But her lady's maids and her dressmakers were exceedingly chatty and informative, as were the multitude of ladies looking to make the new Duchess' acquaintance. Jane never failed as a good source of information, and Lady Candace became a close friend, and her counsel was always wise.

Eleanor's world was smaller, in some ways. Gone was the daily bustle of city streets, waking at dawn to the sounds of the early criers and the seagulls that screamed at their breakfast. Instead, she found the estate at Chatsworth to be a quiet respite. The descriptions Eleanor had heard seemed beyond reality--mythical, almost-- but the property itself was even more beautiful than the stories told.

She filled her days with a different kind of work and socializing--those early days, she scandalized the cooks by showing up, unannounced, to bake treats for the village children. The oddity of it dumbfounded them at first--a Duchess, with flour to her elbows! But the novelty wore off and a convivial comfort took its place. Soon, she was banished to her own corner, a marble-topped bench along the wall, with her own set of tools and stoneware bowls, so she wasn't underfoot of the great, churning activity that kept the denizens of the manor well-fed.

Edward was alarmed, that next spring, when his head gardener, James, had appeared suddenly on the threshold of his study, wringing his wide-brimmed hat in his leathery hands. When the nervous man stuttered that the matter concerned the Duchess, but would barely utter another word, Edward demanded to be shown what was the matter and chased the man to a sunny clearing.

There, instead of the cataclysmic, mute-inducing accident that Edward had expected, he found his wife swathed in a common gardener's smock over a cotton day dress. She had pressed two of the gardeners into service, and was tilling the soil in four large raised beds alongside them with a hoe. She'd looked up, adorable with a smudge of dirt upon her cheek, smiled and waved--oblivious to the panic that she'd instilled in Edward.

He quickly surmised that James somehow thought that he or the gardeners would be in trouble because of her antics. Edward shook his head with an amused smile, and explained to the man that the Duchess was to be allowed to do whatever she wanted, as long as it wasn't legitimately dangerous, and that if her new garden caused them any extra work, they'd simply hire more gardeners.

"Don't expect the new Duchess to always act like a Duchess," he said.

James looked relieved, if a little confused, then shook his head as Edward unbuttoned his jacket, hung it on a nearby branch, rolled up his sleeves, and grabbed an extra hoe.

Eleanor beamed up at him. "I figured I need *something* to keep me busy, and a vegetable garden seemed just the thing. This way, I won't be stealing from the kitchen gardens if I want to bring more food into town. Did you hear that Mrs. MacKinsley is expecting *another*? That will be seven. A family of nine always has use for another basket of vegetables. Seemed the least I could do."

As if the villagers needed another reason to love her, as if the freshly refurbished schoolhouse, the baked goods and the permanent hiring of a good physician weren't enough. But Edward thought there wasn't any downside to his wife's generous nature. And it was her nature to see needs and to fill them.

"Quite right, my love," Edward said, pecking her on the forehead. "It's a genius idea, and you amaze me with your thoughtfulness."

They proceeded to muck the day away happily, planting what turned out to be a very prolific vegetable garden that became his wife's favorite spot. Even when she became pregnant with their own child a few months later, Edward could find her checking on her plants, or, some months later, sipping tea on the chaise lounge that he'd ordered for her, the saucer balanced on her belly. Those evenings were his favorite, when he'd come down from the account books in his study to find her smiling at him, wearing that ridiculous straw hat that she'd pilfered from one of the gardeners.

"Look at the squash," she'd tell him.

And he always did his duty and looked, then complimented their progress--not because *he* cared about the squash. But *she* did. And if complimenting vegetables made his wife happy, he would do it; he loved to see her smile, because he loved her.

THE END

THE MOST IMPORTANT THING YOU'LL READ IN THESE PAGES:

There is a little girl in a basement. It is cold and damp down there. The bare mattress pushed to the corner of the room smells. They don't let her out, so she has gone pale. But even though it is dark and cold, and she can hear things scurrying down there, it is better when she is all alone. Better when the video camera is off. She is waiting for a sound at the top of the stairs that doesn't make her shudder. She is waiting for you to save her.

I wish this were fiction, but it's not. There are more slaves today than in any other time in human history. Human trafficking is growing, and the United States is the largest consumer of sexual exploitation.

What can you do to stop it?

- Go to ourrescue.org/join-the-fight and donate. For the cost of a latte, you can help free enslaved children!

- Learn the signs of human trafficking, then call and report them.

- Stop supporting pornography. Many of those images haven't been created by willing people. Even if they have, watching pornography causes changes in the brain. Consumption of pornography directly feeds the demand for the sexual slave trade. Don't believe me? Go here: fightthenewdrug.org

- Stop giving children smart phones/smart devices.

Let me tell you a true story. When I was about eleven, I got really mad at my parents. I can't remember what they were doing, but I do remember that they were getting ready to have some friends over for dinner that night. They were distracted. I was mad and I decided to run away. I packed my bags, and staunchly headed down our (quite long) driveway. I reached the country road. I looked right. I looked left. I couldn't decide which way would be best. If I headed left, I would end up at my grandparents' house, and I thought they would send me right on back. If I went right, I wasn't sure what I would find. I took a fortifying handful out of the box of cereal I had taken for my grand voyage, decided it would be much better in a bowl with milk, and trudged back up the driveway.

I am so, so very grateful that I grew up before the time of smartphones, social media, and unfettered internet access.

Let me rewrite that 11 year old me scenario if I had been unlucky--if I had been the SAME kid with internet access. Maybe I'd met a friend online. Someone a bit older, an age I really thought was cool, like seventeen. (Seventeen was the name of a magazine that looked really cool in the stores, but that my mom had informed me I was too young for. Seventeen as an age appealed to me, for that reason.) And let's call her "Kate". Now, Kate and I talk online. She listens to me. Encourages me. She's there for me when my parents aren't. I like her. She likes me. It's so nice to be liked, and so flattering that someone that age listens to me! On this day, I get mad. I tell Kate that I am running away. She says, "What a great idea! I'll send my Dad to come pick you up. You can come over to my house and we'll watch movies and eat popcorn and talk about how rotten your parents are. What's your address?"

And because I'm eleven and mad and think I'm far smarter and more worldly than I am, I tell her.

Except, of course, Kate doesn't exist. And the man coming to pick me up isn't her father.

This happens ALL THE TIME. The National Center for Missing and Exploited Children estimates that one out of every six runaways is a probable trafficking victim.

When you hand your kid a smartphone, you are giving creeps and perverts access to your children.

For more information on this issue, go here: savethekids.us

Out of all the issues facing us today, human trafficking is perhaps the most evil. If there is an issue we all can agree on, can it please be this one? Here's a challenge to you...next time you are tempted to tell someone about your diet or your new couch, next time you get so angry at the partisan lines and want to post about it--post or talk about this instead. Point people to resources. Raise awareness. Let's get all those little girls and boys and young people back to safety. Let's fight this!

Acknowledgements

As always, I have to thank my husband first and foremost. I am so blessed that my husband believes in my dream and supports me in every way as I chase it down.

My second thanks has to go to my brilliant cover designer and primary beta reader, Kari Joy Hodgen. I'm so thankful that you are so generous with your amazing talents! Thanks for being a great cheerleader, and for talking me down off all the ledges.

Thanks also to my other beta readers:

-Jenny James, who shows the most impeccable attention to grammar, syntax, and word choice. I know my books would have so many more flaws if it weren't for you!

- Jamie Weatherfield, who asks great questions about character motivation, plot holes, and pacing.

-Heidi Hollander, who pointed out grammar errors, unanswered questions, and pacing issues.

- Babs Veneman, for all the encouragement, suggestions, and pointing out the parts that made you laugh.

You guys are the absolute best, and I couldn't do this without you!

About the Author

Jill M Beene lives in the Central Valley of California with two of the sweetest guys on the planet--her husband, Adam, and her English Mastiff, Rupert. She's the author of the Elayna Miller series, and the young adult fantasy novel, A Sharpened Axe. She'd date ice cream, marry coffee, and kill editing.

Made in the USA
Middletown, DE
14 February 2021